WILD AT HEART

A KINCAIDS OF PINE HARBOUR NOVEL

ZOE YORK

Mom, I didn't understand then. I get it now. Thank you for moving us closer and closer to your Pine Harbour. You keep teaching me new things, every day.

I miss you.

He's the guy everyone loves, and she's the outsider who knows better than to fall for the town's favourite golden boy.

Everyone in Pine Harbour loves Will Kincaid—except the one person he cares about actually impressing. Can grown men have crushes on their frenemies? When Catie joins the small town's Search and Rescue team, Will finds himself spending every Thursday night swapping glares with the hairdresser while they get in each other's way.

Catie Berton has a long list of reasons why Will is an arrogant jerk. But the more time she spends with him, the more she's forced to admit sometimes they make a good team. That doesn't change the fact that Will has always been her *right crush, wrong guy*.

When the SRT goes on a road trip to a competition, she surprises herself by agreeing to ride shotgun in his truck. The long drive could be a chance to repair a shredded friendship, if Catie can get past her complicated feelings for the too-attractive-for-his-own-good school principal.

Because Catie knows all too well how cold a small town can be to an outsider who wants too much happiness from one of their own.

Return to Pine Harbour, in this frenemies to lovers small town romance about two people looking to find themselves in the shadow of community expectations.

LAND ACKNOWLEDGEMENT

Pine Harbour is a fictional town located in a real place, the Bruce Peninsula, which I want to acknowledge as the Territory of the Anishinabek Nation: The People of the Three Fires known as Ojibway, Odawa, and Pottawatomie Nations.

I also give thanks to the Chippewas of Saugeen, and the Chippewas of Nawash, known collectively as the Saugeen Ojibway Nation, as the traditional keepers of this land, a place where I grew up and return to with joy each summer.

I appreciate this resource from the Saugeen Ojibway Nation (saugeenojibwaynation.ca/resources) for providing guidance on how to acknowledge this land I'm writing on, and explaining why land acknowledgements are an important step in reconciliation. Specifically, "A land acknowledgement is a reflection process in which you build mindfulness and intention walking into whatever gathering you are having."

I built a land acknowledgement into this story, in chapter nine, and I hope readers are encouraged to look into the Indigenous territory in which they might read this book.

For example, I now live and write in London, Ontario. This is the traditional territory of the Haudenosaunee and Anishinaabeg, the Wendat, Lenape, and Attawandaron people. At the same time I was writing this book, Indigenous nations across Canada were finally receiving confirmation of what they had known for a long time: children taken from their communities and placed at residential schools, who never returned, had died in those schools and were buried in unmarked graves. The last of those residential schools closed while I was in high school. I grieve the loss of those children, and am angered at the generational harm done to their communities on many levels.

May we all be more mindful of the history of how we came to be here and grateful for the sharing of this space today.

With thanks,
Zoe York

1

Pᴉɴᴇ Hᴀʀʙᴏᴜʀ ᴡᴀs a place full of memories: good, bad, and confusing.

In the few years since Catie Berton moved back—her second time as a newcomer to the town—she'd devoted herself to leaning into the good. Trying to see what her mother had loved about the village nestled high on a hill above the glittering waters of Lake Huron. And whenever possible, she helped make it a better place.

She had allies in that project, too. Other newcomers, like Isla Peterson, who owned *Bake Sale!* across the street from Catie's hair salon and real estate office. The bakery usually closed at mid-afternoon, but today it was open late, like all the businesses on Main Street, for a "Doors Open Pine Harbour" event leading up to the town meeting tonight.

Catie didn't book any hair clients during the event, leaving herself free to talk to anyone who wandered in the door. And right now, while there was a lull, that meant she could dash across the street and grab a latte and a snack for later.

Also, a snack for right now. Double snacks were really the secret to surviving a fourteen-hour workday.

The *Bake Sale!* treat of the day was a cardamom chai cake, so she ordered two of those—one for breakfast tomorrow—and a raisin butter tart.

"Has it been busy?" she asked Isla as her friend efficiently made a perfect latte.

"Pretty steady. Lots of chatter about the town meeting." Isla gave her a curious look over the gleaming chrome of the vintage-looking espresso machine. "Adam didn't know what the big fuss was. He says Pine Harbour rarely has town meetings?"

"This will only be the third since I've moved back." Catie paid for her treats, then leaned her hip against the counter so she could keep one eye on her shop across the road. "Nobody will give me a straight answer about what it's really about, or why there's so much whispering buzz. Just a lot of questions about who is going."

"Which in turn means we need to go," Isla teased.

"Of course we do." Catie took a sip of her coffee. "If we leave the cottagers and the born-and-breds to their own devices, who knows what terrible decisions they might make."

"They're not all bad." Isla was referring to her husband, of course. Adam Kincaid was a prince among men, to be sure. But he also focused on what mattered: keeping his wife happy, and doing his job as Pine Harbour's newest firefighter.

His older brothers, on the other hand, needed to be watched carefully. They had the best of intentions, like a lot of residents. At the last town meeting, they'd even saved the day for the Pine Harbour library. But there was something about them... Catie took another sip. "No. Not all bad," she agreed. "This town just has so much potential."

"You sound like Bailey."

"Bailey's a genius." Catie spotted someone slowing down outside her salon and grabbed her to-go bag. "See you in an hour! I'll save you a seat."

But when she arrived at the community centre fifty-five minutes later, it was already standing room only. Pine Harbour only had a population of six hundred people. Were they all in attendance tonight?

The town meeting notice had been vague. *Community Information Night,* it had been specifically called. Shocking lack of information on offer, though. Apparently, that fact hadn't gotten past every other curious soul in town. She scanned the overflowing room, taking stock of who was in attendance. A few friendly faces were up front—like Olivia Minelli, who had fought hard to keep the Pine Harbour Library open. But Catie's nosy neighbour across the road, Frances Schmidt, was also sitting in the front row, sure to have a half-formed opinion about whatever tonight's topic might be.

And right behind her were two of the Kincaid brothers. Owen, the oldest, the EMT supervisor who had helped Olivia with a plan to save the library. Josh, the second youngest, sat next to him. The mechanic was a brash hothead, just as likely as Mrs. Schmidt to go off half-cocked, but his instincts were at least in the same direction as Catie's, all for change and innovation. No sign of the second oldest Kincaid brother, though.

Will.

Mr. Kincaid, he would probably correct her, which would be yet another blow to the secret fact that she'd once had a crush on the guy. Two crushes, really, separated by fifteen years.

Catie's first crush on Will lasted from when she was twelve years old to right before her fourteenth birthday. He'd recently left Pine Harbour to go to university, and brought a girl home his first weekend back for a visit. Even at fourteen, Catie knew better than to pine for unavailable men.

Her second crush bloomed on her return to Pine Harbour at the age of twenty-eight, and quietly hummed under her skin, a secret she liked enough when she was alone, but that made her a bit nervous if she thought about it too much—or ever considered acting upon it.

But the thing about crushes, she learned over the winter that she turned thirty, was that they weren't real. They were one-sided, a figment of her imagination, and based entirely on the *idea* of a man.

And her idea of who Will Kincaid might be ran smack into the reality of who he kept showing her he was: an irritating rule-stickler with zero capacity for fun. The worst of the five Kincaid brothers by far, although she didn't know Seth very well. The middle brother was a float plane pilot who lived north of Manitoulin Island, and flew home to have breakfast with his brothers at the diner once a month.

Or at least, that was Catie's casual, outsider observation. She tried not to spend much time thinking about Will these days.

You scanned the room, looking for him as soon as you arrived.

Sure, but that had been unconscious. Conscious thoughts about him were limited to how annoying he was. The last time she'd had a real conversation with the community school principal, he'd basically told her to her face that he thought the best idea she'd had in a year was stupid.

Well, she thought his face was stupid. So there.

Ugh.

Why did he bring out the most childish responses in her? She hated that.

As she settled against the back wall, grateful to have her latte and butter tart to keep her company for the wait before the meeting started, she pulled out her phone to check her email.

Which pinged yet another subconscious thought about Mr. Kincaid. Email was the only way she communicated with Will these days.

It started last October, with a story posted online about her new vision to save the tired bachelor auction event to raise money for the Pine Harbour Animal Shelter—a vision Will had basically told her wouldn't work, and then she'd gone and done it anyway.

From: Will Kincaid
To: Catie Berton

Catie,
Congratulations on your new position as the chair of the
Pine Harbour Cares weekend fundraising event. It
sounds like you're taking the bachelor auction to the next
level! I've been a bachelor on that stage before. Count
me in.

The gall of him to just assume he was the type of bachelor she was looking for. And after he'd told her the Pine Harbour Cares pitch wouldn't work. She'd replied, of course.

From: Catie Berton
To: Will Kincaid

Hi Will,
Thank you for your interest in the auction! At this time,
I'm only looking to recruit one or two more eligible
auction participants in a different demographic, and I'm
not sure you're the right fit. We could find something
else for you to do. Maybe the Master of Ceremonies
instead?

He, on the other hand, did not reply.

And then, in November, she had reason to email him about another matter.

From: Catie Berton
To: Will Kincaid

Mr. Kincaid,
It was quite the surprise for the Main Street businesses
to have a wave of children descend on us today from Pine
Harbour Community School, offering demanding willing
to wash our windows with a lot of enthusiasm. There was
some feedback from the business community that a cold
day like today wasn't the best…frozen bubbles all over
the place, a bit streaky. In the future, please consider
reaching out to discuss ideas like this before execution.

His reply was…brief. Curt, even.

From: Will Kincaid
To: Catie Berton

Ms. Berton,
Thank you for your feedback.

After that, it was easy to put Will Kincaid entirely out of her mind, so it was a surprise when she got a new email from him in February.

From: Will Kincaid
To: Catie Berton

Please be advised that PHCS students will be delivering
Valentine's Day singing telegrams today through the
Main Street area.

That one felt like a shot across her bow. She fired back immediately.

From: Catie Berton
To: Will Kincaid

Noted. As you might be aware, the Pine Harbour Cares
committee is doing the same thing to help promote the
bachelor auction.

And he returned passive-aggressive fire.

From: Will Kincaid
To: Catie Berton

I was not aware. Room for us all.

She had been tempted to engage further. She refrained,

of course, and bought herself a treat from *Bake Sale!* to reward herself for her decorum and professionalism.

In March, after the Pine Harbour Cares weekend was a roaring success, and everyone appreciated her new twist on the bachelor auction—everyone except Will, who didn't attend, or even acknowledge that the event had happened —Catie decided she needed a new crush.

It wasn't at the top of her to-do list. That was running her real estate business, alongside her hair salon business, and volunteering for a number of community organizations. But dating was definitely on there, and she thought about that a *lot* over March and April.

She didn't think about Will in the slightest, having left him completely behind in the Winter of Unexpectedly Sharp Emails.

And now here they were, in the Mother of All Town Meetings. She glanced to the door. Still no Will.

"Thank you all for coming," a voice said from somewhere, the words echoing out of speakers set up in the corners.

Catie craned her neck, but there wasn't anyone at the podium yet. Her attention pivoted back to the doorway, and then Isla appeared. Catie waved from where she stood against the wall. "Sorry, no seats."

"Adam texted me as I was closing up the bakery. Apparently this is about parking. A memo came in to the station from the municipal government just a few minutes ago."

Catie's stomach fell. Ah, crap. That hadn't occurred to her, because Pine Harbour didn't have a significant parking problem—but they were one of the only towns on the peninsula that could say that.

They were also the only town on the peninsula without

a tourism plan or much of a social media presence, Josh Kincaid's TikTok account about car renovations notwithstanding. The only time of the year they had parking problems was the annual County Country Music Festival that shut down Main Street, but the town just waived parking limits on all the side streets and the residents good-naturedly—for the most part—made do for three days, because Nashville superstar Liana Hansen had married a local boy and was having his baby.

Which made Catie roll her eyes a little, because they weren't that welcoming to all newcomers, but it also made the more romantic part of her heart do an epic swoon.

But also, summer was coming, and that meant tourists. Each year brought a new burst of city folk discovering a new part of the peninsula, and this year could be Pine Harbour's year—which, like everything else, would be good, bad, and confusing.

"We're going to get started in a minute, please take your seats." Again, the voice came from nowhere, and clearly every seat in the room was taken.

Catie took a restorative chug of latte instead of rolling her eyes. She needed to keep her cool. Whatever happened tonight, there would be time to reply in an appropriate manner. She'd learned a lot as a business owner—about things like consultation periods and requests for proposals. And how to tell someone to fuck right off, but in a polite way. The Bruce County version of *bless your heart*: *We'll agree to disagree*, which definitely meant, I'm taking this up the chain.

There was a scrape of wood on waxed floor, and then a head appeared behind the podium. The voice, it turned out, was attached to the body of someone Catie didn't recognize, who had maybe unfolded herself from a chair directly behind the podium, and now was introducing some representatives from local government. The reeve of Pine Harbour—a ceremonial role, really, since the communities had amalgamated back when Catie was a kid—and the mayor of North Bruce, as well as a representative from the neighbouring community of South Bruce.

This meeting was definitely about parking.

As Catie took another glance around the room—where was Will? This was his type of thing—she realized it was packed to the gills with seasonal cottage owners. There were a good number of year-round residents, too, but the cottage owners had been tipped off.

Was there a maximum number of times a girl could roll her eyes in one night before it became a health hazard?

The stranger started a PowerPoint presentation and Catie went back to checking her emails. She had a few clients actively house hunting right now, so she needed to stay on top of messages from fellow realtors about new properties on the market. Or at least, that's what she told herself as she refreshed her inbox.

Then she gave up and focused back on the presentation. Apparently Pine Harbour had a total of ninety-seven public parking spots in town. And just as Catie suspected, the municipal government was proposing that they go to a paid parking model, similar to other towns. There were some valid reasons in favour of doing it on a trial basis, the strongest being that visitors to the region would pay a potentially fairer share of the costs of maintaining those parking spots.

The room erupted in loud protests, apparently unimpressed.

Catie took another long sip from her latte.

Beside her, Isla winced. "This won't be great for us, will it?"

Catie made a matching face. As a Main Street business owner, she knew she'd be hearing about this for weeks to come. "Nope. But we'll have time to make our concerns heard in a way that isn't yelling at top volume over other people who share the same opinion."

"Promise?"

She sure hoped she could make that promise. "Time will tell."

After a few minutes of squawking, the crowd organized itself into lines behind microphones, and Catie did her best to listen to everyone.

"Are they all saying the same thing, from different viewpoints?" Isla asked at one point.

"Yep."

Her friend sighed and handed over another bag. "I brought you another butter tart."

"Do you know how much I value our friendship?"

Isla laughed loud enough that people turned and glared. She waved her hands. "Not about the topic at hand, folks. Promise."

"Speaking of our friendship, and everything you've done for me." Catie took a big bite of the tart and felt immediately more peaceful. "The search and rescue team try out is on Friday. And if I make it—"

Isla cut her off. "You're going to ace it."

Her friend had helped her train for this over the winter. Catie knew she was strong enough and fast enough now, no doubt. But still, hubris was an important part of life. "*If* I make it, the team training will be every Thursday night. So that won't work for—" She cut herself off as Frances

Schmidt leaned into the microphone and said something disparaging about cottagers.

Wrong room to say that in, she thought to herself.

The room proved her right with a grumpy roar.

"Folks, let's try to keep it productive." The presenter put on a brave face. "Let's consider it a friendly challenge."

The next four comments failed miserably. Nobody liked the idea of paid parking spots in town, but for very different reasons.

"With those thoughtful comments concluded, we're going to have to move on," the presenter said. "Further submissions for or against the parking measures can be filed online. We want to hear from all of you, both in the initial thirty-day consultation period, but over the summer as well. Now, while we're here, I'll turn it over to your reeve to share some town news."

The crowd settled down, and Catie thought about ducking out to get ahead of traffic, but just as she was weighing whether she could slide away quietly, there was movement at the entrance to the room that caught her eye.

A tall, imposing figure in a green camouflage uniform. Will Kincaid—school principal, pain in the ass, and army reservist—scanned the room, lifting his chin in acknowledgment to his brothers first, then the reeve, who had just taken his spot at the podium, and finally, to Catie and Isla.

Her friend raised her hand cheerfully. Of course she did. Will was her brother-in-law. Catie had no such familial allegiance, so she opted to ignore him.

When she turned her attention back to the podium, Will was quietly apologizing to whoever he was standing in front of. The army boots gave him another inch on his already too-tall six-foot-two frame.

"I know this change is going to spark a lot of discussion, but I just want to thank everyone for coming out tonight. We don't do this often enough, so I just wanted to take this opportunity to share some good news as well. This will be posted online tomorrow, but you're hearing it first tonight. The annual Pine Harbour Canada Day picnic will be followed by an evening bonfire at the harbour, a first this year. Thanks so much to August Howe from the marina, and Josh Kincaid from the garage, both of whom have done a lot of the heavy lifting to make this happen."

A polite round of applause was well earned. Catie gave a thumbs up to August, who was sitting next to her sister, January. She liked the Howe sisters a lot.

"Finally, on behalf of our favourite school principal, who has just joined us at the back of the room—"

Ugh, Catie had gone a solid twenty minutes there without an eye-roll. Will was their only school principal! Pine Harbour only had one school, for all grades kindergarten to grade twelve. Will had zero competition for the post of favourite principal. What ridiculous pandering.

"—the business club for grades nine through twelve is seeking a new advisor for the next school year. Qualified community members are encouraged to reach out to Principal Kincaid for more information."

Beside her, Isla's elbow poked out, jostling Catie. "You should do that."

"*You* should do it. You're his sister-in-law."

"That's nepotism. And my schedule isn't flexible like yours is."

"It's only nepotism if you get paid or there are perks." There would be zero perks to spending time under Will's bossy dictatorship.

"Remember the window washing disaster?"

Oh, she remembered all right.

"You could do your thing. Sweet talk them into competency."

"Is that my thing?"

"Yes." Isla nodded emphatically. "That is very much your thing, and they need it. You could really help Will out."

Or sort him out. The more she thought about it, the more it sounded like a volunteer opportunity for which she would be uniquely suited. As the meeting came to an end, she opened a new email message and started typing.

From: Catie Berton
To: Will Kincaid

Will,
I understand the PHCS Business Club needs a new
Advisor next year. ~~*Count me in.*~~ *I'd be happy to help.*

She scheduled it to send an hour later, once she was safely ensconced at home. Then she put her phone away. When she looked up, the favourite principal himself was looking at her again. As soon as their gazes connected, he crossed his arms and looked stern.

Catie would bet even money she wouldn't get a prompt reply from him. That was fine. She had a parking debacle to sort out.

Pine Harbour needed her, even if Will Kincaid didn't.

2

A WEEK after the town meeting, Will scowled at the single email remaining in his inbox.

It was the only message he hadn't responded to yet, and had been sitting there for days—an anomaly for the principal of Pine Harbour Community School, who was a big fan of the principle of both Inbox Zero and also being courteous and prompt in replies to members of the community.

He could pretend the reason he was ignoring the message was that he was swamped, of course. That was true.

The last three weeks before the end of the academic year at PHCS were a wild ride for teachers, students, and staff alike. Plus they were experiencing an unusually early heatwave.

He wiped a drop of sweat from his forehead, glared at the air conditioning unit that had inexplicably decided to stop working on the hottest day of spring so far, and took a deep breath. One of his teachers was sending a kid down to his office and he needed all the calm, centred energy he could muster.

Tonight, at the search and rescue team's weekly training, he would get to burn off whatever frustration was about to rumble through his door. Until then, he would be the fearless leader of the combined K-12 school.

They were still working out the kinks of having both the elementary students and secondary school students under one roof. He had been an elementary school principal for five years before the merger. Now, two years in, he was still feeling his way with the older kids, who all reminded him a little too much of his own teen years. The precarious hold on a life plan still blooming, the very real chance of it all falling apart because of emotions or unfair circumstance.

"I said, don't effing touch me!"

Will winced at the language. The grade ten boy, Sam Otto, had spent more time in Will's office than any other kid in the school.

Sam was not a fan of his new principal. He was new this year, having moved to Pine Harbour from a few towns away. His parents were separated, and he was living with his dad full-time now. His dad had a busy job, and Sam was left to his own devices most of the time.

Will kept trying to push Sam into some of the after-school activities. He glanced at his watch. Ten minutes until the end of the day. Wouldn't even be long enough to get Sam to talk about whatever had happened to get him sent to the office.

But after school, there was a drop-in basketball program until six. The rhythmic thump of a basketball against the floor, the pause before taking one's shot...that had been a big part of Will's teen years. On the court, the stress of being enough faded away.

Will's afternoon plans had just changed.

The door to his office swung open and the sullen fifteen-year-old dropped into the chair on the opposite side of Will's desk. "This is fucking bullshit," Sam said.

Will gave him a bland, unaffected look at the escalation from *effing* to the straight-up f-bomb in his face. "What time is your dad home from work tonight?"

Sam groaned. "No way, man. You can't give me detention."

Will shrugged. "Actually, I can. We don't use disrespectful language, right? You know that. And I know you know that. So it's fair for me to hold you to that expectation. There are consequences for beaking off. You and I are going to shoot some hoops as soon as the bell rings. Until then, you can sit there and take some deep breaths."

"You're a terrible principal."

"I try." Will checked his email as Sam seethed. He sent January a note that he had her wayward student in his office, and they could discuss it the next morning, because he had plans for the kid after school.

It took eight of the ten minutes before Sam cracked. "Look, I didn't know I had homework, all right? Ms. Howe is pissed at me that I didn't do her stupid assignment, but it wasn't in my assignments folder. I swear."

Swearing was part of the problem. "How did you communicate that to Ms. Howe?"

Sam made a face. "She should know she fu—made a mistake."

January Howe was a great teacher. Will had no doubt she would own the error if she had made it, but it didn't excuse a belligerent response. "We don't use disrespectful language, Sam. Full stop. Find another way to deal with your problems, or we're going to have to put a plaque with your name on it on that chair."

"You'd like that. A way to remember me." Oh, that false bravado. Will could relate.

The bell sounded overhead, signalling the end of the school day.

Time to let this kid kick Will's ass at basketball. "Come on. We're going to the gym."

"I don't want to."

"Why not?"

Sam shrugged, but wouldn't meet Will's gaze. Less bravado now, more naked fear.

Will leaned against the edge of his desk. "The kids who go to the basketball drop-in are all nice."

"Too nice," Sam muttered.

Maybe the kind of nice that came with an edge—Will would bet his brand new kayak that kids were being wary of the mouthy, belligerent new guy.

There was a lesson to be learned in that experience, but it wasn't an easy one to be dragged through, or to repair from, either. Will needed to be more mindful of that side of the coin. Sam deserved space to learn how to be a grown-up and handle the boundaries other people put up. But he was still a kid who needed friends.

"Let's go," Will said firmly. "I was going to let you play against me, but I think you'll need some help."

"Whoa, whoa, I don't need any help beating you at basketball," Sam protested, jumping up. "I can take you."

"In your dreams," Will said with a practiced cheer he didn't completely feel.

Just like Sam, he was now a little worried about their reception in the gymnasium. And sure enough, when they strolled through the doors, the gathering chatter ceased as everyone noticed the principal joining them.

Will made eye contact with the most senior kid in the gym, DeShawn Willis. Class president, about to graduate as valedictorian, and accepted into the co-op education program at Queen's University. In five years, DeShawn might just come back to Pine Harbour and work for Will— if he was lucky.

The young man was going to make an amazing gym teacher one day.

Today, Will needed him to be a peer mentor for Sam. To lead by example and model a kind of grace kids sometimes came by naturally, and other times had to be dragged to reluctantly. The hardest part of being a teacher was figuring out which path to take. Let them sort it out? Or push them to get over their differences before things festered to a point beyond repair.

DeShawn nodded to Sam, then cleared his throat. "All right. Let's go. You playing, Mr. Kincaid?"

"I sure am." Will grabbed a ball from the rack at the side of the gym and tossed it to Sam, who held it for a second, then muttered something that sounded suspiciously like *fuck it* under his breath before dribbling the ball a few times.

Will waited.

Sam sighed, glanced sideways at DeShawn, then back at Will. "What do you play? To nine points?"

"Sure, that works."

Sam made a half-assed attempt at the basket, and Will got control of the ball. But as soon as their positions were swapped, and it was Will's turn to take the ball back behind the free throw line, Sam's attitude became an advantage. His mulish obstinance lent itself to defence. It didn't matter that Will was taller and broader than the kid.

Will had to go back and forth a couple of times, looking for his opportunity to shoot. Sam trash talked him, but inside the bounds of school appropriate language, so Will gave back a bit. "What are you gonna do next, son?"

"Not gonna let you make this shot, that's what."

And he didn't. The short little son of a gun blocked Will twice, then stole the ball.

From in front of the next net, someone applauded, and then slowly everyone came over to watch them play.

Will had intended to let the kid win.

He didn't realize how hard it would be to not be absolutely trounced by Sam.

"Why aren't you on the basketball team?" he asked when Sam reached the nine points needed for victory.

The kid shrugged.

DeShawn tapped his arm. "You want to play me next?"

"You as easy to beat as the principal?"

Will groaned, and DeShawn laughed. "Almost."

Which wasn't true, at all, and their evenly matched skills made it an entertaining game to watch. When they finished, a grade eleven girl challenged Will to a game, so he played with her, keeping an ear out for the conversation between the two boys at the same time.

"Next year, someone else will have to show these guys how to shoot." DeShawn flicked the ball to Sam. "That gonna be you?"

"Depends how often the principal gives me detention in the form of a group participation event."

"If you show up voluntarily, you get credit for it and shit. Looks good on a resume."

Sam snorted. "I'll never get a job in this town."

"Not with that attitude you won't." DeShawn slapped the ball away. "Come on. Show me what you've got."

That part of their conversation stuck with Will, and came back when he headed outside after the students were all gone.

He usually didn't have any problems connecting to kids. But something about Sam—well, Sam wasn't a kid. That was the problem. He was older than his years, and Will didn't know how to deal with that. He probably wouldn't sort it out before the end of the school year, and then the kid—young man—would have all summer to resent having to come back to these halls and be seen as not ready for anything yet.

As Will walked to his truck, he added two things to his to-do list for the following morning.

- get to school early enough to practice his free throw in privacy
- look into summer jobs for fifteen-year-olds

He hoped search and rescue training would be boring as hell. He wasn't sure he had the bandwidth for anything else to land on his plate right now.

———

CATIE HAD twenty minutes before she needed to be at the Search and Rescue Training Centre. That meant she had time to squeeze in one more appointment.

This one was both personal and professional.

Mac's Diner sat on the outskirts of Pine Harbour, taking up a sprawling chunk that bordered on a forest. Just inside those dense woods was a popular snowmobile trail, giving the owner a rare, steady supply of winter customers. In the summer, it was a popular stop for locals and tourists alike.

And once upon a time, it had been Catie's first workplace. She started with bussing and doing the dishes, then graduated to being a waitress when her mother got her real estate license and left the position.

Of all the residents of Pine Harbour, the man in the kitchen was by far the one she was closest to. Frank Jenkins was a cross between a mentor and a father figure to her.

And today, she had the slightly awkward but mostly delightful task of finding out how his love life was doing now that she'd played matchmaker.

Frank had been the unlikely (to some, not Catie) star of the recent bachelor auction. In her first year organizing it, she'd tossed out the previous guidelines and gone in a different direction entirely. Fewer boring hot guys, a wider range of ages, gender, and personality types on the auction block, and a hell of a lot more money raised for the Pine Harbour Animal Shelter.

A win-win for everyone, but especially Frank, whose date on auction had been five nights of dinner, personally prepared by Pine Harbour's favourite cook, and served in the winner's choice of locations: the corner booth at the diner, a special guest table in the diner's kitchen, or at the winner's residence on Frank's nights off.

While Catie had maintained a certain distance from observing how all that went down, she'd kept her ear to the ground, and town gossip reported the winner—Moira Calhoun—had taken Frank up on all three of those options, in progressive order, and then Frank had taken two extra nights off.

Frank never took extra nights off.

Catie had swallowed her curiosity, but two months had passed without any further gossip about Frank and Moira. Even the unkind whispers from people like Frances had faded away. That part was a relief. Catie hated the way Frances layered unnecessary judgement on otherwise understandable curiosity. And she would know how it felt —it had been pointed her way more than once.

But if Frank was the reason things with Moira were going cold, Catie wanted to intervene. It was time to bring it up with the man himself.

She took off her hot pink blazer and hung it on a hanger she kept in the back of her car. Then she touched up her lip gloss before heading inside.

In the diner, she waved at the waitress, but didn't break her stride as she headed straight to the kitchen.

"Hairnet," Frank barked when she stepped inside.

She rolled her eyes, but complied with his request. "Nice to see you, too."

"I've been swamped." His lips twitched in an almost smile. "Ever since that bachelor auction of yours, there's a whole new wave of regulars here."

"I'm so sorry to hear that," she mocked gently.

"That wasn't very subtle, the way you did that. High-lighting local businesses."

Other people she had talked onto the auction block included her friend Lore D'Angelo, a bartender at The Green Hedgehog; Esther Kim, a local radio personality who also owned an art gallery on the highway; and Campbell Mills, who owned a moving company that employed army veterans.

"I wasn't trying to be subtle. Then, or now. I came in to ask how things are going with Moira."

"What kind of things?" He moved to the window that overlooked the dining room and pulled a new order off the carousel.

"Have you talked to her recently?"

"She comes in sometimes."

"Frank!"

He wagged his finger at her. "Catie, I see you playing matchmaker. That's not subtle, either. It's not necessary. Don't you worry about me and that woman."

"You were our top bachelor because *that woman* wanted to have dinner with you five nights in a row."

"It was fun."

"Frank, the rumour mill is churning." A slight exaggeration for effect. "She *likes* you." No exaggeration there.

"And I like her."

"So maybe you should call her."

"Why?"

"So you can see her again."

"I don't know if I want to." He shrugged.

She threw her hands in the air. "What am I going to do with you?"

"Not fix me up with anyone else." He tossed some onions on the grill. "I didn't mind doing the auction. That was fun. And it was also fun spending a week feeding Moira. Sure. But I don't want a girlfriend. At my age?" He laughed. "Listen, missy. You want for others what you really want for yourself. The sooner you realize that it's *you* you should be setting up on dates, and not everyone around you, the happier you will be."

Catie propped one hand on her hip. "Don't worry about me. Finding someone to crush on is on my to-do list. But I can't force the issue, not until Mr. Right moves to

Pine Harbour. Whereas your Ms. Right spent fifteen hundred dollars to hang out with you."

"It was a tax-deductible donation that Moira would have made anyway, in honour of her three cats."

"We'll agree to disagree, and I'll follow up next month."

Frank laughed. "You've got me in your calendar for welfare checks, have you?"

"Someone has to!"

"All right." He jerked his head to the front. "Go on, get out of here. But come back soon, because I like your face. Are you staying to eat?"

She shook her head in the negative. "I have a thing."

"You always do."

"I like to keep busy." She stopped at the door. "Hey, can I put you on the auction block next year?"

"Maybe."

"Moira might bid on you again."

"And if she does, I'll be happy to spend another five days with her at that point."

3

———————

CATIE HAD BEEN inside the Search and Rescue Team's training building three times before. Once, when she picked up the application form in the fall, again when she returned it two months ago, and last Friday for the official try-out.

Each of those times, the only person there was Tom Minelli, the park ranger who also served as the SAR manager. Now that she was officially joining the team, she'd be introduced to everyone else.

She wasn't the only new member today. Her friend Lore had also been specifically recruited by Tom, both of them being added to increase the gender diversity on the team.

It was the latest commitment Catie had made to this town where she grew up, this town she had once fled from, and had now come back to almost by accident. And ever since she returned, she'd found herself volunteering to change everything that she didn't like about Pine Harbour growing up.

Not that twelve-year-old Catie had any opinion about

the SAR. But when thirty-year-old Catie heard last fall that the team was overwhelmingly male, and they were looking to change that, she reached out. What would it entail? And could she find volunteers for Tom?

She liked making connections for people. It served her well as a real estate agent, and helped her as a hairdresser, too. As she showed people through homes and when they sat in her chair at the salon, they opened up and told her their problems.

If she could provide a resource that would lead to a solution, that made her happy. But more importantly, it made life a bit easier for those people, which in turn made the town better, and in a long chain reaction of events, more welcoming and therefore appealing to new residents.

Deep down, she knew what she wanted most of all in Pine Harbour was fresh blood, and to welcome those newcomers with open arms.

Which reminded her—she needed to set up a meeting with the defunct Welcome Wagon coordinators and see if they could get something started in that arena again.

Her calendar groaned at the thought, because all those months ago, Catie hadn't been able to find many women or non-binary friends to volunteer for the SAR. So she threw herself into a winter-long physical training program, with the help of Isla, who used to be a captain in the army.

At least Catie wasn't bored. That was the glass-half-full way to look at what she was juggling over the summer.

Inside, Tom greeted her and pointed her in the direction of the kitchenette, where she was pouring herself a cup of coffee when Will walked in. She was prepared for this moment, because she had the advantage—*she* knew he was on the search and rescue team.

He, on the other hand, had no idea she was part of the

new trainee class.

It was probably a bit of dirty pool, keeping this information from him. On the other hand, it wasn't like he was a big fan of getting updates from her. And at some point over the spring, when he got tight-lipped and cool towards her, she decided she didn't need to go out of her way to be fair.

If she bent at all in the direction of fair, when he didn't go out of his way for her in the slightest, it would get all off-balance and weird. And her feelings about him were weird enough already.

He looked like he had come straight from work, wearing a dark blue polo shirt over slim-cut khaki pants. It was weird how she had a catalogue in her head of his different looks. This was what he wore to school most of the time. He wore a suit some of the time, but usually not. She didn't have a percentage, precisely, but maybe only ten percent of the time. (Definitely not more than fifteen percent. It wasn't once a week, which would be twenty—)

She cut the Hot Guy Math off in her head before she got to the part where she thought he looked best in the faded blue jeans and worn band shirts he wore on weekends.

It wasn't helpful for her brain to spend any time on the ways in which Will Kincaid's thighs filled out denim—or straight-front khakis, or his army uniform, for that matter —because the truth of the matter was, he didn't want her attention. Will didn't like Catie.

Once upon a time, he had been friendly. In the way he was friendly with every other person in town. And she'd inflated that general kindness to strangers into the potential for something else, something dangerously like the childhood crush she'd once had on him.

He was seven years older than her, so he'd barely known she existed as a teenager. She'd been in the same grade as his youngest brother, Adam, and there had always been something about the studious second oldest Kincaid brother that did it for her, even before she truly knew what that phrase meant.

Now her latent attraction to him—*past* latent attraction, she corrected—was bizarre, especially because he went out of his way to be downright rude whenever they shared the same space.

For example, the way his eyes flared wide as he approached the coffee carafe and found her lounging next to it. "What are you doing?"

"Having a cup of coffee."

"And why are you doing that here?"

"I'm a new volunteer." She liked the cool, crisp way she said the last word. It made her sound unaffected by his presence.

"You can't—" When every other set of eyes within earshot turned in his direction, he set his jaw tightly and nodded. "Great."

"I'm looking forward to it." She nodded, too, then straightened up and sauntered past him, taking a chair.

The seats were arranged in an open circle, so everyone could see a white board on the wall—and still see everyone else sitting around the circle at the same time. Which meant she had a front row seat to observe Will, all tightly wound and bitter about God knows what.

He pulled a small notebook from his pocket and studied it carefully until all the seats were full and Tom stepped up alongside the whiteboard and wrote on it, *12 Weeks.*

Beneath that, he scrawled *August—OSRTC.*

"Today is the first day of a twelve-week training programme, as we onboard the new trainees. At the end of the training period, you'll complete your Basic Searcher certification test, and join the team for real. But as you all know from your intake interview with me, we are also actively recruiting team members who can compete in the Ontario Search and Rescue Team Competition in August. I'll pass it over to Will to explain a bit about that."

Will nodded curtly. As he talked, he looked at everyone in the room except Catie, although his voice didn't carry any of the tension from the coffee exchange. He sounded smooth and confident. "This seven-event test of skill, ability, knowledge, and endurance is like a heptathlon for SAR, and some of it requires experience, but we'll pair up new trainees with veteran team members to cover that off. This will be our first year competing, the first year we've had a big enough team to enter, so we have no expectations."

"But we do want to win," Tom interjected.

Will laughed, his mouth splitting wide into a white-toothed, laugh line bracketed grin, and everyone else joined in, even Catie, to her surprise. The way he chuckled, and kept going warmly, was infectious. "We will do our absolute best, but anyone who doesn't want to deal with our fearless leader's disappointment if we don't win should plan to carpool with someone else."

That led into an interesting overview of the logistics for the competition, and suddenly twenty minutes had zoomed by. Tom cut himself off as he was about to go into providing documentation for employers granting time off, and pulled up a chair.

"I'm getting ahead of myself. Can you tell I'm excited to have this many new trainees at once? I'm thrilled. We're a small town, and you all showed up. This is awesome. So to get us back to the twelve-week training schedule, tonight is a chance to get to know each other, and once we do that, I'll go over the gear we recommend you collect in the next three months. But first, we have a tradition when we welcome new members. We go around the room and share what made us want to join."

Tom went first, then nodded to the person next to him. One by one, everyone shared their story.

When it came to Will, Catie expected a variation of what she had just heard: a love of the outdoors, giving back to the community, or the appeal of learning new skills.

And it was all of that, in a sense, but not in the practiced, makes-for-great-PR kind of way the other origin stories were.

Instead, he looked at the floor and cleared his throat awkwardly. "I'm here because I lost a kid once. He went on an adventure, from school, in the dead of winter. It was the worst day of my professional career, and one of the worst in my entire life."

Tom gave all the new recruits a funny expression which made sense as soon as he interjected. "My nephew, in fact. But we found him, and got him back to his mom in one piece."

Will sighed and nodded. "It was impressive how Tom and the rest of the crew here worked together. Nothing I learned in the army or as a teacher quite compared to it, even with all the similarities in terms of training and professional guidelines. So I joined the Search and Rescue Team the next day. And it's been…what, five years?"

"Yeah, you're one of the old-timers now."

"I'll never forget the moment that Eric's teacher

reported him missing after recess." Will paused for a moment, raw emotion tightening his face. "I knew in my gut that he wasn't just in the bathroom, that he had left the school property. First I called 911. And then, after I handed that phone over to someone else in my office, I had to call his mother."

She could have heard a pin drop, the room was that still.

"Those moments are burned into my memory in a different kind of way. And understanding that kind of trauma is an important piece of doing search and rescue work. I resisted my first group debrief after a search. It felt unnecessary and invasive. But thanks to this group training, I knew it would help, and I knew my initial feelings around it were part of that trauma response. As searchers, we experience that differently than the family members or friends who report a missing person. I feel strongly about this piece of our work, and it has changed me as an educator as well, so if anyone has any questions about that, at any time, just reach out to me."

Obviously, Will cared about children—that was his chosen profession. But this was a deeper level of empathy, one that Catie hadn't expected from him. She'd thought he would be more about the business of education, rather than Mr. Big Feelings. It was nice to hear, and see.

Tom nodded. "Thanks, Will. That's great."

There were three people sitting between Will and Catie, and it took all three of their introductions for her to swallow around the lump that had formed in her throat. But when it was her turn, she pulled it together.

"How about you, Catie?"

"I heard you needed women for the competition," she admitted. "I feel like I should have a better reason than that, though. I really appreciate what everyone else has shared, and relate to many of the stories. I know what it's like to be an outsider, new to the Peninsula—I've done that twice, I guess—and how a newcomer's enthusiasm for the wild nature can get them into trouble. So if we're talking about ways to relate to the people we help, I understand that part of it."

"That's great, thank you." Tom crossed the room and picked up a backpack, stuffed to the brim. "Tonight we're going to go over gear. I'll cover what's in the pack, and then Will can go over tips and tricks for clothing."

Catie pulled out her phone and took notes on that as Tom started to pull items out and explain them. Some made sense—a survival blanket which doubled as a shelter, extra socks and toques, a fire starting kit, and a GPS locator beacon—but some were real surprises to her, like a handheld saw, which Tom said very matter-of-factly was great for patient extraction.

From the side of the pack, he held up a small notebook just like the one Will had his notes in, and explained—as Catie scribbled yet another note in her phone—that technology couldn't be relied on and batteries drained, but paper and pencil were pretty reliable.

She made a note to stock up on both.

"And now, we'll talk clothing."

Will stepped forward and picked up the backpack. "Our first clue about what works best in clothing actually comes from this pack. We highly recommend this particular brand because of the colour of the rain cover on it." He unfurled it, a bright blue flutter of nylon. "In addition to keeping your bag and its contents dry while you're on the move, this cover also makes it easy for your teammates to keep track of you in the brush."

He showed them the helmets they would wear on searches, complete with zebra lights, and the different kind of flashlights they also recommended.

"So we can make ourselves visible like this, but the easiest way is to be dressed for visibility when you leave the house to respond to a page. No camouflage clothes. No all black. We're the opposite of tactical gear here. We love bright clothes, brightly coloured gear." Even though he wasn't wearing that himself—and nobody was, really, because this was a classroom training night—Catie still felt like he was making a pointed comment about her outfit, which was basic black from head to toe.

She'd worn a bright pink blazer over it all day, she wanted to protest. But she'd taken it off when she visited Frank, and then left it in the car, because her cheeriest real estate agent outfit hadn't seemed appropriate for SAR.

If he wanted bright, next week she would give him *bright.* Next week, she'd come dressed in Day-Glo orange and glittery clown shoes.

Will handed over the floor back to Tom. "The last thing we want to do today is get everyone's contact information updated. Once you're a fully trained member of the team, you'll get a pager to wear twenty-four/seven, but until then, if there's a search we can safely bring trainees on, you'll get a text message or a call from a teammate. So make sure everyone's name and number is in your phone, so you don't ignore any important calls. Got it?"

There was a chorus of *got it,* then the noise settled down to a low hum as they took turns moving around the room, exchanging contact information with everyone.

"I'm Jeong Kim," one of the other newcomers said. "Nice to meet you. I recognize you from the bachelor auction. My cousin Esther was one of the bachelors, so to speak?"

"Right! Nice to meet you. Catie Berton. My number…" And so it went, around the room.

The second last person she exchanged information with was Will. He didn't even do any perfunctory introduction, not that any was needed.

Hi, I'm Will. You went to school with my brother, work across the street from my sister-in-law, and are a general pain in my ass.

So glad to be on a team with you, Will. I'm Catie. You might remember from such hits as Hey, you could be the MC, *and* Can I help with your school thing? *I remember the stone cold radio silence to both requests. Awkward, huh?*

But they didn't say any of that. Instead, she nodded at his phone, and when he jerked his chin in acknowledgement, she rhymed off her phone number. She noticed he put it in his address book as *Catie SAR*, so she did the same when she created a contact profile for him.

Will SAR.

But as soon as he headed for the door, his long legs getting him away from her as soon as humanly possible, she changed that to *Mr. Grumpy.*

Which Lore saw as she pulled alongside. "Who got that name, Will Kincaid?"

"It's a long story."

"You think he's grumpy?"

The truth would invite more curiosity, which Catie didn't want. She waved her hand. "It's kind of a joke, really." She changed the name back on her screen. "See? It's all good. Can't wait for next week. This is going to be great."

4

———

A WEEK LATER, Will made sure to arrive ten minutes early for training.

He was surprised Catie beat him there. She was waiting outside the training building, which was still locked. For at least the moment, they were alone.

Maybe he could kill a few minutes doing something in his truck. Except as soon as he turned it off, she looked his way.

She'd been typing something into her phone, but now she slipped that into a bright pink running belt around her waist. She was also wearing neon-yellow running pants and a teal long-sleeved tech shirt. Someone had done her reading on the gear, although the skin-tight pants had a noticeable lack of pockets.

Not that Will was trying to notice anything about Catie's lower body.

He was, in fact, trying *not* to notice the way she looked in those pants—*fucking hot*—and instead tried to assess her as a new colleague. Eager, enthusiastic.

Sharply critical of everything he did. Well, there was

that, too. It wouldn't be long before she tried to take over SAR, but unlike everything else she shoved her bossy little fingers into, the SAR was properly managed by Tom.

And it was Tom's leadership that had brought Catie into yet another part of Will's life, on his absolutely correct mission to recruit a more diverse crew.

So Will could not, would not complain, even to himself, about the presence of Catie's brightly clad ass in front of him. Even if it annoyed him to his core, for reasons he knew were petty and wrong and beneath him.

He pushed open his truck door and climbed out.

She gave him a look, a curved eyebrow, that was part surprise and part sardonic critique of his choice to get out when it was only the two of them there. *Why aren't you waiting in your truck?*

An excellent question.

"Nice to see you here early." He had to force himself not to wince at the way it sounded. Absurdly judgmental.

"Same to you." She said it like it wasn't nice at all.

The barb hooked in his skin, making him advance on her, until he could see the bright blue flecks in her otherwise dark blue eyes. Until he noticed the little wisps of blond hair at her temple that couldn't be tamed super flat and sleek like the rest of her bob.

He was tempted to tell her straight-irons didn't work in the wilderness, a truly unnecessary thing to point out. For one thing, she definitely already knew that. For another, this was a training night, and she'd come from work, where straight irons definitely did work, because that was her whole job.

He cast about in his mind for a better, sharper critique. He couldn't find one. So he grabbed onto sowing doubt, another jerk move he couldn't stop himself from making.

"You know, SAR is a big time commitment. There's no shame in saying it's too much at any point in the process."

"I'm aware. I've been thinking about doing this for six months. I talked to Tom and did my research. I even trained with Isla, so I knew the physical side of it wouldn't be too much."

"You've just got a lot on your plate."

"Pot, meet kettle. Kettle, this is Pot. His name is Will and he is a school principal, as well as being in the army reserve, the volunteer fire brigade *and* a Search and Rescue team member. Plus he has four brothers who, while all grown men, seem to—"

"Hey, leave my brothers out of it. And I quit the volunteer fire brigade when Adam became a full-time firefighter." He frowned. "Point taken, though."

"I hadn't even gotten to the point, yet." She crossed her arms over her chest. "You owe me an email."

Oh. That. "About the business club."

"Yes."

"Speaking of having too many things on one's plate."

"It's not until the fall, when this weekly training will be over. And isn't my schedule *mine* to worry about? Look, if you don't want me to do it, just have the balls to say that."

"It's not—" Could he handle having her in his school every single week? Could he admit that he wasn't sure he *could*? "Right now, we're focused on the end of this school year. We won't be making a decision about the business club until the middle of the summer."

"That's not what January said." Catie's face practically lit up as Will felt himself scowl.

January was—

Just doing her job.

Before he could reply, two more vehicles arrived, and

they were no longer alone. Negotiating this awkward tension with Catie was hard enough when it was just the two of them, he didn't want to do it in front of an audience, so he drifted off to speak to Jeong, and she went back to her phone, one bright yellow leg crossed over the other, her chin set at a determined angle.

Once they were seated around the circle, Tom asked everyone to share their progress on their gear checklists: what they had found they already owned, and what they had put on their to-acquire list. It was each person's responsibility to kit themselves, but the SAR had loaner items to fill the gaps during training.

Catie proudly shared that she'd already ordered the recommended backpack with the bright blue rain cover, and she looked pointedly at Will when she mentioned the colour. He tried not to roll his eyes.

"And you're setting a great example for the brightly coloured clothing," Tom said cheerfully.

Catie beamed.

This time, he definitely failed in his efforts to stop the eye-roll.

Tom pointed to the whiteboard, where a list of their training objectives was posted. "All right, I think it's time we head outside. We'll pair up for a training exercise."

From across the room, Lore gave Catie a conspiratorial smile, and the two of them headed outside together.

Will trailed behind, watching the yellow leggings, and the pink running belt, and the straight-ironed hair that swished perfectly against her shoulders.

"All right, so the seven events in the competition are as follows: ground search technique; rescue mission planning; team communication—and this one is about radio comms; equipment test, so this will be a hike out and then needing to use what we have in our bags; rope rescue; carry out; and first aid. Today we're going to work on two of these. I'll split you into pairs, and you'll be given either a rescue mission planning assignment, or a radio comms script. For the latter, it's basically about memorizing the standard comms language. For the first one, there's an order of operations, but it's also about taking your time. So we'll want to pair up, new trainees with veteran team members, and then I'll hand out the practice cards."

The group rearranged itself, and since Will was at the back, the pairing up happened in front of him. The two last newbies were Lore and Catie, and as Catie realized who their options were, she looked Will up and down, then shoved Lore in the direction of Yolanda Clarke.

"Looks like it's you and me, Kincaid," Catie said a little too brightly.

If he had said it, it would have been an overture. It should have been him who said, "Well, Berton, I guess we're left."

No, he should have welcomed her first. Before anyone else paired up, he should have said, "Hey, Catie. Do you want to practice with me?"

That would have been an overture, a gesture of good faith.

Accepting her challenging dare when there was no other choice was hardly the same.

Somewhere along the way, he and Catie had lost the kindness that was the core of what being a good, upstanding citizen of Pine Harbour meant. And Will prided himself on being a good, upstanding citizen. It was the driving force of his life. It was the lesson his father had taught him. It was the example he set for his brothers. And with one single exception, he had done it his whole adult life.

With everyone except for Catie.

That had to stop now.

"Sounds like a plan," he said gruffly. It sounded resentful, even to his own ears.

———

WILL WAS A PILL, even when he was trying to be nice. Nice-ish. That's all he could manage to be around her. By the end of the training night, Catie considered re-naming him Will the Pill in her phone, but with her luck, someone would see it and it would get back to him.

So when training finally ended, she didn't head straight home. Instead, she went to the diner, the only place she could get a slice of Isla's pie at this hour. Even though she'd worked all day, she was vibrating with a tired kind of energy, too.

Pour some sugar on these weird feelings. That's almost certainly going to help. She ignored that sensible self-talk, and pulled into the gravel lot.

She parked next to Frank's car—the same car he had been driving for fifteen years—and went inside.

Her former boss was in his usual spot in the kitchen, visible through the pass-through window. She waved, then joined two familiar looking faces at the counter. Bailey Patel and Kerry Humphrey both played soccer with Lore, and Catie had gotten to know them both through that social group. Bailey also worked part-time at Isla's bakery, and Kerry was married to Will's older brother, Owen.

Small town life to the max.

Six degrees of Kincaids, and most of the time you never made it past one degree of separation.

Catie slid onto the stool next to Bailey. "What are you guys doing here so late?"

Kerry patted her pregnant belly. "Owen is working tonight, I'm on call, and baby wanted French fries."

Bailey grinned. "I wanted French fries, too, so I'm keeping her company."

"She's telling me about her plans to take over the world."

The waitress came over, an apology written all over her face. "I'm sorry, hon. The kitchen's closed, but we've got some pie."

Through the pass-through window, Frank barked a correction. "The kitchen's never closed for Catie."

She appreciated the offer, but she waved him off. "I actually came here for a slice of whatever is left."

"It's rhubarb custard."

"Oh my God, *yes*. Perfect." And she nodded to the coffee carafe behind the waitress, the one with the blue handle, which had indicated it was decaf since before she was a waitress here back in her teens. "I'll take a cup of that, too."

"Long day?" asked Bailey.

"Managing fragile personalities is a lot." Catie hadn't intended to confess anything to her friends, especially not Kerry. But she didn't need to get specific. Generalities were more than sufficient for venting her frustration.

Kerry's pager went off, though, a small gift from the universe, and the midwife excused herself, leaving Catie and Bailey alone at the counter.

"Tell me about your world domination plans."

"Actually, they require your help." Bailey's eyes

sparkled. "What do you know about the motel behind the marina?"

"It's abandoned." Catie accepted the steaming cup of coffee from the waitress and added cream and sugar. She took a long, restorative sip before continuing. "It hasn't been listed for sale in the three years I've been here. I can look up the property history when I get home. Are you interested in buying it?"

"My cousin is looking for an investment property. Boutique motels are popping up all over, it feels like a good trend to get ahead of, and I've studied the vacancy rates at other motels on the peninsula—they're all doing just fine, even without significant online presence. That's where the right team could have a huge advantage."

"I like it. Very exciting. I'll get you some numbers in a couple of days and we can talk strategy for approaching the current owner with an offer."

"Thank you." Bailey pointed a fry at her. "Now, your turn. Who is the fragile personality today?"

"I shouldn't say."

"I swear it won't leave this counter."

"You promise?" Catie took a deep breath. "I have this ongoing…thing. A feud, you might call it, except it's more subtle than that. It actually sounds silly to say out loud, but I keep bumping heads with Will Kincaid via email, and now it's super awkward in person."

Bailey made the same face Lore had made, disbelief mixed with confusion. "Really?"

"I know, it's weird, right? He has the nicest reputation. Literally everyone loves him. And then with me he's a grumpy ogre. Like he's mad I walked over his bridge or something." She stabbed at her pie, which didn't deserve the aggression. It was a very good pie.

"What were the emails about?"

"He wanted to insert himself into the bachelor auction. I wanted to improve the way kids from the school cleaned windows. He ruined my singing telegram fundraiser by doing it with cuter, smaller telegrams."

"Kids?"

"His ace in the hole." Catie groaned as Bailey laughed. "I know, it all sounds so terribly petty, doesn't it? And now I've joined the Search and Rescue team, which he is on, and tonight we were partners. It was, once again, petty and awkward. It's like we've both lost the ability to be reasonable grown-ups."

"Did you know he was on the team when you joined?"

"Yes." Catie made a face and stabbed her pie again. *Sorry, pie.* She ate the last bite with more tenderness, savouring the creamy and tart combination before offering what she knew sounded like a weak explanation. "They needed women."

"Ah."

"What, ah?"

"You just can't resist a good cause," Bailey said.

"She's right," Frank yelled from the kitchen.

Catie pushed her plate away. They weren't wrong. "So I need to find a way to smooth things over, but I'm not going to pretend like I started this. I didn't. That's on him."

"Of course." Bailey gave a fierce nod. "I'm on Team Catie."

"We don't need teams. We're all on Team Pine Harbour." It was a bit of a line. Catie didn't really believe that Will shared her vision for the town. Not exactly. But his vision for the town probably aligned with hers in at least a few ways, so she could work with that.

"Sure, but if it comes to fisticuffs in the street…" Bailey giggled. "I'm high on French fries, I'll see myself out."

"Another slice of pie, honey?" The waitress pointed to the display stand. "There's one more."

"Box it up and I'll take it home." Catie slid off the stool as Bailey paid her bill. "I'm going to help Frank clean up."

"Go home," he barked through the window. "Get some sleep and don't let that Kincaid boy bother you."

"He's a thirty-eight-year-old man, not a boy, and you shouldn't be listening to private conversations."

"Then don't have them in my restaurant."

Catie grinned.

As they walked to their cars, Bailey resumed the conversation. "Seriously, good luck with Will. And if he proves to be too much to handle, there's no shame in changing your mind. You've got a lot on your plate. Two jobs, volunteer commitments…you don't need to manage a man child at the same time."

"He's not a—" Catie cut herself off. Will didn't need her to defend him. "It didn't help that I had a long day of work first."

"Maybe you need help in the shop, then." Bailey got a gleam in her eye.

Catie laughed. "I don't think I can afford you, Ms. World Domination."

"No, I don't want another part-time job. But is there anything that could be offloaded? Summer break is around the corner. I bet there will be lots of students looking for work."

Catie thought about that idea as she drove home.

When she first moved to Pine Harbour and opened her salon, there wasn't enough foot traffic or repeat customers to cover the mortgage on her store and her house. It had bothered her that she'd let her optimism uproot her from the city, where she'd thought she'd never be able to have her own salon and a home, only to land back in Pine Harbour and still need her real estate license—something her mother had helped her get into—to make ends meet.

Although this time she wasn't just paying rent on an apartment and a chair in a salon. This time she was investing in herself, and she had to admit, she liked dabbling in real estate on the side. The challenge Bailey had given her tonight, for example. She loved the spontaneous project of digging into the history of a property and crafting the right offer pitch to take to the owners.

And now, both her businesses were stable and she was doing well.

Bailey was right. Catie needed help. Someone who could clean up while she was with clients, and who could answer the phone and fill in appointments, so she wasn't constantly getting back to people and spending an hour tidying at the end of each day. The problem was, she was so used to doing it all herself. Truthfully, she assumed that she would always have to go it alone. But she liked the idea of hiring a high school student, someone who she would be helping in return. She'd never forget that Frank gave her a chance when she was just a kid, and the hours she spent working at the diner made it that much easier to get out of town the second she graduated high school.

Her street was quiet, most houses already dark for the night. Across the road, Frances Schmidt's living room light was on, but it turned off as soon as Catie got out of her car. Was she just as much of a creeper as her neighbour for noticing?

She let herself into her tidy little bungalow. Once upon a time, this had been a rundown rental property, and the landlord had given them a deal on the first month's rent because Catie's mom had agreed to clean it herself. It was their home for thirteen years, rented the whole time, until Catie moved to the city—and Suzanne followed not long after.

Catie rubbed her chest and made a face at the wave of feelings. Maybe she should eat the second piece of pie now instead of saving it for breakfast. She wandered into the kitchen, with the oversized butcher block island. It was the first change she made after she bought the house.

As sometimes happened when she was alone in her kitchen, that first weekend visit back to Pine Harbour rolled through her mind. She'd come up to fulfil a promise to her mother, only to discover while at Mac's for lunch that the house they had once rented was for sale—and at a price she could afford.

It had been a sign.

It was small and simple, but it was hers.

She'd meant for it to be a weekend getaway place, but only a few months after she took possession of the house, the storefront she now used as her salon was listed.

Another sign, Frank had said. That one was more of a stretch, financially, especially after she gave notice at the salon in the city.

Somehow, suddenly, she had become a Pine Harbour full-time resident again. There were a few nosy questions about her return from people like Frances, but most of Catie's own generation didn't question her reappearance.

It had been a good three years. For the most part, she hadn't looked back. It felt right to be back in Pine Harbour, in a bittersweet way. Right, but there was still a lot to do before it felt like the home her mother once imagined for her five-year-old daughter.

She ran a hot bubble bath and sank into it, thinking about Bailey's advice.

Climbed into bed thinking about Will Kincaid and their stupid feud.

The next morning, she put a sign in the window at the salon, then snapped a picture and posted it on social media, too. Catie Berton was officially hiring part-time help for the summer.

High school students were encouraged to apply.

5

WILL WENT OUT of his way to not be on social media, because in a small town, there was a slim-to-none chance of avoiding seeing what his students were doing on the weekend, and they all benefited from him just not looking in the first place.

And yet somehow, by Saturday morning, no fewer than six separate people had told him that Catie was looking to hire a high school student for the summer. His brother Josh, Bailey Patel, his sister-in-law Isla, Olivia Minelli, and both Frances Schmidt and her daughter Ashley, who had just graduated from nursing school, and was suddenly everywhere Will looked.

He replied to Josh, Bailey, Isla, and Olivia with his thanks. He left the messages from the Schmidt mother/daughter duo unread, and didn't feel bad about it. The two of them needed to learn that he wasn't accessible to them like that.

Will prided himself on his ability to draw clear boundaries—especially with mothers who had decided Will might make a good son-in-law.

He wouldn't. He had his hands full with his own family.

It wasn't that he didn't want to get married. He always had, but in the future.

Of course, now he was well and truly into whatever theoretical definition of *the future* his 25-year-old self might have had, and he still hadn't met the right woman yet.

When he did, though, it wouldn't be someone who brought her own family drama to the table. It would be someone like him, with healthy boundaries and a focus on their career.

It was easier to describe who it wouldn't be. Anyone like Ashley Schmidt, who was sixteen years younger than him. He wanted someone his own age, someone gentle and calm. A balm to come home to at the end of the day.

His mind flipped immediately to another *definitely not* example. Catie Berton. It occurred to him that she might be hiring a high school student to make a point or get back at him for the awkward training session two nights earlier. Not that hiring one of his students made sense as retribution, but nothing that had gone on between them made any sense.

Not only was she a strong example of what he didn't want in a partner, but her very existence as a thorn in his side—a complete and utter distraction—made the thought of trying to date utterly impossible.

He pulled out his phone and added *figure out Catie's motives* beneath *email Catie back about the business club* and *tell Sam to apply for a job at Catie's salon*. She had her own sub-list on his to-do list, and Will didn't like that it was growing.

The sound of propellers cut through the still early morning air, and he glanced up at the sky. After watching

Seth's float plane circle around to land, he sent Josh another text message.

Will: He's here and I'm sitting across from your garage, wake the fuck up.
Josh: *hits snooze on the brother texts*
Will: Seth needs to be back here by nine to pick up his passengers.
Josh: I need a shower.
Will: Fine, meet us at the diner.

He met Seth on the dock, then followed as his brother popped into the marina office, where August Howe, January's sister, was yawning over a cup of coffee. One of her kids, Summer, had a steaming cup of what Will was assuming was hot chocolate, and waved at him. "Hi, Mr. Kincaid."

He leaned against the counter. "Helping your mom this morning?"

Summer nodded solemnly. "She says I can work for her this summer."

"That's exciting. What are you going to do?"

"I don't know. I haven't started my training yet."

Seth glanced over from where he was signing papers. "Maybe you'll help my passengers check in."

"You're the pilot who's going to be flying out of here?" Summer gave Will's brother the once over.

Seth nodded his head sideways. "And Principal Kincaid's brother. My name is Seth."

"I'm Summer."

"Nice to meet you. What grade are you in?"

"Six."

"Ooh, good grade." Seth grinned. "All right, I'll be

back in an hour and a half. If they show up early, Summer, you're in charge."

As soon as they were outside, Will spread his arms wide. "Uh, is there something you want to share with the class? You're going to fly out of the marina now? I thought today was a one-off charter."

"Turns out there's some demand for flights from the area. And…" Seth shrugged. "August can use the rent. So we're going to test this out. I've opened my schedule for three times a week for the summer."

"That's awesome." Will grinned. "Motivation to get my Duster road-worthy. You can drive my truck while you're here."

He was slowly restoring a vintage two-door Plymouth coupe with his brothers. It was one part lifelong dream, two parts brother bonding fuel.

But Seth shook his head at the offer. "I'm not going to be here long enough to need wheels. I'll be here more frequently, but just like this. A few hours at a time. I can hang at Josh's garage if nobody else is available for coffee or whatever."

Will didn't bother pushing the conversation around Seth moving home. Josh had moved home after more than a decade in the States on the racing circuit. One day, Seth would come back for good, too.

It didn't pay to put any pressure on them. Every Kincaid had to find their own path, and it took each of them a different length of time. "At least we get to have breakfast together more often."

"Family bonding time. Priceless." Seth smirked, but it was true.

Their relationship, the five brothers, meant absolutely everything to Will. He knew it did to each of his brothers as well. They all showed it in different ways, and needed different levels of attachment, but when push came to shove, it was always a brother who would be there. Even when you just needed someone to reflect back to you that yeah, you were being a jerk.

They were the first ones to arrive at Mac's. They snagged the corner booth that was big enough for five grown men to sprawl out in, and ordered coffee.

"How's school? All the munchkins restless for summer break?"

Will snorted. "The munchkins, the teachers, and the growling teenagers, too."

"Do you have any plans? Want to hitch a ride to a fly-in lodge one week?"

"Can't. I've committed to helping train the new Search and Rescue Team trainees." He made a face. "Although that's turned into a shitshow, too."

"Why?"

He hesitated. Adam, Josh, and Owen had all razzed Will about Catie in the past. But Seth didn't know about any of that. He gave his brother a brief, objective overview. "She's a pain in the ass. Constantly wanting to fix shit that isn't broken. But I should be able to handle her better than I do." He considered the situation as a whole. "It's possible I was a jerk to her. And now we're teammates, and it's awkward."

"Are you asking for advice?"

Will wasn't sure, but he didn't like the surprised tone in Seth's voice. "Why do you sound so shocked?"

"Because you're the one who gives advice." Seth shrugged and stroked his jaw. "What would you tell one of your teachers?"

"To leave personal stuff at the door, and deal with each other as professionals."

"There you go."

"But—" He cut himself off.

Seth's eyebrows lifted in blatant curiosity. "But *what?*"

"Nothing."

His brother narrowed his eyes.

Before it went any further, they were saved from that debate by the arrival of their three other brothers.

"What'd we miss?" Owen asked.

"Will has woman problems—"

"Seth doesn't want to move back to Pine Harbour—"

Owen reached between them and grabbed the menu. "Never mind, I don't need to know."

Adam nodded in agreement and waved to the waitress.

Josh snorted. "You traitors. Just because you're both happily married now doesn't mean you're above gossip. We clearly missed some good stuff."

"Is it good gossip, though?" Owen shrugged. "If it's the same old, same old, I'd rather order."

"And if you wanted to be in on the conversation, you could have caught a ride with me," Will pointed out, eager to jump on the *Owen's Stomach Saves the Day and Ends the Conversation* train.

Josh snorted. "Hard pass."

They all ordered, then Seth filled the others in on his new business plan.

"That's great. We'll get to do this more often," Adam said. "And Will can harass you about moving back home."

Josh nodded. "Will just misses having us crashing at his house."

"Will is sitting right here." The subject of their joking started to give his brothers the finger, but two of his students walked through the door and he converted the gesture to shoving his hand into his hair. "And I already pushed the issue earlier, which I tried to tell you all when you showed up."

"But the more important issue is that Will's empty house reminds him that the only woman who gives him any attention is his nemesis," Seth said.

Fuck.

The conversation around the table came to a screeching halt. Josh narrowed his eyes. Adam leaned back against the booth and crossed his arms over his chest. And Owen leaned in, which was the most dangerous of all—Owen going into Dad Mode with a ready lecture.

Will much preferred it when *he* was the one with the ready lecture. "My house does not feel empty."

"So you're not denying that Catie is your nemesis?"

"Wait," Josh growled. "The woman problems Will is having…we're back to Catie again? What's going on?"

"We're not back to— There's nothing going on here."

Seth looked at Josh. "I didn't know that we had covered Catie before. Why don't you fill me in on what you know and I will tell you—"

Will cut him off. "You won't tell him anything. I asked for your advice in confidence."

Owen frowned. "Why are you asking for advice from him? Why wouldn't you come to me?"

Adam thumped himself on the chest. "Or me. I'm great with women."

"You're a child," Will barked.

"I'm a married man. I'm 30 years old."

"In the context of the five of us, you're the baby. I'm not coming to you for advice. I'm not coming to anyone for advice. I didn't even ask Seth, it just sort of— I will sort out the Catie problem myself. Thank you. We don't need to talk about this again."

"So there *is* a Catie situation." Josh narrowed his eyes. "Is this still about how she didn't think you were hot enough for the bachelor auction? Your fee-fees are still bent out of shape because you like her and she doesn't like you?"

"Wait, you *like* this woman?" Seth shook his head. "Come on, man."

"It's complicated." Did he *like* Catie? He was attracted to her. And he liked how much she cared about Pine Harbour when her laundry list of things that needed to be changed weren't dumped on his own to-do list. He liked her earnestness. But he didn't like... Other things. None that he could specifically name at the moment, but there was a very long list of individual moments where she had annoyed him in the past, and there were certainly common threads to be found between those moments. But he didn't want to dwell on them, which is why he couldn't precisely name her egregious faults. "And it's a moot point, because she doesn't like me. It takes two to tango."

"You sound like a sixty-year-old when you say shit like that."

"That's part of my presentation to the kids about boundaries and respecting the fact that no means no, and I don't like you means no, and silence means no."

"*It takes two to tango.* I'm starting to see why you're struggling to connect with the high school kids."

"Fuck off."

Josh pointed at him. "There you go. That's more their language."

"Let's get back on topic." Seth was enjoying this way too much. "Will likes Catie—"

"Will does not like—" he tried to interject, but it didn't sound true, and his brothers didn't believe him anyway.

"—and he wishes he could have a do-over on their recent encounters."

Oh. Yeah, that part was very true. He nodded. "Somehow, I've turned into this grumpy shithead around her."

Owen scowled at him. "Being a grumpy jerk isn't attractive."

Seth howled, and Josh choked on the toast he'd just shoved in his mouth.

"Kerry seems to disagree," Adam drawled.

Will sighed. They'd derailed again. It was for the best. But now all he could think about was how Catie Berton had some thoughts about the codependent relationship he and his brothers had, and how it was sort of true, but mostly so much better than that sounded.

———

CATIE WOKE UP EARLY, for her, to meet Bailey at *Bake Sale!* for breakfast and real estate talk.

When she arrived at the bakery, Bailey was behind the counter, playing barista. "What can I get for you?"

"Extra-large flat white, please, and one of those savoury breakfast rolls. Oh, and a strawberry tart."

Bailey put two of everything on a tray, then they moved to a small table in the corner. Isla took over at the cash register.

"Here's what I know." Catie passed over a neatly printed page. "The property is abandoned, as you know, but up to date on property tax. Those taxes are being paid by a law firm in Port Elgin who represent the owner. It hasn't been listed for sale in the last decade. It's already zoned appropriately for commercial development, so it's unlikely they're holding out for the town to change that. I recommend a fair market value offer."

She handed over another sheet. "These are comparable properties that have sold in the last three years. None were abandoned for as long, and we would need a thorough inspection, but my guess is this property might sell for about the same as this one—" She pointed to the second on the page. "Or maybe even less."

"Can they get an inspection before making an offer?"

"We can ask."

Bailey bounced in her chair. "Excellent. My cousins are going to visit for the Canada Day weekend, and if they see the potential, we'll want to proceed."

"How involved are you going to be in the project?"

"I'm not sure. I like the idea. But I like a lot of ideas. And I don't see myself actually being the proprietor of the motel. Motelier?"

"Ooh, that has a ring to it. But not for you?"

"I don't think so."

"Fair enough. I can relate to wanting to tackle new projects. I have the salon and real estate to pay the bills, and the volunteer positions are the ones where I play musical chairs." Catie wrinkled her nose. "Not that I'm flighty about it. Just…I like change."

Bailey bit into her breakfast roll and nodded happily. It was a refreshing change to talk openly about changing things up—personally, or community-wise—and not get immediate push back. Catie joined in her silently devouring their breakfast.

As they finished, Isla approached, taking off her apron, her attention on the street.

"Bailey, can you take the counter again if anyone comes

in? Adam's here." The way Isla's face lit up when she caught sight of her husband's truck was a thing of absolute beauty.

Their friend had a rough first marriage and a rocky divorce. If anyone deserved the unreserved adoration of a hot firefighter—a younger man, no less—it was Isla. And a year into their marriage, it seemed like their love was only growing.

But Catie secretly believed that kind of true love was meant to be for most people, and the way Bailey's gaze followed Isla as she darted out the door and launched herself into Adam's arms made Catie want to play matchmaker for the younger woman.

"Speaking of community charities, it's not too soon to start thinking about next year's bachelor auction. Can I talk you into putting yourself on the auction block for a good cause?"

Bailey made a face.

"Think about it. Lore's still dating the woman who bid on her."

"I know!" Bailey grinned. "I'm thrilled for her. I don't know. Maybe. If I'm not dating someone by then..." She glanced out the window and sighed. "Look at them."

Catie followed her gaze. Adam brushed Isla's hair off her face, holding it out of the way so he could kiss her forehead.

If they were in a cartoon, hearts would appear above them.

"Forehead kisses are so sweet."

Catie snorted. "Forehead kisses are foreplay. I mean, yes, they're also very sweet, but that brush of lips on skin...the way he lingers like that? That's a deeply intimate promise of something to come." She stood up. "All right, I need to get to work. That hair won't cut itself. Let me know what your cousins think about the motel."

Outside, she waved hello to Adam, who looked like he wanted to say something to her, so she slowed to a stop. "Morning."

He nodded. "Yep."

Well, if he *had* had a thought, he was keeping it to himself. "See you 'round."

"Wait, Catie." He looked faintly embarrassed, the tops of his cheeks turning pink. "I don't want to get involved, but Will's a good guy."

"I'm aware." She cocked her head to one side and crossed her arms in front of her chest. "Don't want to get involved with *what*, exactly?"

"Nothing." Except clearly Will had said something to his brothers, about her.

"Your brother worries too much about what I think about him."

"We agree on that."

"And he should spend more time actually talking directly to me, rather than using intermediaries who have better people skills than him."

"Whoa, no. Hey. Uh, no. That's not…accurate. On the skills things, or that I'm some kind of intermediary. I'm not."

"Mm hmm." Across the street, she saw her first customer approach the front of the salon. "I have to go."

"I think you have him wrong, that's all."

"I have him exactly as he presents himself. Did he tell you about ignoring my emails? Business related ones?"

Adam visibly cringed. "No."

"Then maybe you don't know what you're talking about."

"All right." He frowned. "I can tell him—"

"Nope. Do not." She took a deep if shaky breath. "I would prefer if we pretended we didn't have this conversation, because you're a good guy."

"Sure thing." Adam shrugged.

She knew the feeling. This weirdness didn't make much sense. "Look, Will just needs to get over…well, all the things he thinks about me. But this is between him and me, and it's fine. Truly. Now I have to get to work, so excuse me."

"He didn't actually say anything. I was just inferring some shit. I'm sorry." Adam looked genuinely pained now.

Catie thought about offering him her strawberry tart, but he could just go inside and get his own. He had the inside track with the baker. "I believe you."

And the funny thing was, she really did.

Her feud with Will felt a bit like a mutual secret. Maybe a poorly kept one, because this was Pine Harbour after all, but she didn't want anyone else taking sides, as she'd said to Bailey the other night. For one thing, nobody else would believe her if she told them Will was a jerk. For another, as much as *she* liked to critique the principal, the thought of anyone else picking on him made her queasy.

Plus people would start picking sides, and he already had a built in hockey team with his immediate family. Exhibit A, Adam, trying to smooth things over, even when he didn't know what exactly had been ruffled out of place.

But an hour later, when Will strode into her salon in the middle of a busy Saturday morning, she thought it might be worth revisiting the secret nature of their quarrel. He scanned the space, searching for her, and when he found her, his gaze locked on her face. Serious, demanding. Like he wanted her to drop everything and tend to whatever urgent inquiry he had.

She jerked her head at the waiting area. *Take a chair, bud.*

He did. She finished the blowout she was doing, checked on highlights developing under the dryer, then made her way back to him. "Can I help you?"

"I'm here about the job posting you put up."

That was funny. "I don't think you're qualified, frankly."

He smirked. "I have a student who I think might be a good fit. He's a bit of a hot head. If I send him to you, can I ask that you treat him with care? I'm not asking you to hire the kid necessarily, but give him a good—"

"Wow, Will. What a backhanded way of telling me not to be mean to a *child*."

"He's fourteen."

"As I was saying." She rolled her eyes. "Tell him to send me his resume. If you think someone is a hot head, they might just be perfect for me."

"Yeah?"

"What? Do you think I'm going to punish some kid because you don't know how to be nice to me?"

"I can be nice to you."

"Evidence suggests otherwise."

He nodded. "All right. Challenge accepted."

She snorted. Sure, and pigs could fly.

"DO YOU TAKE WALK-IN APPOINTMENTS?"

Catie wanted to say yes—she never liked turning away a potential customer—but tonight was search and rescue training. Also known as, poke-the-bear night.

She couldn't be late to trade zingers with Will. "I'm sorry, I'm just closing up."

The customer made an appointment for the next day, then Catie locked the door behind them and quickly hustled through her clean up duties.

But when she arrived at the park, there were no zingers exchanged. Will didn't approach her before training, and he didn't roll his eyes at her once during the introduction to ground search techniques, even when she pulled out reflective wrist bands and a tie-dye neck gaiter to add to her already bright outfit for the night.

"Wouldn't want to blend into the trees," she said brightly.

No reaction at first. A slow blink, second. Then a smile. "Smart."

The same pattern repeated itself when they split into

small groups to discuss the different behaviours people exhibit when they get lost. She made a point of calling teenagers kids, twice, and both times he agreed with her without any hint of being annoyed. As if he didn't even remember their conversation in her salon.

He was going out of his way to be courteous. Polite. Reasonable. She might hate reasonable. Grumpiness felt like he cared at least. This polite professionalism was cool, calm, and probably fake.

She wanted him to be annoyed by her. Outwardly. Then she would know where she stood.

Tom gathered everyone back together. "Let's get outside and put this into practice. The person we're looking for today is a twelve-year-old girl named Yolanda." Everyone had a good chuckle at that, as Yolanda was in her fifties. "She is camping here in the provincial park with her family, and wandered away from their site a few hours ago. We've been assigned this quadrant to search."

As Tom gave them their instructions, Catie remembered the order of operations they practiced the week before. She was able to anticipate what he would say next, which gave her confidence that she was picking this up after only a few weeks.

They lined up in a row, alternating experienced searchers and trainees. Will was at the far end, next to Jeong, then Tom, then Lore, then a guy called Tobin—his last name—then Catie, and a few more people after her. Tom's clear instructions for what Yolanda was wearing rang in Catie's mind. She didn't have enough experience yet to recognize footprints or a newly broken trail, but she could keep her eyes peeled for movement, or clothing, or lost belongings.

As they moved into the brush, her thoughts wandered, annoyingly, to the man at the end of the line.

It was unrealistic to expect everyone in town to like her. That was a lesson she learned early in life, soon after they moved to Pine Harbour. Whispers about her mother —about why Catie didn't have a father (he's never been in the picture, apparently) about how flirtatious Suzanne was (gets around, that one does)—and then later on, about her, too.

She hated how much it mattered to her, even now, what other people thought of her. How deeply she wanted what had been denied to her as a child. She would give almost anything to make Pine Harbour into the ideal space her mother imagined it to be, but she knew now that wouldn't mean universal acceptance.

Her goals were smarter, now. Majority acceptance, and fuck the rest of them.

It worked for everyone except Will Kincaid.

She was saved from examining that too deeply by a glint of purple plastic ahead. "I have something here," she said loudly.

The whole line stopped, and she described the water bottle in front of her. They moved forward again, until she was close enough to pick it up. The vinyl name sticker on it read *Yolanda Clarke.*

SAR members were good about labelling their stuff.

"Let's radio that back to the search coordinator," Tom said, and Tobin went through those motions. That language was less familiar from the previous training, and Catie made a mental note to practice radio protocols more.

Then they resumed their ground search. The next person to find something was Jeong, who spotted a clear set of recent footprints, roughly the right size for Yolanda.

"If we map these two clues out, what does it tell us?"

"She might be moving in a diagonal direction north-west," Lore said.

Catie clapped for her friend when Tom confirmed that was exactly his thought, too.

"The most important thing to remember right now, in this moment, is that we need to ignore the instinct to turn and go in that direction. The search coordinator will dispatch a hasty team to follow that potential lead. We need to finish clearing our assigned area, because it's also possible she's moving in a zig-zag pattern, confused or disoriented, or just trying to self-correct."

If Catie were standing next to Will, she'd say something about it being more fun to go in search of the missing girl—to try to get his back up. But she didn't want to sound foolish in front of the others, so she swallowed the joke.

It was an interesting test of their focus, to keep searching per their instructions, and trust that another part of the search effort would take what they found and try to find the girl elsewhere. And it underlined for Catie that she'd never really been one to rely on a team for anything, and that made it interesting to her that she'd embraced SAR.

Their dedication paid off, because less than twenty yards ahead, they found Yolanda pretending to be asleep next to a tree.

Catie got to be the one to gently approach her, "wake up" the girl and give her back her water bottle. Then, declaring the practice a success, the line broke up into a spread out group for the trek back to the training centre.

After they debriefed, the last task of the night was supply inventory. While each searcher was responsible for their own gear, consumables like batteries, first aid supplies, and ropes were purchased with SAR donated funds.

She helped Yolanda with the first aid checklists, then drifted to where Tobin was testing batteries once that was done.

There were only four other people left when the batteries were all sorted again. Tom was going over gear with Lore and Jeong, and Will was working with a pile of rope on the other side of the big room.

She thought about leaving.

She *should* leave, but then Will glanced up, like he felt her watching him. His expression didn't change, but he held her gaze, and she found herself moving in his direction.

When she stopped next to him, he made an unexpected offer. "Do you want to learn about the rope? We'll be practicing with it next week and the week after."

Her response was uncharacteristically basic. "Sure."

No sarcastic retort, no bristle. She barely recognized herself in that single syllable, but as he launched into it, she shook off that confusing thought. He gave her a brief overview of the equipment, most of which she wouldn't remember, and then recommended a couple of YouTube channels to watch.

"Thanks."

He gave her a polite nod before returning to his task. A momentary flutter, a weird panic to hold his attention a little longer, rose inside her, and she pushed it back down.

Maybe it wasn't that Will *didn't* like her. Perhaps it was more that he just didn't *like* her, a subtle distinction. One she would learn to live with, because it was *fine* for someone to not *like* her. Expecting everyone to think she was the bee's knees was an impossible standard. She could only expect Will to do what everyone else on the team had done—make her feel welcome.

She moved to leave, and he looked up again. "Catie?"

"Yeah?"

"It's good to have you on the team."

She knew he was probably saying that because she was the fifth woman they needed to have a balanced slate for the competition. But it also felt a little bit like he had just read her mind, and a tinge of heat popped on her cheeks.

Catie knew she wasn't anyone's first choice for actual search and rescue. She was still working on her strength, and it would never be what the stronger people could bring. She ignored the way Will's arms flexed as he started pulling rope again. Spare, efficient movements, his biceps bouncing with each pull.

How did a school principal stay that buff, anyway? Catie worked on her feet all day and he put her to shame. "I know I'm not as strong as…"

He didn't seem to mind that she trailed off. He just shrugged. "The most important thing you might do is spot a water bottle. Or if you're in the hasty team, and can move quickly to a coordinate, you might be the first one on scene with a survival blanket and some ibuprofen. Don't underestimate the value of being fast, observant, or nimble."

"Thanks." But the warmth that came from his reassurance faded as he turned away, and this time kept his attention firmly on the ropes.

Will was done with her after two brief attempts at conversation.

———

THE NEXT AFTERNOON, Friday, brought two unexpected people to the salon.

The door swung upon, and in stepped a big, heavyset man who buzzed his own hair off on a standard number one clipper setting. With him was a teenage boy with a slightly longer buzzcut of his own. If it weren't for the white piece of paper clutched in the teenager's hand, Catie would wonder if they were lost.

"Hello," she said cheerfully. "Are you here to apply for the summer position?"

The kid nodded.

"Maybe," the older man asked. "His teacher suggested it."

Ah. So this was the student Will mentioned. She held out her hand. "I'm Catie. And you are?"

"Sam." He shoved the resume at her, then his hand, in an awkward one-two move.

She shook his hand and took the piece of paper. No job experience, but basketball team at his old school and some volunteer experience.

"He's new in town. I'm his dad."

Catie took in the dirt under the father's fingernails, the grease stain on his workpants. "Do you have any concerns about the position?"

"He's just a kid."

She nodded. "I get it. That's why I only posted for a part-time position. My first job was at Mac's Diner, when I was in grade nine. You're in grade ten, Sam? So around the same age."

"He doesn't know anything about hair cutting."

Dad could stop talking for Sam any time now, but she figured that would be easier if Sam spoke for himself, too. Catie caught the eye of the teenager. "You don't need to know anything about hair. Do you know how to use a broom?"

He laughed a little, caught by surprise. "Of course."

"That's what I need help with the most. Sweeping up as I'm cutting hair, and then at the end of the day, too. I'm looking for someone who can come in three hours a day, Tuesday through Friday, and four hours on Saturday and Sunday. I'm closed on Mondays. If you want two days off, you can have Sunday off, too."

"I want to work."

"Okay." She glanced at the resume. "I can call you at this number?"

"That's my Dad's phone. I don't have a phone yet."

"That's fine. I'm collecting resumes until the end of the week, and then I'll make a decision." She gave him what she hoped would be received as an encouraging smile. "I'm glad you came in, Sam."

———

WILL SPENT the last day of school, a Thursday, going classroom to classroom, listening to excited chatter about summer plans and watching his team make a celebration out of the final echoes of the curriculum. In January's grade ten math class, he was thrilled to hear Sam had a summer job, and even happier when he learned where it was.

He owed Catie a beer. Or a bag of trail mix.

At dismissal, he headed out to the front walk, and high fived as many kids as he could on their way to their bus.

Sam was one of the last kids out. He pointed to a pickup truck in the parking lot. "My dad's picking me up today. He wanted me to thank you for the job referral."

"It was my pleasure. Have a good summer, okay?"

"I'll try." Sam grinned. "You should come in to the salon when I'm working there. It would be fun to see Catie give you a new haircut."

"You mean Ms. Berton."

Sam laughed. "She said I can call her Catie."

Of course she did. "That sounds like her."

That conversation was the first thing he thought of when she arrived at training that night wearing bright green leggings and a blue buttoned-down workshirt that had her name spelled out on the back of it in big, silver letters.

He couldn't resist. He cornered her by the coffee urn. "Where do you get these outfits?"

"WillWontLikeThis.com."

"I like it. I don't understand it, but..." He shrugged. "What's not to like?"

"You made a big deal about not wearing all black." She gave him a look like she thought he was dumb. "When I was wearing all black. So..."

Oh. He *was* dumb. "That wasn't about you."

"No, I mean, I know that. It wasn't *just* about me."

"It wasn't about you at all."

"You looked right at me."

He looked at her all the time. But he probably shouldn't say that. "Then I owe you an apology. But don't stop wearing the outlandish outfits. I like them a lot."

She rolled her eyes, but she smiled, and that made him smile, too.

Then she looked at him expectantly.

He stared back. "Do I have something on my face?"

"No."

"Why are you looking at me like that, then?"

"Because you owe me an apology."

"I...gave it to you."

"No, you didn't." She huffed. "You said, *Then I owe you an apology.* And moved on as if you had delivered that apology, without actually doing it. Which is—and I realize at this point I'm making quite a big deal about a thing that was not actually a thing, from your point of view, but I'm just saying, this is very on brand for Will Kincaid."

Then she turned and walked away.

Not angrily. The little huff was the only part of that which had actually sounded annoyed. The rest had sounded...resigned. And the walk was dismissive. Like she was done with him.

Ah, shit.

The chances of her accepting beer or trail mix from him were slim to none now.

But as soon as the training night was called to order, she acted as if nothing had just happened between them. Tonight they were running exercises similar to what Tom expected for the gear assessment in the competition.

All the trainees had brought their backpacks, and while Tom answered their final questions about the best way to pack them for this exercise, Will, Tobin and Yolanda headed into the woods, each taking a separate path. Today the trainees were going to work together in pairs to simulate a hasty team response. They knew the estimated location of the person being rescued—in this case, Will lying on a boulder at the mouth of a small rocky cave.

When he was a kid, this cave had seemed massive, and he'd loved exploring it for hours with his brothers.

He was deep in a memory of his mother laughing in delight as she watched them play when he heard footsteps approaching rapidly.

Speed wasn't always a factor in SAR evaluation, but for purposes of the competition, this event would be timed. Catie and Lore apparently took that seriously, running at top speed to the edge of the rock field that littered the mouth of the cave.

Will slipped into his role. "Help," he said, trying to raise his left arm before letting it fall back to the boulder.

"We're with the Pine Harbour Search and Rescue Team," Catie said quickly. "Hold still and we'll come to you."

They carefully but quickly made their way to him, then took off their backpacks. This was where they would decide what gear they could use to help him successfully.

"We should do a focused spine assessment first," Lore said, pulling out her booklet. She asked him his name, where he was, what time of day it was, and then what had happened to him.

"I was climbing down from there..." Will tried again to use his left arm, and moaned. "Ah. Ouch. There. And I fell against this rock."

"Did you hit your head?"

"No. Just my side."

Catie focused in on his arm, as intended. "The left side? I'm going to check your fingers, okay?"

She checked his fingertips for oxygen, finding them "nice and pink." Then she moved around his body, taking off his shoes to check his feet and other hand as Lore stabilized his neck.

By Will's estimation, it took them two minutes to be confident he didn't have a spine injury and focus in on a possibly broken arm. They worked together to help him sit up, then Lore gave him some water and pretend acetaminophen while Catie pulled out her first aid kit.

"Oh shit," she muttered. Avoiding Will's curious gaze, she looked at Lore. "I only have a small sling. How about you?"

Lore checked her bag. "Damn it. Same."

Catie stretched the fabric out wide, but her initial assessment was correct. It was too small to be used effectively to stabilize his arm.

She propped her hands on her hips, glaring in turn at him and her backpack, like she wasn't sure who to be grumpier with—her pack for not magically having the right size sling, or him for being too damn big.

He didn't bother to point out that she was the one who stocked the first aid pack, and this was exactly why they did these exercises. Also, it was a classic mistake he'd made at least once, too. Murphy's Law demanded that if supplies were sized, you wouldn't have the right one at the wrong time.

And Kincaid's Law demanded that if you had cocky thoughts about a woman who got under your skin, she would immediately find a way to scatter those thoughts and leave you tongue-tied.

Catie stripped off her shirt, leaving her in a tight tank top, slick against her skin. "Here. We can use this as a sling instead."

After knotting it, she leaned in, close enough he could feel her warmth and catch the faint scent of her skin. All thoughts were definitely scattered now, because she smelled good and felt even better as she carefully fit it around his neck and under his arm.

That was inconvenient. *You have a broken arm, you're a hiker with a broken arm,* he repeated to himself.

They checked his legs, double-checked his head and neck again, before letting him stand with their assistance.

"Take it slow. We've got you."

"But not too slow," Catie muttered, trying not to smile. "I think we were the first to find our victim."

"Missing person," Will corrected automatically. "Victim makes it sound like you murdered me."

"Maybe that's the plot twist." Catie sounded far too delighted at the possibility, so he kept his mouth shut as they helped him over the rocks and down to the smooth path. Then they scampered back for their backpacks, before escorting him back to the training centre.

As they had hoped, they were the first ones back, and Tom was pleased with their after action report.

Then he turned to Will, whose arm was still braced in Catie's shirt. "How'd they do?"

"Other than needing a different size sling, they had what they needed in their bags, and they worked quickly and efficiently together."

"I thought we would need to use more stuff for this exercise," Lore said. "I thought about pulling out the survival blanket to keep you warm, for example. Should we have done that?"

That was a good question. Will should have thought of that feedback, but from the second Catie hooked her shirt around his neck, he'd been a bit distracted. "Yep, good idea." He cleared his throat. "The focus on speed may have been a distraction."

Catie's flushed face fell.

Shit.

"Hard to know in a competitive space," he tried to recover, but Tom agreed with his previous statement.

"No, I think Will's right. This kind of head-to-head set up is a bit of a trick. Not an intentional one," he added when Lore protested with a laugh. "But taking the time to do the field assessment carefully is more important than the speed of the recovery. If you are with the found person, and they are stable and safe, going through all the motions is probably going to score you higher than moving quickly. But it's a judgement call."

"They did a good focused spine assessment," Will offered, but Catie didn't seem to hear the compliment. She was chewing on her lip, and he felt like shit for dumping on her clear success. He eased his arm out of the makeshift sling, and found himself inhaling the scent of her shirt as he lifted it over his head.

She wants to murder you already, don't give her legitimate reasons to think you're a pervert as well as an insensitive non-apologizer and *an overly critical teammate.*

He handed it back to her as an excuse to get her attention. "Seriously, that was a great job."

"I feel awful that I didn't have a sling," she admitted. "And I was the one who was focused on speed."

"I would have been, too. It's the nature of the exercise. But don't feel bad about the sling. You used what you had and you got the job done. That would have scored well, too, but more importantly, it would have helped someone in real life. Good job."

She finally beamed at him, and Tom, then gave Lore a high five.

"That deserves a drink to celebrate," the bartender said.

"Do you want to go to the pub on your night off?"

"I don't mind, if you're up for it." As the next team returned from the woods, the women moved away, making plans to go to The Green Hedgehog. Will focused on the next successful recovery. This team had used their portable saw to help get Tobin out from under a fallen tree.

He'd made them carry him back on a makeshift stretcher, and their ingenuity was impressive.

Once training was finished, Catie and Lore announced their plans to go out for a drink, and invited everyone else to join them.

Will wanted to. He almost said yes, but it was a work night. Even though school was done for the year, teachers and administrators had a busy day ahead. Besides, something told him Catie would have more fun if he wasn't there. Instead, he hung back to help Tom tidy up after everyone left.

"You didn't want to join them?" his friend asked.

Want had nothing to do with it.

"I have an early meeting tomorrow. I should get home and to bed." He stacked the chairs to the side of the room. "How about you?"

"Kids are teething. And I haven't seen Chloe all day." Tom grinned.

Will understood. His friend was married to the town's librarian, and they had twin toddlers. "Then let's get out of here. You have a family to get to."

Whereas Will had an empty house, as his brothers would say.

Once upon a time, he'd been proud of his house. He'd bought it not long after becoming a teacher, safe and secure in the knowledge his career path was set. It had been a new build at the time, in a small subdivision of similar new homes on the edge of town.

He had enough room that Josh lived with him in the winter, when it was cold in the apartment at the garage, and Adam had too, after he finished firefighter school but before he bought a house of his own.

Now, though, it was quiet.

He headed upstairs to his bedroom, peeling off his clothes. It was only his imagination that his shirt carried the scent of Catie's makeshift sling on it. He dropped it in the hamper outside his bathroom, and climbed into the shower.

As the steam seeped under his skin, he closed his eyes and pictured her at the bar, laughing and commiserating with her fellow trainees about what a critical ass he was.

And he wished he was there, so she could throw those barbs right at him. Stare him down and make him apologize for real, because she deserved it.

7

THE HIGH OF a good training session lasted exactly thirty-six hours. It fizzled out, hard, when Catie closed up shop early on Sunday, because it was a gorgeous day and she didn't have any appointments for the last two hours.

So she set off by herself in search of a newly popular cave near Lion's Head.

It was a perfectly reasonable plan. She was going on a marked trail that wasn't too advanced. Except when she arrived at the trail head, the small parking area she expected to use was marked as resident-only, with the threat of a hundred dollar fine.

She snapped a picture of that egregiousness, and got back in her car. A quick review of the map on her phone showed a couple of other options, so she headed off, looking for another access point. When she found one with a good size lane that had no visible signs prohibiting her parking, she added a pin to her map, marking her GPS coordinates.

As far as she could tell from this direction, the cave was just off the trail. Except "just" was an exaggeration.

This wasn't a big deal at first. But then the weather turned, and the terrain looked totally different as the sky darkened, an unexpected thunderstorm fast approaching —so she took cover under a rock outcropping.

And the rocks blocked the weak phone signal she had had before.

When she returned to the path—well, this was where she had to admit it was a bigger deal than she'd first assessed.

Up until that point, it was just a sequence of bad luck moments. But then she violated the number one rule of search and rescue.

She kept moving. Instead of stopping where she was as soon as she realized she wasn't sure of her location, she kept going, trying to regain her phone signal. She managed to restore it, but not a strong enough signal to make her maps app work again. So when she finally admitted to herself what she'd known deep down for a while, she didn't have any reliable landmarks to convey to anyone she might call.

Which meant that she not only *really* needed to call someone, it would be a humble pie phone call on top of that.

She tried Lore first. No dice.

Then she scrolled through her phone book, trying to pick the next best candidate. One of the other newbies, Jeong, was a top contender, but she could just imagine the stern, disappointed look on Will's face if—when—he found out she dragged another trainee into her mishap.

Also, if Jeong or Lore called her in this exact same situation, she would make an emergency SOS call to Tom, do not pass GO, do not collect $200. It was a no-brainer.

So she really shouldn't have tried to trick Lore into

helping her on the down low, and if her friend called back, she'd have to dodge the call.

If she was going to rope anyone into helping her in secret, it would have to be someone fully trained. Someone capable, and someone who had his own reasons for keeping Catie's secrets.

For one thing, Will owed her. Well, he owed her an apology, not a rescue, but it was still a debt. And she knew how strongly he felt about other people's safety. She felt a momentary pang of guilt at her instinct to take advantage of his deep sense of responsibility, but it was overridden by her even stronger desire to not be stuck in the forest after dark.

And if Will called Tom, well, she'd have to live with that embarrassment.

She said a quick prayer to the phone signal Gods, then dialled his number. He picked up immediately. "Catie?"

"Hi." There was a lot of noise in the background where he was. "Are you busy?"

He answered with a question of his own. "What's wrong?"

Why did he immediately assume something was *wrong*? "I'm fine. I want you to know that first of all."

"Uh huh."

"And I don't want to have to ask you for a favour. Especially if you're busy."

"I'm not." He muttered to someone in the background. "What's up?"

"I need—" She cut herself off and glanced back down the trail. No, there was no other option.

"What is it?" He already sounded annoyed.

"You can't laugh."

"I won't."

"I'm lost in the woods near Lion's Head. Please don't call Tom," she added in a rush.

He didn't say anything for a long moment, and the noise in the background got quieter.

"Will—"

He exhaled in her ear. "Okay, you've got a phone on you. That's good. Roughly speaking, where are you?"

"I want you to know first of all, that I have lots of battery power on my phone left, and I have a power bank in my backpack, too."

He sighed. "Mm hmm."

"There's tons of daylight hours left still, too."

"Good. Let's not waste it. Where are you?"

"I don't know. If I knew that, then I wouldn't be lost, would I?" She closed her eyes. Snapping at her best choice for a rescue wasn't smart. She should have called Yolanda.

Will made a sound suspiciously like a growl. She decided to think it was a laugh, although she wasn't sure if he would be laughing with her or at her. She was in a bit of a no-win situation so it didn't really matter.

He could laugh at her all he wanted given her predicament. He could growl, even. She'd have to tolerate that.

"Okay, tell me where you started, where you went, and what you know about where you are right now, starting with a general direction I can start driving in."

"Can I just say, off the top, that this is the fault of those people who think parking should be restricted?"

He sighed. "Do I want to know the story there?"

No, probably not. "I'm south of town."

She described where she parked her car and told him her estimated speed, how long she had been out for her destination and when she took the wrong turn.

"How about a GPS location? Can you pull that from your phone?"

"Yes!" Oh, she was so proud of herself for that. "I pinned where I parked."

"Great. Any chance you have geo-location mapping on your photos, and did you take a selfie anywhere along the hike?"

She gasped. Yes, she took a picture of the darkening sky. Was that before she lost her data connection? "Hang on."

After putting him on speaker, she went back to look at the time that she took that photo, then carefully read him the coordinates on it. "I'm about twenty-five minutes roughly north from that point."

"How rough? Do you have the compass app?"

Oh she felt like an idiot, needing to be talked through how to use her phone to rescue herself. "Yes."

"Head back the way you came a little bit. Not so much you'll get yourself further lost, just enough to be sure of your direction of travel. Can you do that?"

"Yes, I can do that."

"Okay. Do that and I'll stay on the line with you. I'm in the truck now."

She fumbled her finger shaking through her phone, second and third guessing her thought that she could ever be on the search and rescue team, but she found the compass and let out a sigh of relief when it worked.

And then she realized it had GPS coordinates on it, too. She kept moving, back in the direction of the small rock cave, and the GPS updated again. "Will, I think I have new coordinates. I think this app is able to get enough of a signal."

"That's great. Text it to me."

She hit send, but the message delivery bar moved so slowly, she feared it wouldn't go through.

He told her that was fine, it didn't matter, he was going to keep her on the phone until he found her. His voice was so calm. So collected, so tight, and so unlike the Will that she found so frustrating.

This must be what he was like to everyone else in his world. A calm, cool professional.

"How were drinks the other night? Did the whole team join you at the Hedgehog?"

She knew he was trying to distract her. "Most of them. We had a good time." On the screen, the text message finally went through. "Will—"

"I've got it. I'll get as close to those coordinates as I can in the truck. Don't move from where you are right now, understood?"

She wanted to say a flippant *yes, sir*, but opted instead for a meek, appreciative acknowledgement. "Yes, thank you."

"Tell me more about the pub."

She did that, then she cracked some jokes. She even offered to sing him a song, which he laughed at harder than her jokes.

Finally, he cut her off. "Good news," he said. "You're not that far from a road."

She heard his truck engine cut out over the phone, then the phone quality changed, and he told her she was on his bluetooth earpiece now. "I'm eight hundred metres away."

It wasn't long before she heard his voice—not over the phone—but actually echoing through the forest faintly and then not so faintly. And then he hung up the phone because he could see her.

She waved sheepishly, and ran in his direction.

He wasn't dressed for a hike. He was in jeans and a t-shirt, and there were grease marks on the hand he raised in a wave.

"You were working on your car," she said apologetically when she realized what she was looking at.

"It's fine." He gave her a curious look. "You know about my car?"

"It's a small town, Will. Everyone knows about your car. Everyone has seen your car broken down on the side of the road at some point. That thing is a menace to our civil society."

He smiled faintly. "Nice to see you, too."

"Do I not sound grateful enough?" She batted her eyelashes at him. "Thank you, Mr. Kincaid. You saved me."

"I did, in fact." He grinned and pointed her in the direction of what she now realized was Josh's tow truck. "Come on, I'll drive you back to your car."

Once they were on the road, though, he brought up the question she was hoping he'd just…not. "Why *were* you hiking alone?"

She rolled her eyes. "Because I'm a grown woman."

"Who got lost."

"And had a fully charged phone, plus a spare battery pack. And a plan."

"It's better to hike with a friend."

"I understand that getting this lecture is the price of being rescued, so I hear you and I accept what you're saying. But have you ever considered turning off the principal thing?"

He swallowed visibly, his gaze locked on the road ahead of them. Then he rocked his jaw back and forth.

All right, maybe that had been too far. "Sor—"

"I don't turn it off, no." He shifted in his seat. "Generally don't get a lot of complaints about that."

"Not to your face."

"How about you, then? Do you ever turn off the Little Miss Charming act?"

"It's not an act!"

"But you don't have any friends to go hiking with."

"Ouch, a direct blow. I have friends," she pointed out hotly. "But I *enjoy* my solitude."

"So no close friends, then?"

"Wow." She could point out that she had more close friends than he did, but that seemed rude after he rescued her. "Okay, let's try this. I am genuinely thankful that you were able to come and pick me up. I really appreciate it."

He shrugged. "Don't overthink it. I figure I owe you one because I wasn't great at replying to your emails."

It was a lie and they both knew it. His ability to reply to emails was just fine when he had something to say. Prompt, efficient. Cutting. His silence to her offer to help with the business club had been a clear message, too.

But he had come to pick her up, and nobody else would know she'd put herself in danger. "Communication may not be your strong suit. You can put it in the same category as…" She glanced at the grease on his forearm. A black, sticky smear that made the corded muscles and visible veins look like they came from honest work instead of hours in a gym.

Not that she knew anything about Will's workout routine.

She really had to stop noticing how hard his body was. It was annoying.

When she lifted her gaze to his face, he had an eyebrow cocked. "As what?"

"Communication and car repair," she said. "Not your strengths."

He smirked. "Never stop putting me in my place, Catie." He parked next to her car. "Have a safe drive home."

"I will."

"Great."

"Good." She opened the passenger door, full of righteously annoyed heat. Which was the wrong tone to leave this encounter on, because he had saved her butt, after all. "And...thank you. Again."

"Don't worry about it. It's our secret." His expression was a careful mask, unreadable and confusing. Made all the more confusing when, as she got into her car, it occurred to her that Will had no reason to keep her misadventure a secret.

It was a pretty good story. And he got nothing out of protecting her. He'd done her a solid favour, as requested.

Had he somehow figured out she'd be mortified if anyone found out?

———

WILL TRIED NOT to watch Catie as she got settled in the driver's seat of her car. She didn't leave right away. She sat very still for a few moments behind the wheel, then pulled something out of her bag.

A chocolate bar.

He grinned as she took a big bite, then dropped her head back against the seat. He liked to think she was groaning in appreciation. He'd like to hear that, too, but no dice. All he got was the silent show, through the windows of two vehicles—and from an angle, because he was trying not to stare.

Trying, failing… He put the tow truck into reverse and carefully backed out onto the road.

That was enough of playing the white knight.

He needed to get his brother's tow truck back to the garage, but he wasn't ready to explain why he'd demanded to take it—in a scrawled Sharpie hostage note, no less.

He'd driven his car to the garage, and it wasn't in any shape to stage a rescue all the way across the peninsula. It was barely roadworthy to get from his house to the garage and back.

When he got back to the highway, where the Pine Harbour Emergency Services building sat, he decided to make a stop there first and see if any of the first responders inside were either of his brothers.

He pulled into the parking lot and fired off a group text message.

Will: Are either of you at work?
Adam: We both are. I'm sitting in Owen's office
right now, in fact.

And then before he got out of the truck another message rolled in from Josh.

Josh: Any ETA on the return of my stolen tow
truck? The Howe sisters have invited us over for
dinner.
Will: Just dropping in on Owen and Adam at work.
I'll raid their ice cream freezer and bring treats for
the kids.

Josh: And the tow truck owner…
Will: And that guy, too.

Now he felt a bit ridiculous delaying his return. Josh had already moved on from wondering why Will tore out of the garage like a bat out of hell, and was focused on dinner. But he'd announced himself to the brothers inside the building.

Maybe he could blow it off as just catching up—as long as they didn't look outside and see the vehicle he arrived in. *Maybe if you stopped acting like a weirdo, people wouldn't ask you why you were acting like a weirdo.*

He knew this building well. For a long time, Will had volunteered there as well, but when Adam joined the fire department, he gave up his position on the volunteer fire brigade that supported the small Pine Harbour full-time firefighters.

The fire department claimed most of the second floor. The paramedics worked on the main floor, and the previously empty third storey was now home to the town library.

Will wasn't going very far into the building. As the EMS supervisor and the manager of the whole building, Owen's office was halfway down the main hallway. The door was propped open, and Adam was lounging in a chair across from the eldest Kincaid brother. Will stopped in the doorway and leaned against the frame. "Afternoon."

They nodded in return.

"I'm on an ice cream mission," he said, which was now true. "Josh and I have been invited to the marina for dinner, and I want to bring a kid-friendly dessert. I'll restock the freezer tomorrow."

"Be our guest." Owen jerked his head in the direction of the kitchenette down the hall.

Will didn't move. He'd get there. It would be rude to rush. "How's work going?"

"Slow day." Adam kicked a stool over to him. "Sit down, stay a while."

"Thanks."

Owen gave him a curious look. "Something wrong? You seem edgy."

"Yeah. I dunno. No, I'm fine."

"You sound fine," Adam said dryly.

Will made a face.

His brothers waited.

Then he sighed. "What I'm about to tell you cannot leave this room."

Owen shrugged. "Sure."

"I'm swearing you both to the highest of confidences."

This time it was Adam who nodded. "Absolutely."

"I think I have some complicated feelings when it comes to Catie."

No response. Owen just looked at him. Adam just looked at him.

Will groaned and shook his head. "Pretend I didn't say that."

"Can't do that." Owen crossed his arms over his chest and rocked back.

Adam leaned forward and braced *his* arms on his knees. "You have to know this is not actually breaking news, right?"

Now it was Will's turn to not say anything.

"How complicated are we talking?"

He shrugged.

Owen sighed. "Complicated feelings aren't fair to her.

Un-complicate them, or learn to hide them better."

"Or talk to her about them." Will recoiled at Adam's very fair suggestion. His youngest brother laughed. "Not at the talking stage yet?"

"There is no talking stage with Catie. That's part of what makes it complicated. We're oil and water. It doesn't matter what I say, she always has a quick retort."

"Half of talking is listening," Owen said.

Adam nodded. "At least. Seventy-thirty seems to be a good ratio in my house."

They didn't understand. They were talking about loving partners, and he was talking about a bossy nemesis. He just wanted to be Catie's friend without the drama, her go-to guy when she got into a pinch like today—without the barbs about him not knowing how to fix a car.

Even if it was accurate. He changed the subject to the re-wiring work he was doing on the Duster.

BACK AT THE GARAGE, Will parked the tow truck, then walked across the road. When they were kids, the marina had been a busy place. But business had changed over the years, and other towns—with more vibrant restaurants and shopping options—had lured away a lot of the boating community.

August and January Howe had recently inherited the land and business after their father passed away.

January had a full-time job as a teacher. August was in the military, a single mom to two kids. Will didn't understand why they hung on to the business. Nobody would blame them if they sold the land instead.

But they didn't want to.

So now they were Josh's neighbours, and it was like a jump back in time heading over to see what they were grilling.

Once upon a time, the five Kincaid boys and the two Howe girls had gotten into a good amount of trouble—good trouble—while their parents had gossiped on the dock, waiting for dinner to prepare itself on the oversized outdoor barbeque.

Today it was August's kids climbing high on the sprawling main building, and Josh, January, and August were the grown-ups getting dinner ready and having a few beers as the sun, low in the sky, glittered off the lake.

Josh was the one to see him first. "Crisis averted?"

Will nodded. "Yep."

January frowned. "Josh said it was something at the school?"

Because when he lied to his brother, he didn't expect his brother to then repeat that to one of his teachers. He winced. "Not exactly."

That made Josh grin. "Ah. Catie."

"What the hell, man? Can't I have any secrets?"

"Not if you don't keep them well," January said with a wink. "Catie, huh? What kind of an emergency was this?"

"A none-of-your-business, but-it-was-outdoors kind of emergency."

"Ah." She wrinkled her nose. "That no-fun kind. Speaking of which, I mentioned the business club to her. We don't have an advisor yet, right?"

Josh spread his arms wide. "I'm right here. How many times have I volunteered?"

"You can't do it, you're my brother. That's a conflict of interest." Will grabbed a chair and pulled up to the table. "What are we making for dinner?"

"Don't change the subject. It wouldn't be a conflict of interest for me to bring my business knowledge to help kids at the school."

Will rolled his eyes. "Fine. I don't think you're the kind of role model we're looking for. Is that what you want me to say?"

Josh pointed a pea shell at him, pausing his dinner prep task of shucking the fresh peas. "You've turned into quite the liar today, Principal Kincaid. What kind of an example is *that* setting?"

"There aren't any kids here."

"We're up here," Levi called out, drawing their attention to the roof. Summer waved from beside her brother. "Listening to everything."

Will craned his neck. "Are either of you going to join the business club next year?"

"Is Josh going to be in charge of it?"

"Unlikely."

"Is Catie Berton going to be in charge?"

That was looking more and more likely. "Would you like that?"

"Sure." Their heads disappeared from view.

"Traitors," Josh muttered.

January grinned at him. "Maybe Catie will have you in as a guest speaker."

"That's probably more my speed anyway."

August handed Will a beer. "We didn't invite you over to talk about work."

"Except I need to talk to him about something else work related for a minute." January scooped the final peas into the bowl, then nodded her head toward the dock.

Will stood up, grabbed her a fresh bottle of beer, and they fell into step side by side. "What's up?"

She took a slow sip of her beer, and more than a dozen steps, before answering. "I heard a rumour that you might not be returning in the fall."

He jerked to a stop. "It's not true."

"If you're not happy—"

"Jan, I swear to you, I haven't told a soul that. You would be the first to know."

She cocked her head to the side, frowning. "Wait. *Are* you unhappy?"

He made a face. "More out of my depth and unsure than *unhappy*. But the rumours are just people observing that and coming to the same conclusion independently."

"You didn't tell the board you want to be moved?"

He shook his head. "No."

He couldn't ask her who was talking about him. That was the line between them as teacher and principal. He was administration, she was staff. They both knew the lines around that. But beneath that professional relationship was a friendship that went back to when they were in diapers.

"I miss being at an elementary-only school. I don't think I know how to be the best principal the secondary students need, and sometimes I think I should never have taken the position."

"It's been three years," she said softly.

"I thought it was going to get easier each year."

"And it hasn't?"

He shook his head. If anything, that first year had been the easiest. There had been an excited shine on the community school coming together.

"Do you want advice, or do you just want to vent?"

Will wasn't sure he liked the way January was looking at him. Like she was so sure the answer was the latter, and okay, maybe it was. Maybe that's what he wanted. But what Will wanted hadn't gotten him very far lately. "I think I need advice—from a friend."

"From my perspective, you're doing a good job. But if you're feeling cracks, like it's more work than it should be to hold everything together, then something has to change. You know the old adage about doing the same thing and expecting different results."

"I struggle to connect with the older students." His chest loosened as he admitted the truth, finally. "I want to go into the new school year with a different approach, absolutely."

"Nothing wrong with shaking up your routine. You know that not everybody responds in the same way, and high school kids are different."

Which hit at the heart of his insecurity that he wasn't the right principal for the job. "Honestly, I think I should have figured out that different path by now. Maybe I *should* let the board bring someone else in, someone who has high school experience. Obviously, people are thinking that if the rumour mill started up."

"A new principal would be in the same position you are. A high school principal would have the same problems coming to a community school, not knowing what works with the younger grades. And you have done the work. You prepped as well as you could, but there's gonna be some on the job adjustments as well. Maybe you're at the peak of that adjustment cycle. But part of being a good leader is leading by example. We can be humble, and own that we don't know what we don't know yet. And it's going to take some trial and error before we can confidently lead, so we're going to lean on other people."

"You mean you. You're a high school teacher. You know what you're doing."

"Yeah." She laughed. "Obviously, I'm an excellent resource."

He chuckled along with her.

"Actually, I think, for this I mean the kids—the young adults. Maybe we can give them more autonomy next year."

"Like with a proper outside advisor for the business club."

January nodded. "Give them real projects, too."

Better projects.

Catie would be perfect for that.

"Do you want me to take that on?"

Part of him did. It would be easier to put some distance there. But they were officially into summer holidays now, and it wouldn't be appropriate for him to ask January to do school-related work over the summer.

Even as a favour.

Besides, if he managed to find the right words, maybe it would lead to him giving Catie a real apology, as she'd rightfully asked for.

That night, he sent a long overdue email.

From: Will Kincaid
To: Catie Berton

Catie,
My apologies for the delay in this response. The PHCS
Business Club would be honoured to welcome you as the
next community advisor.
Sincerely,
Will

8

———

THE NERVE OF HIM. The absolute nerve.

It wasn't Catie's style to not reply to emails right away, but there was something about Will that made her want to leave him hanging. She'd reached out about the business club *weeks* ago. Almost an entire month had gone by, where he'd had plenty of chance to talk about it with her—and where she mentioned it at least once!—and *now* he replied to her with the assumption that she was still available.

What if her life had changed fundamentally in that time?

He sees you regularly, and rescued you on Sunday. He knows your life hasn't changed even an iota.

That was beside the point.

She did like the *honoured* part. That was a nice touch. But she was still waiting before she replied.

It wasn't like he was going to be doing anything with her reply now. School was officially let out, and the teachers had finished their final admin days, too.

Tomorrow was Canada Day, the official start of summer, and because it was a Thursday, also a break from search and rescue training. She wouldn't see Will until next week.

But that didn't stop him from being a constant topic of conversation. First, with Sam, who of course she'd hired. Will didn't believe she would, so she went out of her way to give Sam's application the fairest of considerations—which she would have done anyway.

He wasn't a perfect assistant. No fourteen-year-old would be. But he was funny, caustic in a way she could relate to, and—when he learned she paid twenty dollars an hour—an exceptionally diligent worker.

The only thing that tripped her up were those moments when he told her what an asshole Will was. Not that he used that word precisely.

He'd been working for Catie for three days, and talked —complained—about Will at least once each of those days.

The first time it was an aside about how work was so much more fun than school.

"After being told non-stop by an authoritarian freak that everything I'm doing is wrong, this is a nice change of pace."

Catie had looked at him in alarm. "Who told you that?"

"Mr. Kincaid."

It had been so hard to keep a straight face. *Authoritarian freak* was a perfect label for Will. That would go in her diary if she had one, underlined and with exclamation marks. But grown-ups needed to have each other's backs, so she couldn't let on that she agreed with Sam. Besides, she found it hard to believe that Will had precisely told Sam that *everything* he did was wrong. That wasn't Will's way.

She moved the conversation along instead of engaging.

The second time, she was rocking out to a playlist, cutting Sophie Minelli's hair as her dad Rafe, a local cop, chatted to her about the Main Street closures for the upcoming County Country weekend music festival and the ensuing parking issues, and how that all related to the question of whether to charge for parking. The next song that came on was slightly explicit, so she pulled her phone out of her pocket—which was streaming the music to the Bluetooth speakers—and put on a different album.

Rafe didn't say anything, but after they left, Sam asked why she'd changed the song. He'd been rocking out, too.

"Here's a business tip. *My* musical preferences are not more important than making my customers happy. And a dad with a young daughter? He doesn't want her to hear any spicy language. So if people like that are in the store, I filter what we play. When it's just grown-ups—"

Sam's eyes lit up at the idea that she included him in that, and she modified it a bit. "Or older people, teens and grown-ups, who understand the context of language in entertainment, that's different."

"Now *that* makes sense." He smirked. "You could teach Mr. Kincaid a thing or two about context."

Oh, shit. Once again, Sam wasn't wrong, because Catie *could* teach Will a lot of things about context. But he wasn't right, either. "Are you talking about swearing in school?"

Sam flushed. "Not really."

"But sort of really?" She gave him her sternest look, which wasn't really that stern at all. "Don't take what I said about context out of context, speaking of context. School is a swear-free zone, right?"

He rolled his eyes. She liked a good eye-roll, but not when it was aimed at her.

So she waited him out.

"Sorry," he muttered. "Yes, you're right."

She crossed to her desk and dug out her iPad, then switched the music controls to that device. "Here. You can be in charge of the music today. We need a secret signal if I want you to change a song."

He shrugged. "You can just tell me, *Sam, change the song please.*"

"Okay, I will." But she didn't need to. He selected fun, thoughtful, and appropriate music for the rest of the afternoon, and when they were closing up, she went out of her way to make sure he knew she appreciated him being mindful of their customers.

But then today, the third time Sam mentioned Will, she was forced to come more explicitly to his defence. Because Sam had gone to a house party the night before—something Catie had done when she was fourteen, but she was still slightly horrified at this baby of a young man doing the same—and it was apparently two doors down from Will's house.

Will lived on the outskirts of town, in a newer neighbourhood. The houses were bigger than on Catie's side of town, more modern, but they were also closer together.

And Pine Harbour had a noise ordinance.

When the party was still going at half past eleven last night, Will had apparently come around and told them to turn the music down.

Catie gave Sam a pained look. "I guess that didn't go over well?"

"They thanked him, closed the door, and turned the music up instead."

"Oh no." She shook her head. "Sam!"

"It was funny."

"That is *not* funny. People are trying to sleep at that hour."

"I know. But—"

"But what?" She propped her hands on her hips, then dropped them. That wasn't the right approach here. She took a deep breath and tried again. "I remember not liking my high school teachers that much. Feeling like they were always..."

She trailed off. She didn't want to put words in Sam's mouth, and she didn't want to describe Will in an even more unflattering light than Sam already saw him.

Ugh.

Defending Will was the worst thing ever.

Not as bad as having to listen to a house party rage next door at midnight, of course. But pretty bad.

"Never mind," Sam muttered.

No, that wouldn't do, either. "I think you probably already know a few other ways that could have gone. You don't need to tell me what they were, it's none of my business. But I'm just saying, as one human being to another, it's never funny when people are mean to each other. Principal Kincaid might be strict, and he might be tough, but he's not mean, right?"

"Yeah."

"Did he call the cops after they cranked the music?"

Sam shook his head. "No."

"I might have." She wouldn't. But Frances Schmidt would, and right now, Sam needed a reminder that *someone* would.

He blinked at her. "What?"

"There's a noise ordinance, and after trying to directly communicate with you? I might think that you need to hear it from the authorities."

Sam's face went white. "Oh."

"Yeah. Oh. So next time you think Mr. Kincaid is mean, just remember that he could have been worse, and ask yourself why he wasn't."

————

SHE WAS STILL THINKING about Will marching over to a house party full of his own students and telling them to turn the music down—only for them to turn it up.

That must have burned his ass. She'd have been so mad. Did Mr. Kincaid get mad? Or was he insufferably calm no matter what, even when disrespected to his face?

She'd like to see him absolutely lose it on someone. Not a student, or anyone vulnerable. Like on a grown bully. In her fantasy, maybe he would join her secret cabal against the encroaching paid parking program.

But she'd learned the hard way that Fantasy Will and Real Life Will were not the same person. They looked the same. Dressed the same. But the thoughts inside their handsome, chiseled heads were wildly different.

Fantasy Will spent a lot of time agreeing with Catie, and complimenting all of her great ideas. Real Life Will grunted dismissively and went out of his way to tack unnecessary corrections onto any praise that might slip out.

They both came to her rescue, though. A minor point to Real Life Will's credit. And they both looked good with a smear of grease. Both smelled like Irish Spring, a scent she'd never particularly cared for before, but now found herself considering in the grocery aisle.

Tonight, however, was not for thinking about Will

Kincaid. Real or imaginary. Tonight was for fomenting rebellion—and having a girls' night. Multitasking. Isla was going to be working late tonight, prepping an extra order for the Canada Day celebration, but Catie didn't want to leave her friend out of the fun of a secret meeting on the parking situation. So she talked Isla into hosting the gathering. Everyone else was instructed to bring drinks and savoury munchies, as well as their best and brightest and most out of the box ideas for a made-in-Pine Harbour parking solution.

Bailey was the first to arrive, then Kerry and the other midwife in Kerry's practice, Jenna Kowalczyk, and Chloe Davis, Jenna's best friend. Chloe was the town librarian and also married to Tom Minelli, and she brought her sister-in-law, Olivia, who had also spent a few years working for Frank at the diner, just like Catie. Because Pine Harbour was that small.

Six hundred people.

Sometimes, she really wondered at herself for coming back here.

But Isla, Kerry, Jenna, Chloe, and Olivia were all newcomers to town, too. Of the entire group, Bailey Patel was the only one born and bred, a fact that startled the group when Catie corrected Jenna.

The midwife did a double take. "Wait, I thought you went to school here?"

"I did. We moved here when I was five."

Bailey winked at Catie. "That's almost the same thing."

Almost, but not quite.

"So do you consider yourself a city girl, or a country girl?" Chloe asked.

"I don't know." Catie thought about it as she stretched

her legs out in front of her. "Both, maybe. When I was growing up, I thought I was a city girl, and couldn't wait to return to it. But then I did, and it didn't feel like home, either. I guess I learned that home is where you plant your flag, for better or worse, so I might as well pick a spot and try to make it what I'm looking for."

It was a bit of a practiced answer, but one that felt pretty close to the truth.

The Howe sisters arrived next, bearing a six-pack of beer from Campbell Mills—apparently part of how he paid for his docking fees this month. "This is related to the parking situation," August said after offering the bottles around.

January pointed to the home brew. "So, today, Campbell told us that he's starting a craft brewery. Just down the road from us." She paused for effect. "On land that will have more than sufficient space for a substantial parking lot. Just like Mac's has at the diner."

"Which puts them at a real advantage compared to businesses that depend on public parking spaces," August added, her brows pulled tight.

The marina had a small parking lot on their own land. Tomorrow's big event would see many more people visiting the harbour than they could accommodate on their own. The town-owned empty lot across from Josh's garage was on the list of spaces that could be turned into a paid parking lot—and who would want to park there to visit the marina if a craft brewery with free parking was just down the road?

"In that case, everyone, I think it's time to pivot our conversation to the crisis at hand." Catie snagged a mini apple strudel stick from a fresh tray Isla brought out before continuing. "All right. Over the last month, I've had individual discussions with each of you about the impact of paid parking on Main Street, and in the town in general. And in addition to this disparity that the Howes just outlined, last weekend something happened to me that really underlined the shortsightedness of this move towards limited parking in general." She gave a recap of not being able to park at the hiking trail head, and getting lost. She left out the rescue details.

That wasn't for public consumption.

"So what can we do to shift the conversation in a productive way?" Olivia asked. "We've proven we can fight back, like we did with the library. But it's going to require a made-in-Pine Harbour solution."

"Because the powers that be don't care about our unique concerns." That was Bailey.

Someone muttered something about dictatorial overlords, which made everyone laugh, and Catie secretly thought about Will. *Authoritarian freak.*

The conversation that followed echoed Catie's observations over the last few weeks. There was deep-seated concern in the community about paid parking being imposed for reasons that might make sense to other towns on the peninsula, but didn't make sense for Pine Harbour —their needs, the needs of their little community, were not being put first.

This was the problem of being a very small part of a larger municipal government. But the reality was, Pine Harbour didn't have the taxpayer base to support its own town governance—a fact Olivia Minelli circled them back to more than once.

They didn't want to draw a lot of attention to their campaign, either. Pine Harbour was a secret little gem of a town, and they wanted to keep it that way.

But they still wanted it to be warm and welcoming for those who discovered it.

"Two things can be true at the same time," Catie finally said, trying to draw together all the conversation threads. "We can be wary of the costs associated with increased tourist traffic. And we can also understand that visitors spend a lot of money in our community. However, managing them cannot be put ahead of understanding that we have..." She pointed at Jenna and Kerry. "Midwifery clients, for example. Or my own salon customers, who shouldn't have to suddenly face a three or six dollar charge every time they come to Main Street for an appointment. We need some sort of balance there. And we have to be careful that any solutions that we present, don't come with added costs without also being a revenue generator, right?"

Olivia nodded. "One of the reasons why the municipality likes paid parking is because it is revenue neutral. It covers the cost of itself."

Catie grabbed on to that part. "But it only *just* covers the cost of itself, right? It's not actually profitable?"

"That's right."

"Then that's our task, friends. Let's find alternates that are actually profitable. Something bolder than a few dollars out of someone's pocket every time they want to run an errand."

The conversation spiralled from there, with no idea being labelled as good or bad. The only thing they pushed each other on was to be more innovative, and not afraid of change.

At one point, Catie found herself wondering what Real Life Will would think. Innovation. Change. Not two of his favourite words.

It was a shame Fantasy Will couldn't submit a statement to the municipality in support of whatever great idea they finally settled on. Fantasy Will would think it was exactly what Pine Harbour needed, based on the strength of Catie's recommendation alone.

9

CANADA DAY in Pine Harbour was always celebrated with a family picnic in the park next to the community centre. The celebration started at ten in the morning, and by four in the afternoon, everything was tidied up and people went their separate ways.

This year there were two significant changes to that schedule. For an hour before the picnic started, there was a community event in partnership with the Saugeen Ojibway Nation. The reeve read a land acknowledgement statement, recognizing Pine Harbour as being a part of "the Territory of the Anishinabek Nation: The People of the Three Fires known as Ojibway, Odawa, and Pottawatomie Nations. We thank the Chippewas of Saugeen, and the Chippewas of Nawash, known collectively as the Saugeen Ojibway Nation, as the traditional keepers of this land."

After the statement, there was a moment of reflection and silence, followed by a walk down Main Street. Many in the crowd wore orange t-shirts in solidarity for those mourning recent discoveries of previously unmarked graves at residential schools.

The event was a first for Pine Harbour, and deeply powerful.

For Catie, it was a jarring shift to immediately head from that event to the picnic, so she went home and thought about the land her house stood on, a home her mother had brought her to from the city, and how all of it had once been the territory of Indigenous nations.

She spent a lot of time thinking about Pine Harbour's future, but she owed it to herself and her neighbours to find out more about its past as well. She made some notes for herself, and put writing her own land acknowledgement for her business at the top of her to-do list. Then she checked her phone to see what the estimated time of arrival was for Bailey's cousins, who were coming up from the city.

The other change to the day's official events was the evening at the beach, with Josh Kincaid and the Howe sisters trying to pull some of the picnic party vibe down the hill to the harbour as well for the late afternoon and evening. Lake Huron was at a lower level than it had been at in years, which meant the return of a sandy beach on the north side of the harbour. Josh was sponsoring a bonfire on that newly revealed beach, and the Howe sisters were running a limited menu grill, with desserts from *Bake Sale!* available for purchase as well.

The bonfire would be the perfect setting to show the Patels the potential of the motel.

Knowing it would be a long day, Catie packed a tote bag with all the essentials for a full day of fun. Sunscreen, multiple hats, sunglasses for every level of light intensity, a book to lose herself in if people got too annoying, and a water bottle because staying hydrated was the key to having fun.

She was already at the park with Bailey when her friend's family arrived at lunch time.

"Oh my God," Bailey said as she flew off their picnic blanket and sprinted across the grass. "You made it, you beautiful people!"

And they really were gorgeous. Polished in a way few of Catie's clients were now, cosmopolitan and sophisticated, their arrival instantly transported her back to the best of her time in the city.

She stood and waved as Bailey navigated them around the groups dotting the lawn.

The tallest of the bunch, a bearded, lean, and well-muscled man with a wicked smile, introduced himself as Dilip Patel. "Bailey's oldest cousin. And you are?"

"Catie," Bailey said. "She's a local friend. And the real estate agent who did the research on the motel for us. Catie, Dilip. This is Dilip's sister Aarti, and our other cousin Sandeep."

"So nice to meet you all." Catie shook their hands enthusiastically, then gave them a quick orientation to the picnic. "The food stations are in that direction. Tickets can be purchased in a couple of places. That's where the face painting is, balloon animals are over there... You get the idea."

"And where do we go to talk business?" Dilip asked.

She laughed and sat down, patting the blanket next to her. "Right here."

WILL HAD COME STRAIGHT to the park from the land acknowledgement to help set up for the picnic, so the Kincaid encampment was in a prime spot, under a big oak tree. Lots of shade coverage, enough for all their chairs, and the perfect location to see the entire park.

For example, if someone wanted to track how long Catie had been lying on a picnic blanket with some hot stranger, they could.

He didn't, of course. He was talking to Owen about his adult daughter Becca's plans for the fall, when her boyfriend—who played pro hockey—would be busy, and with Kerry's due date approaching, Becca wanted to be back in Pine Harbour for the arrival of her baby brother or sister. Owen wanted to know if Will could…something.

"Are you listening to me?"

"Yep." He jerked his attention back to his brother. "Just missed the last part."

"How long has Catie been talking to that guy?"

"Almost two hours," he bit out before catching himself. Owen chuckled.

Will sank lower in his chair.

"As I was saying," Owen continued, mercifully returning to the original subject. "I was hoping Becca and Charlie could stay with you when they come up to visit."

"Yeah, of course." Will scrubbed his hand over his face. "My house is their house."

"You'll need to install some gates on the staircase."

He nodded. "That's fine."

"I can buy them if you give me the dimensions."

"I'll get them." He glanced in the direction of the hamburgers—the opposite direction from where Catie was sitting. "I'm going to grab something to eat. Do you want anything?"

Owen shook his head. "Do you want me to keep guard and report if there's any kissing?"

"She's not going to kiss someone in the middle of the picnic," Will snapped, the back of his neck getting hot.

"And if she wanted to…"

"It's a free country."

Will stalked away. At the burger table, he bumped into some of his students, and allowed himself to be dragged into a volleyball game on the far side of the park.

By the time he finally made it back to his siblings, Catie was long gone—and so was her mystery date.

But Will spotted them again a few hours later, when he followed the party down the hill to the harbour. Catie and her friend were hanging out with Bailey on the marina dock. It looked like Catie was giving one of her polished *Welcome to Pine Harbour* spiels.

Maybe he should go over and introduce himself.

That's the worst idea you've ever had. What would he say? Hi there, I'm the man Catie can barely stand. What are your intentions towards her?

Instead, he forced his feet to head in the opposite direction, to the bonfire set up Josh had put a ton of energy into. He had buried two oversized metal rings in the beach, one inside the other, the inner one lower than the outer one. Adam had secured them a number of good quality fire extinguishers, and Owen had a couple of off-duty EMTs there.

Since the fire wasn't going to be lit until the sun went down, right now the EMTs were handing out stickers and flyers for the community vaccine drive. Will took one, and then found a spot of shade to stand in while he took a picture of the flyer and posted it to the school's social media accounts.

Officially, Will Kincaid was not an online person. Unofficially, he had all the apps on his phone and only used them for work purposes. And occasionally for keeping tabs on community members.

Don't look at Catie's Instagram.

He didn't. Instead, he looked at a dating app he'd downloaded last year and never created a profile on. He knew he was in a rut. Had known it for months, but work had overwhelmed him.

Now he had the summer off.

It hadn't been *that* long since he'd been on a date. There had been a nice woman last summer. They'd dated a few times. And the summer before that there had been... He tried to remember. Two women? Maybe that was three years before.

Will dated, anyway. Every summer, he thought, *this is the year I find someone.* Time had started to blur together. Suddenly he was thirty-eight and past the point when younger Will had been sure he would find the Right Woman.

He clicked on the dating app, but instead of opening it, he deleted it instead.

Then he went and looked at Catie's Instagram account. The first photo was of Sam, proudly in charge of the music playlist the day before. Her caption on it was great, encouraging people to come in and book an appointment to see if Sam's music selections matched their mood or not.

It was the kind of playful community engagement Will just couldn't seem to muster.

As he scrolled back, looking at her posts—including the one everyone had told him about, a joyous call for a summer student employee that made Will wonder why he'd ever questioned Catie's intentions about anything—a kernel of an idea started. A proper apology, and a redo. A chance to start over.

Before the idea could properly form, he heard a familiar laugh. Throaty and amused, confident and sexy. Jumping as if his phone gave him an electrical shock, he fumbled it for a moment before managing to shove it in his pocket. Then he glanced up, knowing Catie and her friend were strolling in his direction.

She wasn't looking at Will, but somehow he knew she knew he was watching her. It was in the way her shoulders squared, and the way she slowed down almost imperceptibly. Ready for a fight, always. Even when she didn't want one.

Even when it was just Will being a dick for reasons he could not name.

He forced a smile on his face—why didn't that come more naturally when he was around her?—and stepped out from under the tree.

———

CATIE LIKED the way she had Dilip's complete attention, and hated that she could not say the same about herself toward him in return. She was trying, but everywhere she took the potential investor, Will was there in the distance— glowering, and then pretending to ignore her.

And now not in the distance at all, but right in front of them.

Smiling. Sort of.

"Will," she said smoothly. One of them could be slick no matter what. "This is Bailey's cousin, Dilip Patel."

"The school principal," Dilip said, grinning. "I've heard a lot about you."

Catie's eyes flared wide as Will glanced sideways at her. No. Hell no. Not from her. But now Will was grinning for real. "Oh yeah?"

"My sister is a teacher. The community school you have here sounds like a lot of work."

"It sure is. But it's rewarding, too. Nice to be able to keep school local."

She rolled her eyes, not that either of them noticed.

Will leaned in her direction. "What brings you and Catie down to the harbour today?"

She'd wasted the eye-roll on his humble brag. She should have used it on the world's silliest question. "Same reason you're here?" She put a distinct *are you being dumb?* questioning uplift at the end. "The bonfire."

"Right." Will crossed his arms and furrowed his brow at Dilip. "But why *else* are you here?"

She wrapped her hand around Dilip's impressive biceps. "To see his cousin."

"Also getting to know Catie." And bless his heart, he didn't say anything about the motel.

She liked the way that wiped the grin off Will's face. *That's right, Mr. Kincaid. Some people actually like me.*

Dilip turned around. "Speaking of Bailey, I should go and find her." He glanced back at Catie. "Are you joining us for dinner?"

She wanted to say yes, just to keep Will wondering, but she was also ready to find a spot on the beach and read a book for a while. So she shook her head regretfully. "But thank you for the invite. And we'll keep in touch, yes?"

"Absolutely."

As the lawyer sauntered away, she took her time turning her attention back to Will.

When she finally did, his expression was carefully neutral. "How's it going, then?"

"Great. You?"

"Yeah. Excellent." He did a slow pivot on his heel, taking in the growing crowd. "Nice turn out."

The park they were standing in was at the bottom of a T-junction. With the lake behind them, the marina sat to their right, and the beach stretched out towards the forest on their left.

Across the road, on one side of the T junction was Joshua's garage, and on the other side was an empty, abandoned parking lot. Except today it wasn't empty. It was full, but not overwhelmingly so.

And it was to that orderly, well-sorted group of cars that Will pointed. "Someone should take a picture of that and send it to the powers-that-be. Point out to them that Pine Harbour doesn't have a parking problem most of the time, even for a big holiday event."

The powers-that-be. Will—the authoritarian freak—was echoing the conversation from the night before. Was he more open to innovation and change than she had given him credit for? "How would you feel about that lot being modernized and having paid meters installed?"

He made a face. "Nothing wrong with how we do it."

So maybe a *no* on the innovation and change after all. She made a noncommittal noise. Time to go find a spot on the beach.

"You don't agree?"

She lifted her gaze to meet his—only realizing when his bright eyes locked onto her attention that she'd been avoiding looking at him quite this...directly. "I didn't say anything."

"Which isn't your usual style."

So she made the same noncommittal noise again.

He gave her a faint smile, this one different than the others before. Not cocky, not unsure. A bit cool, and a lot distant. Then he nodded and shrugged at the same time. "You're probably already on it."

No way was she being goaded into revealing her secrets. She dug into her tote bag and pulled out her book. "I'm going to grab a spot on the beach before it gets too crowded."

"See you later?"

What kind of a question was that? They always saw each other, whether she liked it or not. "Maybe?"

"Are you staying until the bonfire?"

"Yeah."

Another nod/shrug combo. "Then I'll see you later."

She forced herself to walk past him, and not look back. What she really wanted to do was stay and dig into him about his unnecessary fear of change and what he really meant when he guessed that she was *already on it*.

But this wasn't the time or the place. Maybe there would be a chance to bring it up at next week's training. *"Hey, by the way, last week you said something to me and I've been stewing about it ever since."* No, okay, she wasn't going to bring it up. She was going to do her best to put Will out of her mind, and just enjoy the rest of the day.

Once she was settled on the beach, though, she couldn't get into her book. Even the snack she'd bought earlier, a handy to-go quartet of Isla's *Bake Sale!* treats, didn't help her relax.

Maybe she needed to wander back over to the marina and get something more substantial for dinner. *Maybe you should have tagged along with the Patels for dinner.* She stood up, carefully packed up her tote bag, and made her way back to the park, stopping to chat to people along the way.

She enjoyed ninety percent of those conversations.

The last one, though, was with her nosy neighbour, Frances Schmidt, who never had a nice word to say to Catie, and today was no exception.

"Miss Berton," her neighbour said, commanding her to stop.

Maybe that's where Catie's dislike of Will's preference for formal address came from. She pasted on a smile. "Frances."

"I noticed your sprinkler went off this morning."

Nosy. Fucking. Neighbour. "Yes?"

"It's a no-watering day."

Catie pressed her lips together and counted backwards to one. "That's for municipal water usage, Frances. I have a rain barrel and that's the source of my timed sprinkler."

"How am I supposed to know that?"

The gall of her to sound offended, when it was none of her business in the first place. "You could just not worry about it?"

"We have rules for a reason."

"And I follow them." Catie went to step around her neighbour, but stopped as she realized Will was directly in front of her, talking to a group of people—including Frances's daughter, Ashley.

The older woman's gaze followed the line of Catie's attention, then swivelled back. "Did you know Ashley was home from college? You should go say hello."

Catie didn't have the same negative thoughts about the younger woman as she did about the girl's mother, but she didn't want to go *say hello*.

Which meant she had to stand here and find something

else to talk to Frances about until the people directly in her path moved on.

Of course, she could just move on with her life and not worry about what Frances thought, but that wouldn't stop her neighbour from whispering about her non-stop, exactly as she had about Catie's mother, too.

"Just ignore her. That Schmidt woman is a nosy bitch who doesn't have enough fun in her life." Twenty years later, that stinging observation remained painfully true.

"Frances," Catie said smoothly, a practiced approach that doubled as a shield against evil. "About the rain barrel system. Since you seem to have a good handle on who is watering their lawns excessively, perhaps you could help me spread the word about this alternative?"

"People don't need a new system. They only need to stick to watering on the allowed days."

Catie had expected that sourpuss response. She didn't really care about Frances's opinion, anyway.

All she cared about was Will getting out of her path, and Ashley, too.

Preferably not together, she thought darkly as Ashley grabbed Will's arm and pulled him from where he was standing near the deck at the side of the marina's main building, toward the dock.

The girl was almost young enough to be his student, for goodness' sake. A few years younger and she *would have been* one of his students.

Will, being the least spontaneous and fun person in Pine Harbour, didn't move far. He slowed down, glancing back at the group they'd just split away from. Ashley pulled harder, prompting Will to say something under his breath that Catie couldn't hear.

Whatever it was, it prompted Ashley to pout. Even

from a distance Catie could see her lower lip jutting into the space between them. The play for Will's emotions worked, and he closed the gap between them and ducked his head, mollifying her.

Catie couldn't hear their conversation, but it wasn't exactly private. They were standing next to a group of people. After a few exchanges, Ashley tossed her hair over her shoulder, gave Will a hug, and spun away. But the girl misjudged how close she was to the edge of the dock, and the final turn of her spin completed with a splash into the lake.

Frances shrieked. "That's my baby!"

On the dock, everyone pointed and laughed. Everyone, that was, except for Will, who without a second thought handed his phone to the person beside him and jumped into the lake after the panicking woman. The whole exchange had been annoying to watch, but that part was pretty impressive. He quickly got Ashley oriented to the ladder and urged her up and out of the water.

As soon as he hauled himself back onto the dock, she was clinging to him, like a sad, drowned rat plastering itself to a…

"Oh, he's just so handsome," Frances said, fluttering her hand against her mouth in a weird mix of worry and admiration. "Good job, Ashley."

Catie narrowed her eyes at her neighbour—good *job*? "Aren't you going to help?"

Frances scowled back. "She doesn't need my help. She has Will. Look at them."

Catie jerked her attention back to the display on the dock. Will had his arms around Ashely now. Although on second thought, it was less of a hug and more like he had his hands on her upper arms. Catie liked to think he was peeling the other woman off him, but it wasn't clear from this angle. Then he scanned the crowd. His attention finally landing on January, rushing towards them with towels.

Beside her, Francis said, "My daughter is going to marry that man," at the exact same moment Will shoved Ashley into the towel January was holding out.

"Can you deal with her?" He asked his colleague, and that was loud enough to carry across the crowd.

Catie smothered a smile as Frances made a huffing sound. Will glared at the person who had been holding his phone, who immediately handed it over, and then the soaking wet principal stalked away, water still sluicing off him.

No, she didn't think Ashley was going to marry that man after all.

And the weird fog that had settled on Catie's shoulders lifted.

When she got home that night, she looked at the email from Will. Maybe it was time to write back.

From: Catie Berton
To: Will Kincaid

Will,
Thank you so much for the belated reply. Since my last email some time ago, my schedule has filled up. What day does the club meet on? I'll see if I can fit it in.

Regards,
Catie

10
___

WILL LAUGHED out loud when he received Catie's email. He wondered how many drafts it had taken her to once again put him in his place.

He replied immediately.

From: Will Kincaid
To: Catie Berton

Catie
My apologies, again. In the past, the club has met on
Thursdays, but you are welcome to pick another weekday
afternoon. Whatever works for you.
Yours,
Will

He spent the next week checking his email—no reply, she was taking her time and making him sweat—while he also hid at Josh's garage. Working on his Duster was infinitely preferable to fielding the unrelenting romantic inquiries of Ashley Schmidt, who had dropped by his house once and called twice—but thankfully hadn't figured out that he liked to spend time with his brothers.

The universe was having a good laugh at his expense. He'd had a few passing thoughts about looking for the right person to settle down with, and now he was in the cross hairs of someone who he couldn't be less interested in.

Ashley was a nice enough girl, but there was a hard emphasis on *girl*. And it didn't seem to matter to her that he didn't share her enthusiasm for the thought of dating each other. When Will thought about finding the right person, he knew deep down it would be like the kind of love his brothers felt for their wives. All consuming, intense. Scary, even, because once that love took hold in his chest, it would require sacrifice and change.

Once he fell in love, if he was ever that lucky, he would be changed forever.

He would know if he was falling in love with Ashley Schmidt. He wasn't. He couldn't even bring himself to fall into like with her for an afternoon.

Other than that minor personal situation, which he was doing his best to avoid entirely, and the upcoming SAR training on Thursday night, he didn't have anything else on his schedule for the week. The ideal lazy summer vacation, after a tough school year—but the calm was disrupted by two very real callouts for the Search and Rescue team, back to back.

The trainees weren't ready to participate in searches yet, so they didn't join the veteran members at the Red Bay Lodge parking lot, which had been converted to the second command centre in as many days.

And once again, they were right on the edge of the water, which added a layer of complexity to the search.

The day before, the subject had been a little boy, and he'd been discovered within an hour, much to the relief of his parents. Today it was a woman in her eighties, who may or may not have taken medication that could cause confusion and disorientation.

The search took hours, and was complicated by the insertion of community volunteers—although Tom did a good job of redirecting most of those folks up and down the shore road, keeping them out of the water.

When they found the search subject, she was alive, but not conscious. They had to work together with emergency services to stabilize her and safely get her off the rocky shore and onto a backboard.

That night's debrief was longer than the day before—and they all stayed together at the training centre until they got a positive update from the hospital, which wasn't always possible. It helped that both Tom and Will had paramedic siblings.

"Probably a sign we should add water search training to the summer's schedule," Tom said as they walked out to their trucks. It was an add-on training course they usually did in the winter, when they could combine it with ice safety. But the more the shoreline was developed, and people unfamiliar with the lake were spending time there, the more often they'd get called out for this type of search.

Will dragged himself home, ready for a hot shower, a beer, and his bed. He frowned when he found a gift bag sitting in front of his door. Inside was a beach towel, and a suggestive note from Ashley that the next time they went for a swim together, it could be part of a day at the beach.

He sighed, set it just inside, and resigned himself to the fact that the next morning's agenda would need to include a direct conversation with the persistent young woman about how he just wasn't interested.

He bumped the beer up the action item list, stalking into his kitchen and finding a cold bottle in the fridge. Then he climbed the stairs to his bedroom, started the shower, and stripped out of his clothes. He smelled like the lake, and pine trees, and a day of stressed-out sweat.

A trip to the beach was exactly what he needed, but not with Ashley.

A fleeting thought of Catie flashed through his mind. Stretched out on an oversized beach towel, nose buried in a book. Would she be a bikini type, getting maximum sun? Something bright, like the running pants she wore to training nights? Neon triangles covering her breasts…

He shook his head, trying to dissuade himself from that line of thinking.

Trying, failing.

Maybe she was more of a sporty one-piece kind of girl. A red racing stripe up her side as she chased him into the water, launching herself into the waves. The spandex stretching high up her waist, baring a plump slice of her ass…

Stop.

He was half-hard, though, and his imagination was off to the races. Catie in every *Sports Illustrated* Swimsuit Edition poster young Will had ever pored over. A zippered suit, unzipped down to her navel. Her breasts again, round little swells. Her shoulders, as he slipped one strap off her body, then the other.

Making out in the lake. Slow kisses.

Fuck.

He forced himself into the shower, taking his beer with him. Hot steam, cold lager. It did nothing to scrub his mind of the inappropriate and fucking glorious fantasies, stacking up fast and furious now.

How was he going to look her in the eye on Thursday? His only explanation was that it had been a weird week, and a long two days of searching for people.

He was tired. And apparently, horny for a certain brand of opinionated spitfire. At some point, he'd need to reconcile these unexpected feelings with the fact she didn't like him very much. It wasn't healthy to want someone who didn't want you back.

But oh, it felt pretty fucking healthy to want Catie tonight. She was so much. Endlessly challenging. Her glorious glower. A glare that would win awards. The perfect stare, unwavering and bold.

She was confident and knowing. Is that what she would be like in bed? As she peeled off the neon bikini and climbed on top of him, rubbing her slick pussy against his cock, and then his belly, before climbing onto his face?

Fuck. Fuuuck…

Will closed his eyes and gave in, stroking himself hard as he fantasized about the impossible dream—Catie Berton liking him enough to let him tongue-fuck her into ecstasy.

One of Catie's favourite things about SAR was the phone tree of text messages before training each week, reminding each other about gear and coordinating rides together. The camaraderie and team spirit cheered her up every single time.

Today's training had changed at the last minute, based on real rescues that had happened earlier in the week, and the text chain told them to wear clothes that could get wet.

Catie went with her trusty neon-yellow leggings and a long-sleeved navy blue swim shirt. Not quite visible enough, she thought to herself, so she put a hot pink bandana over her hair, too.

At training, Tom launched right into lecture mode, all business. "For the most part, from our perspective, we're focused on shore-based approaches to a rescue. But on any rescue, if we're looking at a water search, we also have to consider whether motorized watercraft would be a better rescue option, and that means coordinating with local authorities. A reminder that that's a decision that is made at the search coordinator level, and your team leader will update you as appropriate, but if you don't see a boat, don't assume one is coming. For that reason, what we're going to practice today are some simple shore-based approaches. In the fall and winter, we run a separate training course on lake rescue, but all of us need to know how to toss a rope either into the lake or, more likely, a river."

Tom gestured to where Will was over at the rope cupboards, pulling out specific types. He waved as Tom continued. "It looks like everyone got the text messages about clothing. Just to underline why it matters. Before we talked about the importance of visibility. Now we need to consider buoyancy as well. You don't want to wear anything into the water, or even on the shoreline, that could weigh you down. And it's not just clothes—our packs get taken off and left back from the waterline. And when the water is cold—and it always is on the Georgian Bay side, if we get called over there—we need to be considerate of what will help retain our body heat temperature for as long as possible."

Shit. Catie hadn't considered that at all. She put her

hand in the air. "Can you elaborate on that?" She gestured down her body. "I went strictly for swimability here, not warmth."

"And that's fine for today," Tom said reassuringly. "We're just going down to the creek. But Yolanda, can you share your favourite pieces?"

The older woman stood up and took them through a quick tour of the layers she was wearing, including a lightweight wool base layer in bright red that Catie adored.

Then another member of the SAR who didn't usually come to the training nights was introduced. Sharon Dunks ran an open water swim club, and gave a quick overview of how SAR members were welcome at any of their regular swims, and could participate in their training programs for free.

Catie saw another fitness goal in her future.

Tonight, though, they weren't all getting into the water. Only Sharon would be rescued, over and over again, as she floated in a creek not far from the training building.

As Will handed out bright red bags with rope coiled inside, Sharon and Yolanda demonstrated the difference between an overhand throw—more accurate—compared to an underhand or sidearm toss, which were better for distance.

"Practice makes perfect. And tossing a throw bag is hard, so we're going to practice it tonight until our arms fall off."

Sharon nodded in agreement with Yolanda's statement. "And that practice will carry forward to when you actually put it into motion. Every time, before you do your actual toss, you'll want to go through the throwing motion a few times. Visualize where you want the rope to land, ahead of where your rescue target is. The visualization and practice movements both help the throw land on target."

"Ready to go?" Tom glanced around for any final questions. "All right. Lead the way, ladies."

A path behind the training centre led to a well-maintained set of stairs, with multiple landings and benches on the way down to the creek.

"I haven't been down here before," Catie said to Yolanda as they descended.

"Really?" The other woman grinned. "Then you're in for a treat."

Catie heard the rush of water before she saw the waterfall. Wide and layered at the top, and then narrowed by boulders, it split the river into two parts. One curved off into the forest, leaving a wade-able but fast-moving creek at the bottom of the stairs.

Sharon jogged ahead along the creek bed, toward the waterfall, then waded into the middle of the creek where the water was waist high.

Yolanda got into position down current from her. Sharon yelled out an exaggerated "Oh no!", kicked out her feet, and was quickly carried toward them on her back. Yolanda yelled to get her attention, and made the rope toss look easy. Sharon grabbed it the first time and climbed out.

"Mission accomplished," Lore cheered. "We can go home now."

Everyone laughed.

"I think you've volunteered to go first." Yolanda gestured for Lore to join her. "Everyone else, line up."

It turned out, it was not nearly as easy as Yolanda made it look.

Over and over again, Sharon jogged up the path, into

the water, and was carried back in their direction. More than half the time, the rope missed her by a mile.

The only person who made it look as easy as Yolanda was Will—of course. Both of his tosses were pitch perfect, and the way he confidently pulled Sharon to the safest exit point was noted, too.

After everyone had two attempts, Tom split them up into pairs, and tasked them with repeating the same throw ten times in a row while Sharon took a break. "Then move to another toss strategy, underhand or from the side, and give me another ten. Repeat, repeat, repeat, and then we'll take a break. Pick a rock as your target person, and keep going until you can hit that rock three times in a row."

As they always did, the more experienced SAR members spaced themselves out amongst the trainees, and Will ended up between Catie and Jeong. He didn't say much, just practiced alongside them, but when they asked for tips or feedback, he gave them positive suggestions.

No critique. No comparison to his obviously superior skill.

Curious.

"All right, everyone, gather back around," Tom hollered. The sun was low in the sky now, glinting like cotton candy pink and burnt coral through the trees. "We'll take turns rescuing Sharon again, but this time, you'll get more than one attempt. Let's build that muscle memory! Jeong, you'll go first, then Lore, and Forrest. Tobin, Will, Yolanda, and Catie, you can take a break."

The men drifted away, and Yolanda came over to see how Catie was doing.

"I can see how it takes a lot of practice, but when I hit that rock, it felt great."

"You'll get it. You're really picking it all up fast. There's a lot to remember."

"I'm glad I asked Isla to train me before I joined." Catie rubbed her shoulder as they reached the stairs. "That was hard!"

Will, who was stretching on the first landing up the stairs, gave her what sounded like genuine encouragement. "In a real rescue, you only need to do it a few times."

"After hiking for hours, maybe," Yolanda added.

"Let's not scare the new folks." Catie didn't miss the way Will glanced at her carefully, and it clicked in—he was being cautious about criticizing her. Consciously. Huh.

She didn't know how she felt about that. It was good, of course. But also...why? She squinted up to the sky, where a vulture circled.

"That guy knows I'm almost dead," she muttered.

Yolanda chuckled, then turned as Tom called out her name, asking her to come help. "Oops, gotta go help the boss."

That left them alone on the stairs. Catie glanced around. "Where did Tobin get off to?"

Will pointed further down the creek. "Calling his kids for bedtime."

"Ah." She slowly climbed the stairs to join Will on the landing. "Have you had to actually do this? On a search?"

He nodded. "Twice, and both times it was for fellow search and rescue people. We slip and fall into fast running water sometimes."

"Oh. Shit." She swallowed hard and tried to make a joke. "Good thing you're extra competent at saving girls who fall into water."

He frowned in confusion.

"On Canada Day," she offered innocently, leaning back against the railing.

His eyes narrowed as he clued in. "You saw that. Of course you did."

"Did she call you her hero?"

"Stop."

She did, immediately. But she was still laughing on the inside, her whole body shaking slightly with giggles.

He joined her against the railing, his elbow brushing hers. "I'm not her hero, for the record."

"I'm sure that's a great disappointment for her mother."

"Frances?"

"Yeah." The answer was sour in Catie's mouth. She shouldn't have said anything, because now Will was looking at her, really looking at her.

"Not a fan of Mrs. Schmidt?"

She hesitated. If it were anyone else, she wouldn't have even shown this much of her hand. Could she trust Will with the truth? She hedged her bet, but gave him a little. "Not a fan of small-minded gossips in general."

"That's fair." He sighed. "Well, hey, at least you get to work out some of that disappointment tonight."

"True."

"And next week will be just as physical."

Was it just her imagination, or was the way Will said *physical* kind of dirty? She couldn't remember the training schedule all of a sudden. "What's next week?"

"Ropes training." He started to add something else, a joke, and then stopped like he thought better of it.

She leaned in and lowered her voice. "What were you going to say there?"

"Nothing." But there was an edge to his denial.

"Was it a tying me up joke?"

He choked on a laugh.

She grinned. "Was it?"

"Yes." And his cheek darkened a little. Like a very subtle blush.

Just then, Tom called out their names.

She bumped her elbow against his as she stood up. "You should have made it. That would have been funny."

"I'll keep that in mind."

"Excellent. It'll slowly help rectify the vicious rumour that Mr. Kincaid doesn't have a sense of humour."

"If that rumour is circulating, I'll have one guess where it started."

"Frances Schmidt," Catie deadpanned.

Will nodded, his face absolutely serious. "Absolutely."

"I'm so glad we're on the same page." She grabbed her throw bag. "Gotta get back to work."

He followed her down the steps. "Hey," he called out.

She glanced back over her shoulder at him. "Yeah?"

"I'm still waiting on an email from you."

Catie was well aware of the message sitting in her inbox. She smiled. "I know."

11

WILL FOUND himself counting down the hours to training the following week. It wasn't that he didn't have anything else to do—he was busy. First, he found Ashley Schmidt and very directly told her he wasn't interested—and returned the towel she'd given him as a gift. And he made great progress on his Duster, to the point where he felt comfortable driving it over to have dinner with his brothers at the Green Hedgehog in Lion's Head.

But the whole time, he felt a low-level hum of anticipation for ropes night.

Climbing had always been a passion of his. Being able to teach Catie how it was applicable to Search and Rescue? It would be a highlight of his summer.

Like a lot of SAR skills, being a rope rescue technician was a specific certification that was beyond their initial training. But the team got the basic exposure during this preliminary course to give them a taste of what further training could mean—a lot of fun, as well as a functional skill that could save someone's life.

Tonight they were doing simple climbs and rappels off

the SAR's climbing tower. The first half of training was an orientation to the rigging and safety protocol, then Will demonstrated how to properly repel down the tower.

Then it was the trainees' turn. They used both sides of the tower. Will and Yolanda took Jeong, Catie, and Lore on one side, and Tom and Tobin took the other trainees on the other side.

They all sailed through navigating down off the tower, so the next thing Will demonstrated was how to use the ascender attachment on their harnesses to go back up—which some people found harder.

Catie seemed a little nervous and encouraged the other two to go first, but when it was finally her turn she bounded up to where Will stood at the base of the tower. Together they did the safety check on their harnesses, Catie shadowing his movements carefully. Then he helped her get the ropes properly threaded through the rocker and the ascender hooked to her harness.

"All set?"

She took a deep breath and grinned. "I think so."

She turned quickly, but not away from him, not towards the tower. In her excitement and nervousness, she twisted towards Will instead, right up against him, and he caught her in his arms.

It was, in many weeks of training, the closest they had ever been.

And maybe it was the unexpected collision, or the way she vibrated with excitement, the vulnerability of her trying something new and scary and trusting him to help her—but in that moment, that split second before he let her go, it was hard to pretend that he hadn't spent an inordinate amount of time imagining all of this—her scent, the feel of her body against his.

And somehow he had almost entirely kept that knowledge from himself. Somehow, he had pretended to himself that he didn't think she smelled like sunshine.

Where had he gotten that idea from? Was it the time she rescued him and used her shirt as a sling? Had she smelled like sunshine then? Is that how he'd recorded that memory? Because now he knew that she smelled like lime and something floral, maybe grapefruit. And that was so much better than sunshine.

What the hell did sunshine even smell like, anyway?

But this sweet, citrusy brightness that was so subtle, the only way to smell it would be to be two inches from her hair, was absolutely perfect.

And then he stepped back, putting space between them. Pretending all of that hadn't crashed through his mind like a pervy Kool-Aid man. In the next moments, he was thankful for years of training that allowed him to continue going through the motions of coolly telling her how to get started, then prompting her as she lifted off the ground and headed up to where the others waited for her on the platform above.

She lost her rhythm halfway up, and got tired.

"You can do it," he murmured to her. "You're stronger than you think. Take a moment to shake it off, then keep going."

She whined a little, then laughed. "Sorry. That's annoying."

He shook his head. "Not at all."

The truth was, he didn't think she was ever annoying—not now, for sure, and probably not ever. Perhaps, deep down, he had always found her captivating and alluring. And it was only because *she* didn't like *him,* that he had stubbornly dug in his heels and said yeah, me, too.

But no. Not him. Not *too.*

He probably should have realized that he'd been lying to himself when his tired brain had dragged him through a kaleidoscope of fantasies about Catie as a Sports Illustrated swimsuit model. But those had been two-dimensional. This three-dimensional reality of frustrated, determined, resilient Catie, covered in a slight sheen of hard-earned sweat punched through the final wall of his denial.

Jesus, he was going to get half-hard during training, in front of a woman who barely tolerated him—and all their teammates.

She swung one of her legs up onto the platform, then rolled all the way on. And as her head popped back out, she gave him a cheery smile and a big old wave, he thought, *say something smart aleck-y, put us back on the footing where we don't like each other.*

But nothing like that came out of his mouth. All he could do was give her a thumbs up.

———

BACK AT THE TRAINING CENTRE, Will checked the lines carefully before putting them away in storage. Catie and Jeong both helped, eagerly, and Will was happy to answer their questions about further rope rescue training.

By the time they were done, everyone else was gone. Tom locked up behind them, then the four of them walked out to their vehicles.

Jeong waved goodbye first, then Tom got in his truck. Catie and Will were still standing next to her car as the others departed.

Why was he sticking around?

Her phone rang, and she pulled it out. He wasn't trying to see the screen, but it was right there. *Dilip Patel.* She answered with a cherry hello—seriously, what had happened to snarky Catie? Where had she gone?—and then turned away from Will slightly.

He started to move towards his truck, but Catie reached out and grabbed his arm. *Hang on,* she mouthed.

Which meant he was forced to listen to her end of the conversation. It wasn't eavesdropping, then. She'd asked him to wait.

And once he finished justifying listening to what she was saying to her new friend, it sounded like it was about…real estate. "I know Bailey is keen on that specific property, but I think it's smart to consider other possibilities, too. I'm meeting with her tomorrow to do a drive around. Would you be interested in a FaceTime call when we get to those sites, or do you want a summary after the fact?" She smiled again. Fuck, her smile was glorious. All hope, like the world was this guy's oyster. "Sounds good. Okay, thanks for calling me back. Talk soon."

"Business?" Will asked when she tucked her phone away. Was that subtle enough?

"Yeah. Bailey is interested in buying the motel."

"The haunted, abandoned motel?"

"It's not haunted." She rolled her eyes. That was better. He liked this Catie, knew how to handle her. "Her cousin is one of her investors. So he's my client, too."

"Ah."

She narrowed her eyes, like there was more to that *ah* than just making small talk. Which there was, but she couldn't know that. Will was not ready for Catie to know anything about what was going on in his messy thoughts. He probably wouldn't ever be ready for that.

"Listen, I wanted to talk to you." She snapped a pair of hair elastics off her wrist and gathered the damp tendrils of her hair into two rough pigtails. "At some point we got on the wrong footing, you and me, and I'd like to deal with it."

It was unexpected, direct, and painfully accurate. "Oh. Well. All right." He glanced around the parking lot. "Do you want to talk now?"

She smacked her shoulder, nailing a mosquito who wanted to munch on her lovely skin. "Can we go to the diner? Get something to eat? Do you mind?"

This wasn't where he thought his night was going to go, but *mind*? Not in the fucking slightest. "Of course."

He followed her in his truck, and when they arrived at Mac's, they had lots of choice where to sit because the dinner rush was well over. Catie led him to the corner booth, a few tables removed from where anyone else was sitting.

"Don't order anything too special," she told him. "Frank will be closing up the kitchen soon."

That was the bossy woman he'd gotten used to pretending to dislike. "Thanks for the hot tip," he said dryly. "I'll do my best to not be a dick customer."

She paused for a beat. "Okay, so maybe I didn't need to say that."

"Maybe." He gave her a half smile. "But you used to work here, and you know how annoying demanding customers are, especially this close to the end of the day."

Her face relaxed. "Yeah."

"It's all right." He only gave a cursory glance at the menu, and was ready when the waitress came over. "I'll have a burger, please, and either fries or a salad, whichever is easier for Frank."

Catie's lips twitched. "Same for me."

Once they were alone, she dove right back to the direct conversation she'd wanted to have. "You have the wrong idea about me, you know."

He took a deep breath, then nodded. "Yeah. I probably do."

She tipped her head to the side. "What kind of idea is that, anyway? Can we just put it on the table without me guessing?"

He poked the tip of his tongue into his cheek, feeling all kinds of foolish. "I don't even really know." Except he did. He just didn't want to say it out loud. He cleared his throat. "You're bossy."

"Ah."

"And you change shit. Constantly."

One of her eyebrows lifted. "Oh."

"And…" He stalled out.

"Please, don't stop on account of my feelings."

Oh, she could be so droll sometimes. "It's not your feelings that I'm about to re-bruise," he muttered. "When I volunteered myself for the bachelor auction, and you turned me down. That stung a little. A lot, maybe. I dunno, that felt like a turning point for us."

"Oh." Her eyes went wide. "Wow. That's…really fragile."

He huffed a protesting breath, but didn't bother to argue. It was fragile, he could see that.

Her shoulders hunched up, her whole body rocking from side to side as she took a slow breath, then she exhaled and cocked her head on an angle again. She was constantly in motion, and he found it all so overwhelming.

Then she gave him a look he couldn't translate, her

expression both challenging and…maybe soft, although he didn't know if that was a trap. "Can we call a truce?"

He raised his eyebrows. "Are we at war?"

"Is that a no?" Her tone sharpened.

"Is that a yes?"

"It's not like when I see you I go to DEFCON 5 or anything."

The correction was out of his mouth before he could stop it. "That's normal readiness."

She blinked in surprise. "Pardon?"

"DEFCON 5. It doesn't mean whatever you think it means."

"High alert."

"Yeah, no. That's not what it means."

"Are you sure?" Oh, the suspicion in her voice.

Will smothered a smile. "Yes. I'm sure."

Her expression promised that he'd definitely moved the DEFCON scale in whatever direction was up. "So what is high alert?"

"DEFCON 3."

"That's the middle of the scale. What's the highest level?"

"DEFCON 1? Nuclear war in progress."

"Oh." She paused. "Well, we aren't at that level."

"A relief for everyone, I'm sure."

She laughed. "What are we doing?"

He didn't know, precisely, but whatever it was, he couldn't stop. "Do you know?"

Her eyes danced, bright and amused, but still dangerous. She thought he was *fragile*. "Are you going to answer every question with another question?"

"Are you—" He cut himself off and grinned. "Yes."

"Why?"

"Because we're at war. Apparently."

She didn't reply to that immediately. Maybe it was his addition of the word *apparently*. Because they weren't at war. Not really. They were at *odds*. Finally, she glanced away, and her next words were muttered. "Everyone likes you."

Most people. But she didn't, and right now, her opinion of him was the only one that mattered. "Not you."

"Apparently." She repeated his word back to him.

They were at odds. That didn't mean they didn't like each other. It meant… He lowered his voice. Like this was top-secret. "Do you?"

That made her lift her head, and she looked at him straight on. "Like you?"

"Yes."

She thought about it long enough to make him nervous. Maybe they weren't on the same page after all. "Enough to offer a truce."

Ouch. A pity truce, then.

But if they stopped this bizarre war of feelings, maybe he could show her he was actually that nice guy everyone else seemed pretty fond of. "Then truce accepted. But I thought we'd been getting along better."

She shrugged. "On the surface, maybe. There's a difference, you know."

He did. But the way she said it made him frown. "Of course I do."

"That." She snapped her fingers. "That, right there. Whatever thought just went through your head? That's the part of you that doesn't like me."

There was no part of him that didn't like her. "I don't like that you think I don't know the difference between playing nice on the surface, and actually being at peace with someone. But—"

"Maybe you know the difference and do it anyway."

Because he couldn't help himself.

But that made him sound like a fourteen-year-old boy, so he didn't say it. "Or maybe I didn't realize how I was acting, or what I was projecting. I promise you, it isn't that I secretly don't like you."

She shifted again, restless.

"I like you a lot, actually." He cleared his throat. "You make me nervous, and that's not a bad thing. I told you— don't stop holding my feet to the fire."

"You mean it."

"Yeah." He shrugged.

"All right." She paused as their food arrived. "I make you nervous?"

"We can add that to the long list."

"Because I'm bossy?"

He laughed. "No. Because you're direct and bold and brave. All good things."

That got him an honest to God beaming smile. "That's kind of you to say."

"Thank you. I'm trying."

She laughed. "I have noticed, by the way. That you're being careful not to be too critical."

Now he was grinning back at her. "Good."

"I wasn't sure if you were being nice to me because you think you should be nice to everyone, or…"

Will didn't know what to make of that thought. Of course, that was why he should be nice to Catie. That was why he should be nice to everyone. "You object to kindness as a civic responsibility?"

She frowned in thought and dipped a French fry in

ketchup. "From people in general? No. From you? Maybe." She ate the fry and her expression morphed through a few reactions, settling on something thoughtful. "I think that there's a difference between being civil—or a truce, for example—and fake niceties."

It was the fake part that bothered her. That made sense. Will leaned in. "I promise that there is nothing fake in my desire to be kinder to you. I will never be fake with you. Maybe—and I know I should not be proud of this—but maybe that's why I was grumpy with you for too long about something stupid. Because I couldn't cover up my initial grumpy feelings with you. And I own that I should have handled that with more maturity. I own that I should have continued communicating with you and then we would have avoided the whole problem. But if there's any silver lining from that period where I was an ass to you, it is that I promise I cannot be fake with you."

Shock rippled across her face. "Well. That's an angle I hadn't considered. I just… I've seen it too many times. Where people say one thing to your face and another when they turn around. When your back is turned, they're scurrying off to whisper rumours."

He frowned. "Is anyone spreading rumours about you?"

The thought hurt him to his core that anyone would be making Catie's life difficult. He hated that.

She made a face "No. Not now. I go out of my way to avoid being fodder for the rumour mill."

So it was in her past.

Will felt like he was getting closer to understanding what drove Catie, what made her so wary of him. But he also sensed that he couldn't push her, that if she wanted to share she would and if she didn't, it wasn't his place to ask. Not yet. Maybe one day. If their friendship grew, then she would confide in him.

And until then…they had SAR.

They dug into their food, and the conversation drifted to the competition next. Then they talked a bit about the paid parking drama, and finally, as their plates were cleared, Will remembered that he owed her a proper apology.

"Listen, you wanted to clear the air, and I appreciate that. But I think I also need to say, directly, that I'm sorry for not handling any of this better before. You told me I owed you an apology—"

"That was before you rescued me." She gave him a crooked half smile. They hadn't talked about that again.

"One does not replace the other. So…I'm sorry."

"Thank you." She sighed and rubbed her belly. "That was great. The conversation and the burger. But I should get going."

"Yeah. Me, too."

Neither of them moved. And then they both did, at the same time, so they bumped into each other as they stood up. Will stepped out of the way, letting Catie go ahead of him.

Outside, he followed her to her car, because it seemed like the right thing to do. She unlocked, then opened her driver's side door.

And still, they lingered, staring at each other. If she were any other person, if he hadn't spent months being an absolute shit to her for no good reason, Will might think this was a prelude to a kiss. A soft, unexpected, gentle kiss full of potential. A spontaneous opportunity to turn a friendship into something more and see where it might lead.

Except he didn't even have a friendship with Catie.

He had a truce. And one did not spontaneously kiss the opponent during a truce, primarily because they were your opponent.

"Listen, I just wanted to say—" Catie started.

"We should keep talking," Will blustered out at the same time. Then he heard her. "Sorry, yeah, you go."

"Thanks for letting me talk to you about the misunderstanding. That meant a lot."

"Of course. Any time. And thank you for letting me apologize."

She smiled. "Any time."

12

———

For Sam's one month anniversary of working for her, Catie asked Isla to bake him a special mini cake. And then she asked him to consider taking on even more responsibility. "In two weeks, I'm going away for five days for a Search and Rescue competition. My plan was to shut the salon down, but Bailey Patel has agreed to work here in the afternoons. So there will be a grown-up in the building, but the store front jobs would be all yours. Do you think you can handle it on your own?"

His face lit up. "You bet."

That was one issue sorted. Another was her response to Will's email about the business club. That was decidedly *not* sorted. She looked at it almost every day, and wondered what he meant with the sign-off... *Whatever works for you. Yours, Will.* Their tenuous new friendship was confusing at the best of times, and then he added in a *Yours?* It triggered a strange, wibbly-wobbly feeling, and made it hard for her to compose a response.

But time was ticking away, and she wanted the business club firmed up on her schedule for the fall. Besides, she'd been poking the bear a bit pretending she wasn't sure if Thursdays would work, when she'd already cleared her schedule for SAR training. The business club would just slide in right before training.

From: Catie Berton
To: Will Kincaid

Will,
After careful consideration, I have decided Thursdays are ideal. Can we meet to discuss the details?
Catie

She sent the email in the morning, then went out to show Bailey a few more investment properties, because she was starting to think the motel was dead in the water. For whatever reason, the legal office that paid the property tax each year was not interested in communicating with a real estate agent about the property.

When she got back to the salon in time for her afternoon clients, there was a response waiting.

From: Will Kincaid
To: Catie Berton

I'm always available for our new community advisor.
Dinner tonight after training?

She was pretty sure *I'm always available for our new community advisor* was an exaggeration. That wasn't something Will would usually say. Although maybe she didn't know what he would usually say to someone he wasn't holding a weird grudge against. The last thing she should do was read too much into basic human kindness. And she needed to remember that for months, he hadn't trusted her enough to have a proper, straight up conversation.

She really had missed an opportunity in the spring to develop a crush on literally anyone else. Dilip had been right there. There were other people around town, too. Campbell Mills, although he seemed cockier than Will and Josh combined.

No thank you.

She sighed. The problem was that Dilip and Campbell weren't her type.

Will was her type.

She pushed away that annoying thought and fired back a to-the-point response.

From: Catie Berton
To: Will Kincaid

Sounds like a plan.

That night, Sean Foster came to talk to the group about nutrition around the competition. The former elite athlete now used a cane, following a debilitating injury while overseas with the military, but he had transitioned into a career as a sought-after coach.

"The Pine Harbour Search and Rescue team is probably his lowest paying client," Tom said during his introduction. "So I hope you guys give him your full attention, because this man's knowledge is out of this world."

Sean gave Tom a lopsided smile. "What he doesn't say is that my brothers—and Tom here—used this training facility to pull me out of a deep depression following the injuries that changed my life forever. I owe a lot to your fearless leader. But we aren't here for a mutual apprecia-tion society tonight. Let's talk about what you guys have in common with elite athletes, and it might be more than you think."

He gave them a brief rundown of mishaps that had happened to him when he'd gone off plan with food as a younger athlete. "What I learned was that while what I ate did matter, what mattered even more was that I ate the same thing for a competition as I did in the workup to that. Which usually means bringing food with me. Even now, when I travel as a coach, I bring food with me a lot of the time instead of relying on restaurants to cover off everything."

Catie wondered if she should mention that her most consistent sources of nutrition, also known as fuel for her athletic body, were Frank's burgers and Isla's pies.

Probably not.

She did find the conversation interesting, though. Consistency as a training principle just made sense. And it would be awful to work this hard on the competition, only to get knocked out by a weird gastro response to the wrong thing.

After Sean's presentation, Tom walked them through what to expect on competition day. There would be three different locations all within walking distance of each other, and each would host two or three events, meaning there would be seven events happening at the same time.

Catie couldn't picture the schedule in her head, but she didn't need to. That was Tom's job as team leader. She just needed to show up where she was told, and do the job asked of her.

When they were dismissed, she found a text message on her phone.

Will: Meet at Mac's?

She glanced across the room to where he was talking to Sean, his phone casually held in one hand.

Catie: Sure... Are we being super stealthy about it for a reason?

He glanced at the screen, then covered his mouth, suppressing a laugh.

Will: No. Did it read that way? I was just confirming. We can drive over together if you want.
Catie: I'm already deeply invested in sneaking around. Business Club discussions are top-secret. There will be a password.

As she kept typing, she tracked him excusing himself from the conversation and crossing the room to where she was still staring at her phone. She hit send as he stopped in front of her.

Catie: The password is maraschino cherry.

He laughed out loud.
She glanced up. "Ready to go?"
"Yep."
She waited.
He sighed, then muttered under his breath, "Maraschino cherry."
Now she was the one laughing as they headed to the parking lot.
But once they got to the diner, Will set the tone—all

businesslike and thorough, giving her a complete history of the Business Club over the last two years, and what he knew of it from when the high school was its own entity.

Catie tactfully decided not to bring up the window-washing debacle, and focused on objectives Principal Kincaid wanted his new community advisor to design a program to meet. "Is the goal here to engage kids who might one day go into the business world? Or to demonstrate every day math and social studies in action? Or reinforce curriculum?"

"Yes, yes, and ideally, yes."

"Tall order."

"You're up to it." He held her gaze for a moment. "And you'll have support. Mine, of course, although that's... well, it's not my forte. But January Howe is also happy to help."

Catie felt her eyebrows shoot up. "Was that a little slice of Will Kincaid humility?"

"Two weeks in a row," he muttered. "We could make this a regular thing, eating humble pie with you is better than therapy."

She laughed as the waitress approached. "Anything else for you two?"

"Just the bill, please." Will stopped Catie's protest that they should have two bills. "We talked about nothing but work. This is on me."

"In that case... Speaking of pie," she said sweetly, holding up her finger to keep the waitress next to them. "I'll take a slice of the cherry pie to go."

Will nodded. "One for me, too."

When they were alone again, he stretched his arms wide across the back of the booth. "Is yours a midnight snack, or a very good breakfast for tomorrow?"

"Breakfast." She jerked her chin up at him. "You?"

"Midnight snack."

"Interesting."

"We're not that different, you and me."

She rolled that observation over in her mind. Did she think they were different? Or annoyingly too similar? "Maybe not."

"In fact..." He paused as his phone vibrated on the table between them. He glanced at the screen. "It's Tom. He wants to know people's preferences for carpooling for the competition."

Catie pulled out her phone, too. "Same message."

"Are you going to drive with Lore?"

She shrugged. "I could. We haven't talked about it."

"I was going to volunteer to drive, because my truck has room for gear. The passenger seat is yours if you want it." He looked at her expectantly.

"Do you want to be stuck in your truck with me for eight hours?" She laughed.

"Well we get a break on the ferry." He groaned. "No, that sounds wrong. Yes, I want to be stuck with you... You know what I mean. We've been working well together. We can spend the drive prepping for the events we're in together. Or talk more about the business club. Whatever you want. We make a good team."

She wanted to not be flustered by the offer. "We. You and me. Tenuous truce people."

He shrugged. "We're teammates. Personal history aside, there's no *I* in team."

"There is no Catie and Will in *we*," she retorted a little too quickly.

Because he frowned at her clumsy response. "That doesn't make any sense. You can say, there is no *I* in *we*, although that's basically what I just said. But Catie and Will is—" He paused, thinking.

"Oh my God, you're counting the letters, aren't you?"

"There are twelve letters that you are saying can't be crammed into two letters. I mean, obviously—"

"I can't believe you counted." She sighed, and laughed, and tossed her napkin at him. "Yes. I'll ride up to Timmins with you."

"I'm in charge of the music, though."

She snorted. "I wouldn't have even suggested otherwise."

13
─────────

WILL PULLED into her driveway at six thirty in the morning. Catie had been watching through the window, and was out the door with her backpack and cooler of carefully packed snacks before he even turned off his truck.

He gave her a big grin as he opened the passenger door for her, indicating where she could tuck her bags behind the seat. "Ready?"

She practically bounced in response.

They convened with the rest of the team at Mac's Diner, where Frank had coffee to fill their travel mugs and breakfast sandwiches made to order.

"Don't eat the food on the ferry," he warned Catie as she gave him a tight hug in the kitchen. "And don't let that Kincaid boy get under your skin."

She didn't bother to correct her mentor over Will's age. Maybe they were all still kids in one way or another. "We're getting on better than before."

"Good." He jerked his head to the door. "Go on. Make Pine Harbour proud up north."

In Tobermory, they queued up in the line of cars, waiting to board the Chi-Cheemaun Ferry to Manitoulin Island. The ferry's nose was up, revealing the vehicle deck they would drive onto, and the horn blared regularly, the loud sound matching the heavy thump of Catie's pulse.

Then the line started to move.

Will navigated his truck into the dark underbelly of the ferry, parking where instructed, and once the attendants put blocks under his wheels, they got out and made their way up to the passenger deck for the two hour crossing.

They found enough seats to sit together as one large group, and from the smell of the coffee from the cafeteria, Catie was glad she had an extra big Thermos filled with Frank's good stuff.

Tom reminded them all of their timings. They would have a team meeting at the hotel that night, then early to bed, because the competition started at eight in the morning, and they needed time to get to the mine site where it was being held. "And don't forget to plan your pee breaks."

"Thanks, Dad," Lore said.

He gave her a pained look. "It's not safe to pull off on the side of the road."

"The Venn diagram for Concerned Dad and Safety-Aware Park Ranger is a perfect circle," Will joked.

Tom held out his hands in a *why are you joining in?* move. "Pot says what about kettle?"

"Anyway, we don't need to worry about sticking in a convoy, but please have your passengers text each other updates from time to time so everyone knows we're all making good progress."

Will nodded and stood up. "I'm going outside to catch some fresh air."

He stayed out on the deck for the entire crossing, only returning when the overhead announcement indicated the ferry had docked safely, and passengers could return to their vehicle.

They went below deck as a large group, but Tobin apparently planned to take the "no need to convoy" instruction seriously. "The race is on," he crowed. "See you there, suckers."

Catie rolled her eyes. She thought she was alone in thinking that was silly, but as soon as they were in the cab of Will's truck, the principal muttered under his breath that Tobin was a fool. "If he wants to get a speeding ticket, that's on him."

Catie tried to suppress an amused smile.

Will glanced at her out of the corner of his eye. He didn't say anything until he'd navigated them off the ferry, and onto the road towards Sudbury. Somehow that little stretch of silence made it even harder to hide her amusement.

"What are you grinning about?"

"Nothing."

"That is the least innocent-sounding nothing I have ever heard."

"I was just thinking about how much of a rule follower you are."

"Oh?"

"Speed limits should be obeyed. Road safety warnings should be taken seriously. Noise ordinances should be respected." As soon as the last example was out of her mouth, she realized she'd said too much.

Will's brow tightened up. "Noise ordinance?"

She could fudge the truth. But almost two months had passed, and she didn't think Will would mind that Sam had told her about the party. "Before Canada Day. There was that party near your house…"

"The gossip mill knows everything?"

"Not exactly."

He looked across at her with curiosity. "Right. You're not one to gossip."

"I heard about it from Sam," she confessed.

Will grunted.

"We had to have a conversation about responsibility and respect after that."

"Really?"

"Did you think I would take the kids' side in that?"

"It's not outside the realm of possibility."

"It *is* outside— Will Kincaid, I am a responsible business owner," she said hotly.

"Nobody said you weren't, Catie Berton."

"For the record, I told him that in a couple of days, he would probably feel bad. And sure enough, it came up again after a while. He didn't go to another party hosted by the same people, because he didn't think they were worthy of his time. Sam's a good kid, Will."

Will gave her another one of his classic side-eyes. "I'm aware. That's why I recommended him to you for the job."

"Good, then we're on the same page about him."

"Good."

A long silence stretched between them, then Will turned on the stereo system. On the touch screen display he selected a playlist titled, *Six Hours From The Chi-Cheemaun to Timmins.*

The Authoritarian Freak had programmed, apparently, six hours of what Catie quickly realized was non-stop country music. And it was all good stuff, Southern rock and folk music. But it wasn't her usual, and she didn't know any of the words.

Which made it hard to sing along, and Catie *loved* nothing more than belting out road trip tunes. Dancing in her seat was a given, too. Even if she didn't know the words, she was all-in. At first it was quiet, very under her breath, but as a Brothers Osborne song came on that she *did* know a bit, that she liked from hearing it on the radio, her version of the lyrics slipped out a little louder.

> *Dancing at the dentist in my old Levis*
> *I got the fuel, yeah all right*
> *I've got the awl, if y'all got the knife*

Will choked a little. "What did you just say?"

"Now you're the one smiling," she muttered, not answering him.

"Did you say, *I've got the awl?*"

"Maybe."

He chuckled. "What do you think that line means?"

She decided to brass it out. "They're incredibly violent men. Armed to the teeth with…awls and knives."

"After dancing at the dentist's?"

"Yep." She lifted her chin proudly and tapped the display. "Let's listen to it again, I think you'll find I'm right."

His eyes danced. "Do you want to play something else?"

"Not at all, I'm loving this."

"Good."

"Great." And she danced again in her seat just to prove her point.

———

HALF AN HOUR on the other side of Sudbury, they made their first stop. They both took Sean's advice and ate lunches they had packed themselves, but they grabbed drinks from a Tim Horton's just off the highway. Then, instead of getting back on the road, Will typed a different address into his GPS. "Want to stretch your legs a little?"

"Sure. What are you thinking?"

"There's a pretty spectacular waterfall near here. I know a secret spot I thought you might want to see." On the short drive, Will gave her a brief history lesson—which doubled as an art lesson, because it was a popular location for the Group of Seven artists a century earlier.

"You know a lot about this place."

"I've come up a few times. Chaperoned two grade eight trips, and then this particular spot I discovered when I came here a few years ago with my brother Seth."

After they parked, Catie asked him more about that trip with his brother.

"Seth had to pick up a plane up in Gogama and fly it home. I volunteered to drive him up there because it was the summer break and I was bored. It was my first summer not doing school of my own, and I was a bit at odds with the extended break."

The path opened up, and ahead of them was a water-fall, wider and more vigorous than the ones around Pine Harbour. Catie slowed to a stop. "Wow, it's pretty."

"Yeah." His voice was lower now, closer, and she glanced sideways. He gave her a slow smile. "Come on, there's something else."

The rush of water got louder as they climbed up the

path along the side of the waterfall, but then it quieted again at the top, and the river flattened out.

Will caught her hand and turned her, his hand sliding up her arm to her shoulder. "There. I know how much you like caves…"

This one was glorious. Big and deep, a dark chasm surrounded by overgrown green. She bounded towards it, then turned around. Will had his phone out. "Go on up there, and I'll take your picture. We have to document the road trip properly."

She twirled in a circle, then posed on a boulder in the middle of the cave mouth. He joined her after taking the picture, and they sat next to each other on the rock, looking back at the river.

"This is a pretty sweet rest stop," she whispered, not wanting to disrupt the quiet.

He nodded. "Glad you think so."

"Any more caves on the map?"

"I think we'll find a couple at the mine site once we get to Timmins."

"Awesome."

"Yeah." He was looking at her again. She could feel his attention on the side of her face, a warm kind of focus. And then it was gone, and he stood up. "Shall we hit the road again?"

"Yep."

"Do you want to put your music on for the next leg?" he asked as they headed back to the truck.

"But you have a six-hour playlist," she teased.

"Maybe I want to shift things up. Try something new."

"Get a little wild?"

He laughed. "I might even make up my own lyrics, who knows?"

He didn't need to, though. In fact, after she synched her phone up to his truck's Bluetooth system, it turned out that Will knew all the lyrics to all the songs that Catie listened to on a regular basis. He might have programmed exclusively country for his own playlist, but he was well versed across a broad selection of music, no matter what she put on next. He was right there with her, especially when she put on a retro pop playlist.

The fact that he knew every word of Debbie Gibson's *Shake Your Love* did something very funny to Catie's chest.

But before she could explore that unexpected sensation, she got a text message. And not just on her phone—but, to her horror, it also delivered right to Will's dashboard, thanks to her having synched up to play her music.

Lore: You managing okay with Mr. Grumpy?

Will made a choking sound as Catie jammed her hand over the way-too-big digital display screen. "Shut up, Lore," she said out loud. Her face was burning. Why didn't she see that coming? *Because she hadn't texted about Will with anyone, ever.* "I'm sorry."

"Why? You didn't say it." His voice was deliberately calm. Extra calm.

Except she had and he knew it. The only reason Lore would say that in a text was if it was a nickname Catie had given the man taking up way too much room in the cab of his pickup truck right now.

She decided to go for the brutally-honest-on-the-offence approach. "I did once, in the past." She lifted her chin. "Because you were, at times, grumpy to me."

He made the choking sound again and looked out his driver's side window. "Uh huh."

"But I'm going to text her back…" She picked up her phone and furiously typed out a response, then showed it to him.

Catie: We're getting along super well. Nothing grumpy about Mr. Team Player.

Will's face turned red, then he turned his attention to the road ahead. And he kept it there for the rest of the song. When the music faded out, he hunched his shoulders up, then smoothed his hand down his denim-clad thigh. "Mr. Team Player makes me sound like a square."

He was a square, though.

But then she remembered that he'd confessed his hurt feelings about her not wanting him to be in the bachelor auction.

As intensely attractive as Will Kincaid was, he was still just as insecure about his appeal as the next human being.

"You say that like it's a bad thing," she said softly. "I quite like that you're a team player. And responsible. That you have big feelings about safety and fairness. I'm sorry if I ever made you feel like that wasn't part of your appeal."

She reached out and caught him by the arm, her fingers wrapping around the thickest part of his forearm and squeezing. His gaze found hers and locked on, his eyes serious. She waited for him to jerk away, but he didn't move.

There was a depth in his expression, like she'd hit a nerve—but one he didn't mind her hitting. He didn't pull away, even after he glanced back to the road.

She squeezed her hand reassuringly, then sat back.

WILL ALMOST SHUDDERED as she drew her soft fingers away from his skin. Something had shifted between them, and he felt that old impulse to exasperate her try to rise to the surface. A misguided self-defence mechanism, but he wasn't going to let himself do that.

Self-defence in this case would be self-sabotage.

Oh, the irony, that the well-trained school principal had discovered much to his own horror that he deliberately acted out to get the attention of someone who judged him. Any attention was good attention. It was true for fifteen-year-olds and thirty-eight-year-olds alike.

But he didn't want to put that wall up between them, just to try to make her climb over it. They were done with that. So he stayed soft for her, even though she probably had no idea what it took. More irony. That the one person who saw through him was probably the only person who didn't want to see that much of him.

As another '80s pop song came on, he cleared his throat and reached for anything to change the subject without sounding like he minded where the conversation had gone. "Speaking of being a team player…"

She laughed softly. "Yes?"

"I have a media lab at the school. It's part hands-on history, part technical library. We have CDs, cassette tapes, VHS movies, even a few 8-tracks—and all the equipment to play them on. It's something that I wanted to offer to the business club last year, but didn't get around to organizing. Right now a few teachers use the material in their literacy classes, and our music teacher has, too."

"That's very cool." Her lips purse together, and even as he kept part of his attention on the narrow highway slicing through rock and heavy pine forests, he didn't miss the way her eyes twinkled. "And still slightly square, I have to say."

His cheeks heated up. "Fair is fair."

"But very, very cool."

"Next week I'm back in the school every day. So if you wanted to come in and see it…"

"Yeah. Definitely. So the media lab… I noticed you're really into all kinds of music. Where did that come from?"

"My dad." His neck heated up. "Not that he knew how much I appreciated it when he was alive. I have a lot of regret around that. I used to tell him I hated his music, and that wasn't true. I found it confusing sometimes, maybe? I think back to that and shake my head. So now, I go out of my way to never say that about music, even if it's not my taste at first. It's one of the things I think I get right with students. I listen to everything they do."

She made a humming sound in agreement. "That's really great. You know, I had a phase where I said I hated things when I actually found them confounding or fascinating." Her nose scrunched up. "I still feel residual shame for some of those moments."

"You too?" He didn't like that she felt shame. That was a heavy thing to carry. "How old were you?"

"Early teens. Twelve, thirteen. I know when it ended, though. I was fourteen when I started working at Mac's, and I told Frank I hated it when people tipped too much. And of course I didn't actually hate it. I just was overwhelmed. He laid into me about appreciating people's generosity from their hard-earned money. I felt like *shit*. Went home and sobbed about it. My mom told me to go back the next morning and apologize properly, and show Frank I understood how hurtful those words had been."

"Did you ever say it again?"

"Never. Not even once."

He could see that fiercely earned lesson in her to this day. It was a raw confession. So when she asked him what his most mortifying memory from that age was, he couldn't deny her the truth.

"Popping a boner in Madame Acton's grade nine French class. And not subtly, either. Everyone laughed and pointed."

She giggled. "Oh, boy."

"Yeah."

"I never would have imagined that you were awkward as a teenager. I mean, now, sure, I can see it—" He poked her knee, and her laugh doubled in size, joyous and big. "But back then, you were so confident. At least, that's what it looked like to a much younger girl."

There was a wistful note there that got under his skin. He tried to think back and remember what he could about little Catie Berton, seven years younger than him. Maybe by the time she was aware of him, he was heading off to university. A young lifetime of experience separating them.

"We never truly know what someone else is going through. But I can't complain about my teen years that much. I had it pretty good." He glanced over at her. "How about you? What was high school like for you?"

She made a face.

Now it was his turn to laugh. "That good?"

"I couldn't wait to just be done. Move back to the city. I was gone the second I graduated."

"And then you came back."

"And then I came back," she echoed.

"Is there a story there?"

"There's always a story." But she said it in a way that warned he wouldn't hear this one, not today.

"We've got nothing but time."

"Yeah." She wasn't ready to open up yet, though. That was clear.

He gave her an out. "Maybe on the drive home."

She made a noncommittal noise and twisted around in her seat and tugged at her soft-sided cooler. "Want a snack?"

"Sure."

It was the end of deep conversation for the rest of the drive.

When they arrived in Timmins, though, and pulled into the hotel parking lot, she put her hand back on his forearm. The touch sizzled his skin and warmed him to his core.

"Thanks for thinking of me with the rest stop choices." She rubbed his arm, and he felt like he was in grade nine French all over again. "You're a good teammate, Will. Don't let anyone tell you that you're grumpy."

14

THE KNOCK on Catie's hotel room door came far too early, but as soon as she heard it she was wide awake, heart racing with excitement. It was competition day.

"One minute," she called out, slapping her hand around to find the light switch. The red numbers on the clock glowing in the dark promised her she should have had at least another thirty minutes of sleep.

Not that she hadn't gotten enough the night before. After their team meeting, she'd come up to her room and passed out hard—because spending eight hours getting into unexpected deep and meaningful conversations with Will Kincaid had been surprisingly exhausting. *And wonderful.*

But there was no time to think about that now.

"I thought you said our call time was six," Catie grumbled good-naturedly as she opened the door.

Will leaned against the doorframe of his room across the hall, his hair standing up in places, his feet bare beneath a pair of flannel sleep pants that sat low enough on his hips she could see a slice of taut abdominal muscles between the waistband and the worn band t-shirt.

He looked rumpled, warm, and—when she lifted her gaze to his face—slightly amused. She shoved a hand through her own sleep-affected hair, which probably looked ten times scruffier than his did. His looked…cute.

"Don't blame me," he said, yawning as he jerked his thumb down the hall to where Tom was knocking on other doors. "That was our mighty commander."

Her attention caught on the mug in his hand. "Is that coffee?"

He straightened up and handed his mug over. "Here. I haven't had any yet."

"It's okay, I can…" She moaned as she caught the scent.

He shoved it into her hands, his amused expression deepening as he looked down at her, his eyes crinkling. "I'll make another cup."

"Thank you." She took a long, restorative swallow, then turned and waved at Tom, who was knocking on Lore's door at the end of the hall. "Do you think he's accidentally woken up anyone *not* heading for the competition today?"

"I wouldn't bet against it."

"I don't know why I thought I'd be able to pretend to be a morning person for this," she muttered. Then she took another long sip of coffee. "This is good."

"I brought my own."

"Taking Sean's advice to the next level."

"I try."

She smirked. "You succeed."

He yawned again, then let himself into his room. He propped it open, so she followed, lingering in the doorway as he turned on the kettle and popped a filter into a small hand-held pour-over coffee contraption.

Her gaze tracked over what she could see of his room. Unlike her room, which had two double beds, his only had one—a king-size—and he'd already made it. His backpack was on a chair in the corner, and in the other corner— "Is that a Jacuzzi?"

"I think this might be what passes for a honeymoon suite in Timmins." His kettle whistled and turned off. He carefully poured a steady stream of hot water over the grounds he'd added to the filter, then tidied up.

Lore and Jeong joined Catie in the doorway, everyone looking a little rough, but it was quarter to six in the morning. They were allowed. Will made them all mugs of coffee, and they slowly ate their prepped "first nutrition break" snacks.

As Catie fully woke up, her excitement mounted. It was gonna be a big day.

After retreating to her own room to get dressed, she gathered with the rest of the team for a final gear check. Then they loaded into their vehicles and headed for the mine site where the competition would take place.

Everyone on the team would compete in two or three of the events. At the end of the day, the team's highest score in each event would be added to their tally.

The math made Catie's head swim and she liked math, but Tom had a clear vision in his mind—the path to victory he called it. As soon as he said that, Will interjected and pointed out that any result was a good result, that this was their first time competing, and whatever they did would set a benchmark for them to beat next year.

"Hard to beat winning," Tom tagged in at the end, making them all laugh.

Her first event of the day was the hasty team response with first aid. It was basically the same thing she and Lore had done well with in training, when Will feigned a broken arm.

Today, Will was her partner, and they were the first duo to arrive to the designated starting spot in Area A.

"The downside of going first is there's no data on how other teams have done," Catie said under her breath to Will as she glanced at the bare whiteboard that would, over the day, have numbers added to it as a makeshift leaderboard.

She had watched a number of videos from previous years on YouTube in preparation for this moment. Now, she laughed nervously. "I'm overthinking it."

"Want me to distract you?"

"Do you have another grade nine boner story?"

He groaned. "That stays between us."

"Oh, absolutely," she teased. "That's too good to share with anyone else."

"Can I trust you with my most embarrassing secrets?"

"Absolutely." She said it extra-breezily, but it was true. He could.

He huffed a laugh, then looked up at the sky. "All right. I'm scared of the dark."

"Oh."

He tapped the headlamp on his head. "I think it's why I like SAR. I've always got light with me. But it's not bad outside. Even when it's really dark, there's an openness outside." His face tightened up. "A dark room, though...terrifying."

"That's not embarrassing." She stepped closer and bumped her backpack against his, a sideways nudge in solidarity. "That's human."

"Thanks."

"Do you sleep with a night light?"

His mouth curved lazily at one corner, but a whistle cut through his answer.

She winked at him as they stepped forward, next to the other teams that had arrived while he was distracting her. It was time to focus.

They were given a briefing, then handed an envelope. Inside was a map and a set of coordinates.

"On your marks, get ready, GO."

Will ripped open the envelope and immediately turned and oriented the map to the ground. She gave him the grid reference, and he plotted a route. He took a bearing, and they were off.

From the start line at Area A, they set out to a logging road, and ran down that for ten minutes. But once they cut into the forest, Will made her slow down. Out of the corner of her eye she could see flashes of pink as one of the other teams cut through the brush. These routes had been tested by the organizers to be roughly equivalent in distance, but not close enough to hear or see what the other team was doing when they found the person they were searching for.

Catie had a compass on her bag, but she didn't need to use it because Will had one on his watch strap, and he barely broke stride when he checked it every five hundred metres or so.

It took them nineteen minutes to reach the coordinates. Unlike when they practiced this drill in Pine Harbour, the search person wasn't in plain sight.

Catie radioed back to the start line, informing them of their position, while Will did a scan of the area. She was about to report they didn't have a visual when he caught her hand.

"There. Nine o'clock."

It was dark blue fabric barely visible beneath thick brush and it didn't stand out at all.

"Stand by for an update," Catie relayed into the radio.

They ran over to the volunteer slumped on the ground beneath the tree.

Will scanned the area, then shrugged off his pack and knelt next to the man. "Are you okay?"

No response.

He tapped on the man's shoulders and repeated the question, louder and in the other ear. Then he shook his head. "Not conscious. Call it in, we need EMS support."

Catie relayed that to the start line. As she did that, Will did a look and listen for breathing, and reported that the person was breathing on their own. Catie passed that on, too.

After a pause, the radio crackled back to life. "Understood. EMS are on their way. What else do you have to report?"

Will went through a complete assessment. As soon as he finished, the brush behind him rustled and a woman wearing a yellow vest moved into view. "I'm the ambulance. You've successfully passed the patient on to me. Return to SAR base now as fast as you can."

Will grabbed Catie's hand and they took off running. She churned her legs as soon as they hit the gravel road again.

As soon as they skidded to a stop in front of the official, their time was recorded on the white board. Forty-six minutes and three seconds. And to Catie's delight, it was the first time listed.

There were two more rounds to go, but they'd beat the other teams against them head-to-head.

She jumped in the air, legs akimbo, and hollered her delight.

Will laughed as she gave him a double high five.

"You were so calm and capable," she said breathlessly. "Well done."

"Right back at you." He jerked his head back in the direction of the staging area. "Shall we go see how everyone else did on that round?"

Lore and Tobin, who had partnered up on a radio protocol event, were already back at the Pine Harbour group spot.

They exchanged stories from the first round, then stretched out for a snack and a rest.

The next round all the partners were rearranged, and Catie went to Area B with Tom for rescue mission planning, while Will headed off to Area C with Jeong.

The rescue mission planning was a role play with an examiner, not that different from the radio communication in the hasty team event. There was a checklist they were being scored against. Tom had those memorized, so his parts sounded like something out of Hollywood central casting. Catie struggled a little with the order of operations, but caught herself and course-corrected enough that she felt confident she had done a decent job.

There was a lunch break after that, and the whole team reconvened in their staging spot. Catie was both wiped and wired at the same time.

"What do you have next?" Yolanda asked her as they tidied up.

"Nothing." Most of them were only competing in three

of the four time slots; Catie and Jeong's break was this one, the third session of the day. "How about you?"

"Rope rescue with Will."

Jeong came up beside them. "I want to go watch that. Do you want to as well, Catie?"

She sure did.

They made their way to Area B, and found a spot to sit at the side of the crowd where they could hear as Will and Yolanda got their instructions from the mock rescue leader for this event.

There was a person stuck on a ledge halfway up a rocky cliff face. They waved happily to Will and Yolanda as the timer was reset, then lay down and pretended to be injured.

As Will and Yolanda harnessed up and discussed their ascent plan, someone else in the crowd watching passed Catie and Jeong a checklist for the event, which made it easier for Catie to make sense of the choices they were making.

Catie hadn't trained at all for this event, and it was interesting to note that unlike her events, time was not a weighted factor in the score. Will was good at taking time to make sure the plan was safe—she was glad that she'd had him as her partner for the first event. Mr. Methodical was a good balance to her own wild enthusiasm.

Yolanda started to climb first, then once she reached the outcropping of rock, Will started his own climb.

Catie's breath caught in her throat. His movements were efficient—quick, but not flashy—and suddenly this looked and felt like a real rescue. There was an urgency to his movements that was profoundly sexy. The low-grade magnetic pull she always felt about him intensified as she tracked his climb. She wanted him to nail this, not just for the team's total score, but for another reason that felt murkier and more complicated.

As much as she clashed with Will, she was drawn to cheer for him and protect him, too, because her feelings for him weren't entirely platonic.

Which wasn't ideal. They were teammates. They were trying to be friends.

And her feelings weren't based on Will, her friend. They were about Will, her fantasy. And Will, the real guy, had trampled on those feelings in the past, so she tried to protect herself by trying to avoid letting the crush reform.

Now, watching him work with Yolanda to put their patient on a portable stretcher and get it safely connected to a rope system already in place—a nod to the fact that in a real rescue, there would be a larger team—Catie realized she didn't want to tamp down those feelings any longer.

It was a lovely, warm, fuzzy feeling. A few months earlier she had told herself it was time to find a new crush.

But she didn't *want* a different crush. She wanted to revel in this secret attachment to Will, if only for this weekend. Because at her core, Catie was a romantic dreamer.

Maybe the problem wasn't the feelings, which didn't feel like a problem at all. Maybe she needed a different framework to hold them inside. She could set aside the romanticized ideal of Fantasy Will, and focus instead of the crush-able nature of Real Life Will, as messy and imperfect as he was.

———

Will knew they had scored well on the ropes rescue. As he waited with Yolanda for their mark to be posted, he caught Catie's attention in the crowd and gave her a thumbs up.

This was his last event of the day, so during the final round, when he had a bye, he'd be able to make the rounds through the different competition areas and figure out where the Pine Harbour team stood in the rankings.

It was important to manage Tom's expectations before the end of the day. He knew his friend wanted to win, but they had a lot of new team members. It was just as important to buoy them up, no matter how their efforts stacked up against more seasoned teams.

Did Catie know how well she'd done in their first event? Was she confident going into her next one, the last round?

As if on cue, she stood up and brushed off her bright blue hiking pants.

Good luck, he mouthed as she headed back to the staging area—and then the crowd shouted, because they'd just been given their score for the rope rescue, and it was the best yet for the day. Catie stopped and gave him an open-mouthed, *look at you* expression as Yolanda punched her fist in the air.

"Yeah," he breathed, grinning. "Excellent."

Their score was added to the top of the list, and they received a copy to take back to their team leader.

By the time he got back to the staging area, Catie was long gone, off to team carry-out with Sharon, Tobin, and Lore. Tom was at the officials' table, so Will and Yolanda turned in their score and then grabbed their boss.

"Is this an intervention?" Tom joked as they headed down the trail towards Area A.

"Not exactly," Yolanda said.

"Yes," Will said.

"We're doing really well, though." Tom's eyes were bright, his smile wide.

"What matters most is the experience." Yolanda jerked her thumb towards Will. "To steal a page from this one."

"Guys—"

Will shook his head. "The last thing we want is discourage—"

Tom stopped walking and turned around so he was facing them both. "We're in third place."

And he was fucking beaming over it.

Will grabbed Yolanda's arm. She grabbed him right back. "We're in third?"

"And it's close." Tom jerked his thumb over his shoulder. "Let's go see how our team is doing in the carry out."

So much for being the voice of reason. Will was just as amped up as his friend now. If their last events scored well, they'd be in the top three. Winning had never been likely, but top three? His pulse pounded.

Area A was where he'd started the day, with Catie, and when he glanced over at that running scoreboard, he noticed their time from that first event was still near the top. Only two teams had bettered their effort.

The other event that was taking place in Area A was the team carry-out. Since the Pine Harbour SAR was in the brush right now, they couldn't be spotted from where Will, Tom, and Yolanda stood, but that didn't stop Will from trying to catch sight of Catie.

And the rest of the team.

But mostly Catie.

While Tom checked on the leaderboard, Will paced back and forth. Then suddenly there was a flash of reflective yellow, and the sound of voices working together. Calm communication, and then what he'd been scanning for desperately—a flash of bright blue.

Catie's hiking pants.

The Pine Harbour team emerged from the tree line and swiftly deposited their rescued, mock-injured party at the feet of the officiants. Then they caught sight of their teammates. The others stayed close to the white board, but Catie headed over to them.

"We were quick," she said to Tom. "It felt tight."

He nodded.

She turned to Will and her eyes lit up. "I saw that our hasty time stayed pretty good all day."

"It was great." Behind her, their team time was scrawled on the white board, and the others had noticed, but she was focused on him. He paused a beat, wanting selfishly to soak up her attention a moment longer. A split-second. Then he told her the good news. "This time was better."

"How much better?"

He pointed. "Look."

She spun around.

His chest expanded again. "Bit better than all right."

They'd taken the top spot in this event. The chances that they would finish in the top three overall were almost assured now.

He was expecting her to jump in the air for her zero-chill victory leap, but instead she froze. And then everyone started to put together the pieces. All the different scores for the day, added up.

"Are you the Pine Harbour team leader?" the Area A official asked Will.

He pointed to Tom.

"You might want to head back to the staging area." The woman grinned. "They're posting the final results now, and your team has something to celebrate tonight."

15

CATIE FLOATED through the walk back to the staging area, the thank you speeches by the organizers, and the reveal of the final points tally.

Pine Harbour SAR, the only new team in the competition this year, came in second.

She could feel how exciting it was for everyone, and was thrilled herself, but nothing would beat the high of Will telling her they had taken top spot in the carry out. The way he'd looked at her—impressed—and how he clearly knew how much it meant to her to impress him.

How hard she'd worked to do her part for the team.

He saw her, right to her most vulnerable secret fears, even when she didn't give him very much.

They spilled into the parking lot just ahead of the team from Bancroft that took first place. "I'm buying a round," Tom announced, then waved his arm at the victors as well. "For everyone. One hour from now, in the hotel restaurant."

Catie groaned as she climbed into the passenger seat of Will's truck. "I hope a hot shower puts me back together so I don't miss that. Right now I just want to go to sleep. Muscles I didn't even know I have hurt. I'm pretty jealous of your jacuzzi tub right now."

Will started the truck and turned his whole body to glance out the back window as he reversed. He braced his hand on the side of Catie's seat. "What's mine is yours."

"No, that's okay." She shrugged, and her shoulder brushed against his fingertips. A tingle started under her skin at the contact.

"Catie." He pushed against her shoulder gently, sending that tingle blazing down her arm and across her chest. His gaze burned bright as she re-focused her eyes on his face. "Let me run you a bubble bath. You kicked ass today. Seriously. You put in a hundred and ten percent. The least I could do is give you my room for a bit."

"You're sure it's not an imposition?"

His expression softened. "Very sure."

She sighed happily.

Back at the hotel, they walked to their rooms together. "I'll just unpack and gather some things."

"I'll take a shower and change, and then I can go sit in the bar with Tom. I bet he's already down there, talking shop with anyone and everyone."

"Okay." She beamed at him. "Thank you again. Maybe text me when you're out of the shower?"

"Sure."

In her room, she dug her last piece of pie out of the fridge, ate half of that slowly—victory pie, well-earned— and then stretched out on the bed. There was no chance she'd fall asleep now, not with the way her whole body was humming with awareness.

Will wasn't her fantasy. He was just a regular guy,

warts and all, who she had a crush on—for the third time. That part was a bit heady.

Was she really doing this again? Letting herself free fall into wanting *Will*?

Yes, yes she was.

When her phone vibrated, she jumped up. She stripped out of her worn-all-day clothes, then put on the bathrobe provided by the hotel, and gathered her toiletry bag and her room key to come back once she was all pruney and well-soaked.

Will was on the other side of her door when she opened it, his hand raised, ready to knock. His hair was damp, towel-dried, and he had changed into a dark grey Henley and soft-looking, worn jeans. "Thought you might have fallen asleep," he said, glancing down at her bathrobe.

Did she imagine that it took him a minute to look back up?

Whew, she needed to settle down. *Admit to oneself that you like a guy, and the heart starts galloping all over the place with want.*

"No chance."

"Good." He looked like he was going to say something else, but stopped and turned back, leading her across the hall to his room. After opening the door, he didn't follow her inside. "I'll head downstairs. Come find me when you're done?"

Come find me. Not us. Him.

She nodded. "Yep."

He glanced past her to the dim of the darkened room. "Take your time."

And then she was alone. She set her toiletry bag on the edge of the tub and tested the water. Extra warm, but not hot. Dropping her robe on the floor next to the bath, she turned on the jets and stepped into the frothing waves.

A groan ripped from her immediately. All of her muscles sighed as she lowered herself. Her feet pulsed, her calves and thighs strained, and her back tensed—and then, as one, they all gave in to the rolling pressure of the jetted water.

She closed her eyes and replayed the day. She imagined Will sitting on the side of the tub, hashing it out with her. Could they have gone faster in the hasty? *We did what we needed to do. We did better than expected.*

"Better than you expected," she muttered out loud.

He would grab her foot and tickle it in response to her mulishness.

Fantasy Will was amused by her more stubborn traits.

When the jets turned off, she was surprised that thirty minutes had passed. She'd spent the entire time lost in an imaginary conversation. She scrubbed from head to toe, then drained the water out of the tub and used a sprayer head next to the tap to wash her hair.

She carefully left Will's room exactly as she'd found it —the ghosts of her romantic dreams lingering, maybe, but she couldn't control that—and returned to her room feeling much refreshed.

As she did her hair and makeup, she caught up on messages and made a few calls, then pulled on a pair of jeans and a soft black sweater. Touchable, one might hope, if one were a silly romantic.

Downstairs, she found almost the whole team sprawled out around two tables. Other teams were nearby, and she saw Lore and Yolanda sitting with the Bancroft team, sharing their pitcher of beer.

Will pulled out the seat beside him. "Do you want a drink?"

"Yes, sure." She took the glass from him, and raised it to Tom. "Thank you for this."

He tipped his glass back in her direction. "Thank you for everything you did today."

As the conversation resumed, a similar debrief to the imaginary one she'd had upstairs, Will rested his hand on the back of her chair.

Would he have done that a day ago?

Had he touched her more today than ever before?

Questions swirled through her mind. She took a long swallow of beer, trying to chase them away, but no use.

"What did you think, Catie?" Tobin leaned in from across the table.

"About what?" She shook her head as everyone laughed. "Sorry. I'm..." Daydreaming about the guy beside me. "Tired."

"And hungry?" Will slid a menu across to her. "We haven't ordered yet, but we can. We should."

She took it gratefully. "Thank you."

"We were just asking about the day in general. Did we prepare you adequately for it?"

"I think so. It reminded me of high school track and field, but like, wilderness edition." She glanced up. "I mean, what did you think, Tobin? It's not like you've done this before, either. We're all newbies at the competition, right?"

That made Will laugh. "She has a point, man."

She smiled sweetly. "But you captained our carry-out perfectly."

Tobin's red face calmed down. "Team effort," he said gruffly.

Tom lifted his glass, and swivelled around to wave at Lore and Yolanda, too. "To a team effort," he called out.

"Cheers!" Everyone clinked, and Catie took another long slug before setting her glass down.

But after that, she nursed that one beer. They ordered food, and other teams came over to introduce themselves and congratulate the Pine Harbour crew.

"Will you be back next year?"

"Absolutely," Catie answered before anyone else could.

That earned her another laugh from the table.

"A verbal statement is considered a legally binding contract in all ten provinces and three territories," Tom said.

"That's not true," Will murmured in her ear.

Her shoulders shook with a private laugh just for him.

After dinner, people switched to harder drinks. But Catie just wanted dessert, not that she could get the waitress's attention.

Will tracked her growing annoyance and leaned in. "You don't have any pie upstairs?"

She shook her head. "I ate my last slice when we got back, to celebrate."

"All alone?"

"Celebratory pie never feels lonely. Besides, I had to call Sam."

"How's the store?"

"Good. He says congratulations, by the way."

"To you."

She elbowed him. "And you, specifically. He said that. *'Tell Mr. Kincaid I said good job.'*"

"Yeah?" Will looked pleased.

"Yeah."

He stretched and glanced around, then lowered his

voice. "You know, there's ice cream in the lobby. You don't have to wait for the waitress to bring the dessert menu around."

"What?" She stood up. "Let's go."

"Where are you guys going?" Tobin shouted, clearly drunk already. "The pool?"

"Emergency ice cream run." Now it was Will's turn to give their teammate a polite smile. "Want to join us, if you can walk?"

Everyone laughed.

Nobody joined them, so they left cash on the table to cover their dinners, and headed to the lobby, where sure enough, there was an ice cream counter in the shop in the lobby.

Catie carefully perused the flavour options. "What are you going to get?" she asked Will.

"Vanilla dipped in chocolate."

Sounded like Will. She straightened up and nodded at the clerk. "I'll have the rainbow sorbet swirl, please."

Once they had their treats, Will pointed to the back door. "Do you want to go sit outside? There's a garden behind the restaurant."

She followed him out, then joined him on a bench. They didn't talk, just quietly ate side by side. Each lick was a different flavour, which Catie loved. Will seemed to take his time with his cone, too. It took them ages to finish, but she didn't mind.

She didn't want this moment to end, either. So right after she nibbled the last bit of her cone, she turned towards him.

"I wanted to—" she said at the same time as he twisted, sliding his arm along the bench.

For the third time that day, his hand caressed her

shoulder, and this time, it wasn't a glancing touch. This time, his fingers wrapped around the curve of her muscle and stayed there.

The rest of what she was going to say died on her tongue.

He groaned, and the heat in his eyes arced between them, setting her skin on fire. "I'm sorry," he muttered, dropping his hand.

Don't be sorry.

"It's okay," she whispered.

Time slowed, the air thickened, and her pulse skittered desperately as he didn't respond. *This was a mistake* warred inside her with *we're just two dumb, horny chickens.*

"Will?" She scooted closer. Now their legs were touching, her knee against his solid, well-defined thigh. She pulled her calf up onto the bench, turning fully to look straight at him.

He lifted his head. His eyes glittered, his temple twitched, but his mouth looked soft. Vulnerable.

———

WILL'S heart pounded in his chest as he forced himself to look at Catie again.

"Fuck it," he muttered.

She was staring at him, wide-eyed, her lips parted.

"I want to kiss you. Sometimes I want to shake you. Not often, but sometimes. But I usually just want to laugh with you, and most of all, I always want to kiss you. And I know that's—"

"Then you should." She squared her shoulders and gave him a defiant look.

Did she think he fucking wouldn't?

But he wasn't. He was still staring at her, even after declaring fuck it, which really felt very strange to him. He was a grown man. He wanted this woman. He should just—

She closed the gap between them, and his over-thinking brain finally, thankfully short-circuited.

She tasted like raspberry and mango sorbet, a bright burst of wonder, and the soft little inhale she took before kissing him back imprinted in his brain. *She likes you*, he realized like a dolt.

Then he grinned.

She laughed, her breath brushing his cheek as he gathered her tighter still, until there was no space between them, then he kissed her neck, her jaw, and her mouth once again. A wild sense of freedom settled over him, like he'd been holding himself in check for months, and now he could show her just how much he liked her, too.

He liked her a *lot*. Deep, hungry kisses levels of liking her, head spinning with desire levels of liking her, and he really hoped—

The door around the corner crashed open and people spilled out onto the patio.

Catie gave Will a wide-eyed look, a nervous, happy smile, and he stood, catching her hand in his. He pulled her deeper into the garden, towards the back wall of the hotel, and once they were safely out of sight, he pressed her up against the wall.

He could feel her heartbeat against his chest, her shaky breath, shallow and careful, then slower as she calmed down.

They weren't going to be caught. Not that it mattered, but they didn't need to share their first kiss with a group of drunk idiots amped up on either victory or defeat. He hadn't even noticed if they were people he recognized.

Once he was sure they weren't going to be disturbed, he kissed her again. Softly this time, lingering. Each brush of her lips and tongue against his skin did something heady to his soul. "We should probably…"

Could he invite her up to his room? Could he form words that properly functioned for an adult conversation about what she might want next?

"Right." She put her hand on his chest, a flat, firm palm that felt almost like she was going to push him away, and his heart lurched. "Will—"

"What happens in Timmins, stays in Timmins," he said in a rush. "We're celebrating. Don't overthink it."

Her fingers curled, fisting the front of his shirt.

Holding on.

His heart lurched again, this time in the opposite direction.

She tugged him in again. "Celebrating," she whispered against his mouth before pushing her tongue in and making him see stars. "How do we get upstairs without being seen?"

It turned out, it wasn't that hard. His room key opened a random door at the back of the building, and the elevator was right there.

They didn't touch on the short ride upstairs, but he could feel her, a hair's breadth away. Her arm swinging loose at her side, her gaze cool in the reflection on the shiny metal doors.

What happens in Timmins, stays in Timmins. Why had he said that? "I—"

The elevator stopped, and the doors slid open.

She stepped off first, and his mouth went dry at the

purposeful stride away from him, the curve of her ass in those jeans, and the straight stretch of her back. "Coming?" she asked without looking back.

Any fucking minute.

He swallowed hard and strode after her, catching up as she turned the corner towards their rooms.

"My place or yours?" he joked.

"Your bed is bigger."

Fuck. She was just as direct about sex as she was everything else, and it drove him wild. He tapped the keycard against the door, and let her in.

The room still smelled vaguely of her shampoo, that citrus-sweet summer scent. He wanted more of it, more of her.

As soon as the door clicked shut, he wrapped his arms around her, not missing how she shook when he pulled her that final inch. Good, that made two of them affected by this chemistry. He molded her to the shape of his body, one hand low on her hips, the other in the middle of her back.

A surge of intense need roared through him as he brought his mouth to hers, slanting their lips together again. How right she felt in his arms, how soft and wonderful and *good* she felt against him. But most of all, how sweet it felt to finally be free to kiss her, to know the quiver of her lips as she smiled against his mouth.

He didn't want to shake her anymore. He wasn't confounded by her anymore. He wanted this, only this. Her lips between his, her tongue, tentatively eager. Her wet, warm, sexy mouth, parting into a gasp as he showed her there was *nothing* tentative about his own enthusiasm for this.

When he finally released her, she gave him a tremulous smile. "Wow."

Then she laughed.

It was a surprised bark, a short, sharp exhalation of giddiness, and before his brain could overthink it, she was back in his arms, her hands warm against the nape of his neck.

Pulling him in for another kiss, this one slower, languid.

And then pulling his whole body deeper into the room.

"I didn't see this coming," she whispered as she pulled off her sweater.

"Didn't you?" Will filled his hands with her bare torso, his fingertips tracing the edges of her bra. "It's all I've been thinking about for months."

"Huh." She tugged his shirt up, and he helped her yank it over his shoulders. "I thought my crush on you was one-sided."

Will startled. "Crush?"

She giggled and tumbled back.

He fell on top of her. "And I thought I was doing a shit job of hiding how I felt about you. You thought…you had a crush on me?"

"It's a long story."

"I thought I was being so fucking transparent at times, and you were annoyed by me."

"Oh, I was." She grazed her fingers over his belly, making his skin pull tight, then she notched her hands around his belt and tugged. "Take these off. I'm not annoyed with you now, not in the slightest."

He caught her wrists and pressed her against the mattress, wanting her to hold still so he could get a good look at her. But he didn't have the words to explain that, or anything else about this moment, and how much he just *wanted* and *needed* her. Then she reached for him, and he wanted that, too. Wanted to fall onto her, into her embrace, and give her as hungry a kiss as she was serving him.

Her scent filtered into his brain, kicking his want into overdrive. He said her name as she kissed his neck, a whisper, then louder again when she shivered in his arms.

"Catie, I—"

"Me, too." Her breathy exhale was followed immediately by her tugging down the cups of her bra, plumping up her breasts and revealing her nipples to him for the first time—an offering that made his mouth water and his knees weak.

If he only had one night with her, he was going to make the most of every single second. If this was some post-competition, adrenaline-fuelled celebration, and she just wanted his jeans off and his mouth on her tits, then he'd give her an orgasmic parade, followed by fireworks, followed by an encore that belied comparison. A filthy fucking show that would make her remember this night every time her head hit the pillow.

He ducked his head and caught one dusky tip between his lips.

Her body arched, a tense bow pulled taut.

With an exhale, he breathed warm air on her flesh, then swallowed more, gently sucking more of her breast into his mouth. Her already tight nipple hardened against his tongue, and he worked against it, imagining how that might feel for her.

He found her other breast with his hand, a small, perfect fit against his palm.

He traced the shape of her, his hands spreading wide across her skin, trying to touch as much of her as he could.

When he'd tasted his fill of her breasts and she was panting, he unzipped her jeans and worked them off her hips. He eased them down her legs to her ankles, then stripped out of his own clothes as he stood at the foot of the bed.

She hooked her thumbs in her panties, and he nodded. "Those, too."

Without breaking eye contact, he grabbed a condom from his bag, turned on a light so he could see her better, and crawled between her legs. He kissed his way up her inner thighs, where she was soft and flushed pink. Then the darker skin at the apex, where curls framed her sex.

The sight of his hands against her flesh here, his fingers big and blunt against her sweet, sensitive parts, lit him up in a new and primal way. It was obscene and wonderful at the same time.

Her fingers tangled into his hair, urging him closer—not that he needed it. Fuck, he just wanted to take his time, but she needed his mouth on her, and he couldn't deny her that.

The first taste of her was tart, then sweet as he slid his tongue between her lips. He traced the curve of her pussy, from the outer lips in to where she was slick, around her entrance, then up to her clit.

She breathed harder when he got there, whispering his name, and then single word guidance. More. Yes. There. Yes, there. Oh.

Will.

He felt it more than heard it, the way she sighed his name as he closed his whole mouth over her clit, his nose buried in her mound, and pulled. A gentle suck, a steady pressure, and then she started to roll, grind against him, rock.

He held still and worshipped her sex and she rode his

face to a shuddering orgasm. He slid his tongue down to where she gushed for him, a slippery release that teased him, lured him to rise up on his knees and sheath his cock.

The first taste of her mouth, raspberry and mango, lingered on his lips as he gazed down on her in silent wonder. Her bra hung around her waist, her legs were spread wide for him. They'd gone from kissing in the garden to being naked on his bed, and they hadn't said very much.

He had so much he wanted to say, and it overwhelmed him.

But how the scent of her was imprinted on his face, his cock throbbed in his hand, and she was smiling shyly up at him.

"I'm ready," she whispered.

It was all he needed to hear—for now.

He slid into her, an inch at first, then as she adjusted to him, more length. Slow, agonizingly good pulses of his hips until he was firmly seated in her body. She shook in his arms and made the best sounds, alternating between panting his name and warning him to be quiet.

He wasn't the loud one in bed, but he grinned nonetheless and covered her mouth with his hand. This time when he thrust deep into her, her groan was for his ears only, reverberating against his skin as he muffled it. He couldn't wait to get her alone in his house, where she could be as noisy as she wanted.

They found a rhythm together, her hand reaching up to brace against the headboard, his arms wrapped around her. His thighs braced against the backs of her legs, his knees wide on the mattress.

A few hours ago, they'd both been exhausted. Now he felt like he could fuck her all night. Harder, faster. Make her come again, then flip her around. He wanted her in every position. The thought of her ass in the air made his hips jerk twice, seeking even more of her tight squeeze.

Her teeth sank into the fleshy part of his palm, just enough to jolt him. His cock liked that, too, flexing and swelling inside her at the fresh burst of sensation.

And then she gasped, her head rolling back. He dropped his mouth to tasted her neck, and he felt her cry through the corded muscle there.

"Come for me," he whispered. "Let me feel it."

She wrapped her legs around his waist, grinding her hips, and he lost it, too, his own orgasm a sudden, barreling-down-on-him surprise.

Darkness crowded the edges of his vision and a roar filled his ears as his whole body came to a frozen standstill, then thundered to pieces. He fell on top of Catie, barely catching himself as she gasped beneath him.

And then she kissed his shoulder. "Is it ice cream that does it for you, then?"

He laughed and tumbled to the side, pulling her with him. "Sorbet, apparently."

"Mmm." She shoved her hair off her face. "How late do you think that shop in the lobby is open?"

16

IN THE END, they decided not to go back downstairs. That risked them bumping into some of their teammates, and while they didn't talk about it in depth—they had better things to do than talk—Catie was relieved that Will agreed with her.

Nobody else needed to know how they spent the night.

So instead of more ice cream cones, they ordered room service dessert, which came with ice cream.

They mostly consumed that in an orderly fashion, although Will did lick a few drops off her breast at the end.

And then they tumbled on his bed again, this time slower than the first. Longer, sweeter. He explored her body, gently massaging the parts that ached from the day, and discovering which parts made her shiver. Then he perched her in his lap and notched them together again.

As she sank onto his length, as he once again filled her up and took her breath away, he dusted his mouth over the curve of her collarbone, then filled his hands with her breasts and feasted.

Will didn't talk a lot during sex. He was the strong,

silent type. Her new favourite type, she decided as she rode him slowly, his mouth full anyway, because he was sucking on her nipples.

Talking was overrated.

And once she came in a clutching, wonder of a climax that milked his release immediately after, she was overcome by a heavy, sudden wave of the good kind of tired.

Will pulled the sheet over her and settled in behind her.

"I'll set my alarm for first thing," he whispered into her hair.

She nodded, her eyes already closed.

———

SHE WOKE before his alarm went off. Before the sun came up, and with a start. Then she realized where she was—and whose arm was draped low over her hips.

Deep inside her, a kernel of regret formed. Not for the sex, but for the sleepover. That made this morning more complicated.

How did you think it was going to go?

She hadn't been thinking, though. That was the problem. She'd been feeling. And it had felt *amazing*.

Before she could crawl out of his bed and sneak over to her own room, he tightened his grip. "Stay," he murmured.

"I should go…"

He kissed her shoulder. "You could. Or you could stay." His hand slid lower, cupping her mound, his fingertips grazing the seam of her pussy. "I could make you feel good again."

It was early still.

She nodded, not trusting herself to speak.

He kissed her neck next, as he played with the growing wetness between her legs. She could feel his erection thick against her bum, but he didn't move. He just kissed her neck and stroked her flesh, working her body into a state of fevered readiness.

Last night, he hadn't been a big talker. This morning was the complete opposite. As he touched her, he gave her a rough blow-by-blow of how hot the night before had been. "I especially liked it when you ordered me to take my pants off."

"It was more of a firm request," she murmured, reaching back to wrap her fingers around his cock.

He groaned as she stroked him from root to tip, then used the bead of arousal there to slick the head of his cock. "Like your firm request for me to be quiet, when you were the loud one?"

"Hmm, I don't remember that…" She sucked in a breath as he slid a finger into her, then two fingers, filling her up. "Oh! God, Will. More of that. Ah."

"Just like that." His voice was low, rough. "When you started moaning, it was over. I needed to be inside you. So hot."

"I wasn't *moaning*."

"Groaning. Crying out my name. At one point, I covered your mouth and you bit me."

"Oh my God." She rolled over to look at him as he reached for a condom. "Do you think anyone heard us?"

"No, because I covered your mouth."

"And I *bit you*?"

He grinned. "That was hot, too."

She rolled her lower lip between her teeth. "You may need to do that again."

His eyes lit up as he reached for her. "Or you could bite down on something else. Like the pillow."

"You want me from behind?" She rolled over, feeling shameless and sexy as he hooked his hands around her hips and lifted her into position.

He sighed her name and smoothed his palms over her ass, then rocked his erection between her legs, finding her clit, making her throb for him.

"Don't you just look incredible like this," he rumbled. And in case there was any doubt about what he was looking at, he got specific in a way that made her face burn and her thighs shake. "Wet and ready for me."

Then he was at her entrance, thick and blunt, and pressing inside.

She groaned into the mattress as he shushed her, telling her to be quiet, telling her to be good. Praising her for taking him, all of him. He'd figured out how much she liked the specificity, apparently. Could read her body's reaction to his filthy words, which she liked just as much as last night's silent intensity.

He described what it looked like, how she stretched around his cock, and she lost it. He'd already gotten her close with his fingers. And now, with each deep push, he nailed that spot inside her that made her mind go blank. She babbled his name a few times, panting as her body coiled tight, then burst.

His fingers dug into her hips, holding her in place as he chased his own pleasure next, thrusting harder and harder until he stopped, suddenly, and then groaned. Loud, long, deep.

"Shhh..." she whispered into the silence that followed.

And he laughed.

God, how fun was it to have sex with someone—good sex, *amazing* sex—and then end it with shared laughter?

What happens in Timmins, stays in Timmins. That was for the best, for many reasons, but now that she'd had a taste of Will and his hands and his…everything…it would be that much harder to maintain a friend boundary with him.

Time to go.

She slipped off the bed as he cleaned up, and already had her clothes on when he returned from the washroom, still buck-ass naked.

He glanced at the clock. "What's the rush?"

"I want to pack up," she said. It sounded weak, even to her own ears. *Add a compliment.* "That was nice. One last time before we return to real life."

"That was more than nice." He caught her around the waist. She tensed up, and he felt it. She knew he felt it, because he stopped talking immediately. "Catie?"

Her pulse raced. "Yep?"

He cleared his throat and smoothed out his words. "Did I misread the situation? Do you not want to…"

She wanted to be annoyed at the cool Mr. Principal voice, but she knew better now. That was just Will trying to stay calm.

Sighing, she relaxed into him. They could hug. "You didn't misread anything," she whispered against his neck. "But I don't think we can do this back home."

The long silence that followed physically hurt.

Why not? She knew the next question that was coming. And she didn't have a great answer. *Because I'm scared to want too much. Because I don't know what would happen if people found out. Because I don't know you, not really.*

And then the worst one.

Because you don't know me.

With a rough exhale, he stepped back and pulled on some pants. That was fair. This wasn't a naked conversation. "I thought...what with the mutual feelings..." He paused there and laughed, a short, humourless bark. "I might be able to take you out on a date when we got back."

This was the problem with crushes. They were never logical or well-thought-out, and just ended up hurting people. Usually her, which was one thing, but now it was Will. She winced. "Then people would know that we're..." She shook her head. "I don't think that's a good idea. I'm a trainee, and you're the assistant team leader. It's...we can't muddy that."

He frowned. "Tom wouldn't care."

That was probably true. Fuck.

His face tightened up into something more like understanding. "But *you* would care."

She nodded.

He glanced away. "And what if we can't forget this?"

The room still smelled like them. But even after they were long gone, there wasn't a chance of her letting go of a single moment. "I don't ever want to forget... That's not—"

"Okay." He bent over and picked up her phone. "This must have fallen out of your pocket."

A clear dismissal. She deserved that.

———

WILL's chest felt like it had a wooden stake jabbed straight through his sternum. He still dug deep for a better note than *here's your phone.* "And thank you," he said gruffly. "For last night. And this morning."

He gave her the phone. Then he held out his hand, because he needed to touch her again, and maybe a handshake would be enough. "Teammates."

She shook on that, then left.

In the silence that followed, he sat down heavily and thought about how fucking awkward the drive home was going to be.

And how he couldn't spend it fixating on the fact that her excuse was bullshit. This wasn't about needing to stay professional on the team together. Tom wouldn't care. He knew Will could separate the two things. Catie, too. Which meant she was purposefully combining them.

Whatever her true reason, she wanted an excuse.

That stung.

She had a crush on him. Her words. But she didn't want anyone to know about it? It was hard not to take that personally, but he had made the mistake once before to assume she was rejecting *him* instead of making her own decisions for her own reasons.

He just wished he knew what those reasons were.

Ask her.

It had been on the tip of his tongue to demand why. Something held him back, and he didn't think it was fear. Caution, maybe. Always better than rash bravery. And when it came to Catie, he'd acted rashly before. Maybe not bravely, although he'd fooled himself into thinking it was something akin to that.

But fuck.

From that first kiss, he hadn't thought for a second that it would just be one night.

Except when you told her that what happens in Timmins, stays in Timmins.

Maybe he had known, deep down, that she'd be skittish. And he'd been willing to gamble on that to get another taste, and then another. To spread her out naked on his bed and be inside her.

He'd tried to show her with his body how right they were together.

That, in hindsight, hadn't been the smartest plan.

From somewhere else in the room, his phone vibrated. Without glancing at the clock, he was pretty sure that was a wake-up text from Tom.

Breakfast in the restaurant, and then time for the convoy of vehicles to hit the road so they could make the ferry crossing later that afternoon.

He threw himself into the shower, hoping that the steam would bring clarity.

It did not.

He packed up and took his bags down to the truck.

Then he steeled himself and went to find the team. But Catie wasn't there. He glanced down the table.

"Looking for your passenger?" Lore asked.

Yep. That's who Catie was. He nodded.

"She just left. Said she was going upstairs to pack, and took her breakfast to go."

"Ah."

"She didn't sleep much last night," Lore continued.

That was a fucking lie. She'd slept like a log. A beautiful, exhausted log. He took that as an opportunity to change the subject. "I crashed out early. How about you?"

He didn't hear Lore's answer. He nodded, and someone else replied, and nobody noticed that Will was deeply out of sorts.

Was it worse that he'd braced himself and then she hadn't been at the table?

Yes, ten times worse.

He pulled out his phone after he ordered some eggs that he wouldn't taste.

Will: I'm packed up already. Let me know when you are ready to get going.

She didn't text him back. But as he finished eating, she appeared in the doorway of the restaurant, her pack on her back and her other bags over her shoulder.

"Hey," he said carefully.

"Got your text." She gave him a look he couldn't read. "I was busy building a better playlist for the drive back."

Oh. It was going to be like that.

All right. It was a peace offering, and he grabbed it with both hands.

He grinned. "All country?"

"Zero country. We're starting with New Order and Talking Heads. The rest will be a surprise for you."

And just like that, she'd established some safe talking points for the drive home: retro music, which could spin into the media lab, and then from there the business club. And she'd deftly pointed them in that direction without her usual blunt directness.

He paid up, and they waved goodbye to their teammates.

They grabbed coffee for the road, then fuelled up and hit the highway south. Twenty kilometres dragged by before either of them started a conversation. Catie finally glanced sideways at him and threw deft politeness out the window.

"Is the music okay?"

"Yep."

"Are you mad at me?"

He choked on a laugh as heat crawled up his neck. "No. Maybe a little mad at myself."

"Don't be. Will's a good guy, be kind to him."

He rubbed his jaw. "Is that what you want to talk about?"

She shrugged. "No, I guess not."

"Can we talk about your secret meetings to discuss the parking dilemma?"

"Who told you?" Even from the corner of his vision, he could tell she was indignant.

"Nobody you need to get mad at. January told Josh, and he mentioned it as an aside."

"And you kept that to yourself."

"So did you!"

Another shrug. "Yeah, well…"

"We've got nothing but time. Do you want to tell me about your options?"

She didn't answer right away. First she fiddled with her phone, changing the music. Then she stared out the window.

But after a couple of minutes, she twisted in her seat to glare at him. It was a nice glare, as far as glares went. "You are sworn to secrecy. Don't tell Josh yet."

He crossed himself. "Got it."

"We have a couple of options in the works. Basically, we think the municipal government isn't thinking big enough. They see it as a problem to solve: parking gets out of control, so they need to hire security to enforce parking rules, and then charge for that parking to cover the cost of that monitoring. But that is a revenue neutral exercise at best. Sure, it doesn't end up costing taxpayers anything financially, but it costs them something in spirit. So is that actually revenue neutral if it quietly has a long-term impact on how Main Street businesses are thought of? I don't want anyone to think it's a hassle to come to my salon, you know?"

"Yep. That makes sense."

"So we need a different plan to cover the cost of parking enforcement. Time limits, of varying length, make sense. Parking for an entire day, maybe we could have a small fee attached to that. But stopping on Main Street to run an errand shouldn't cost anything. One option is to raise business taxes. I don't love that, for selfish reasons, but it makes more sense to me than the negative vibe of passing it on to consumers."

Will thought he could see where Catie was going. "But that's still revenue neutral, right? Just coming from business tax base instead of parking meters?"

"Yes." She gestured wildly. "Exactly. You get it. So what if parking was instead funded through..." Her face went all soft and dreamy. "Like a big event. We could leverage celebrity residents or something like that. Maybe tie it to the condition of hosting County Country next year—that weekend could generate more than enough money to pay for parking and more if we just chocked it *full* of fundraising."

Will could see it. He nodded slowly. "Like you did with Pine Harbour Cares. And I have to admit, I didn't see your vision for that, but it totally worked. If you put that forward as a proposal, you have an example of it already being more effective when tied to another event."

"Oh my God." She fumbled with her phone, stopping the music. "That's so smart."

"It's your idea. I just reframed it back to you."

But she wasn't listening to him. She was buried in text messages. And because her phone was synched to his truck, he saw the replies fire back. From Olivia Minelli, and January, and Will's sister-in-law Kerry.

That was quite the crew Catie had secretly convening to make the town better, right under their noses.

Then her phone rang. He didn't notice who the caller was before she accepted it, and disconnected the Bluetooth so she could just talk directly into the phone. "I *know*. We've successfully merged multiple fundraisers into one focused weekend. Let's do it again and layer in municipal parking enforcement, right? Except we won't call it that. That's not sexy in the slightest. Right. I know. Oh, the *hayrides*. Yes! And also— That makes me think about hayrides for County Country. What if we had a designated parking area, like a farmer's field? Is that doable? Okay, we'll think about options. But then people could pay for a hayride into town. *That's* sexy. Perfect. I'll be back in town by eight, I think?"

Will nodded when she glanced at him for confirmation.

"Yes, eight. I know. Will gets some of the credit. Ugh, I know, they can't keep a secret. But it's okay, I think he's on our side."

He'd prefer if she didn't leave any room for doubt there—because he was on her side so much it hurt—but the vote of some confidence was better than none.

As she kept talking, he replayed their conversation earlier.

"And what if we can't forget this?"

"I don't ever want to forget…"

She'd said that in the same soft, dreamy voice she'd talked about radical parking funding options. He didn't understand what she was thinking in needing to shut down the idea of *them*. But that little thread of hope…and then her subsequent display of trust, albeit guarded...that meant a lot to him.

What happened was their secret. It had brought them closer together.

And when they got back to Pine Harbour? He could figure out what her fear was and tackle that as a separate problem.

———

It was afternoon by the time they made it back onto Manitoulin Island and into the queue for the ferry.

Rejoining with the team for the passage across the mouth of Georgian Bay to Tobermory was bittersweet. Getting back in his truck for the last leg home, the sun hanging low in the sky to their right, even harder.

This was the final leg. As he drove past the sign for The Grotto, one of his favourite spots on the peninsula, he was hit by a powerful fantasy to suggest they pull off. Go camping. Go skinny dipping. *We're not home yet. What happens on the road trip, stays on the road trip...*

He probably had enough camping gear in the bed of his truck. They'd share a sleeping pad...

"Will?"

"Mmm?"

"You slowed down. I asked if you forgot something."

His mind, maybe. "No." He gripped the steering wheel and stepped on the gas again. "Should be home in thirty minutes."

While she might not forget what happened this weekend, he would have to pretend he did.

Lock it down. That was the only way to survive being around her now that he knew what she sounded like when he had her in his arms, how she felt on his lap, and what it did to him inside as he watched her sleep, curled up in his sheets.

At her house, he waited until she was inside, the lights on and the door closed, before he headed across town to his own home.

It was dark, and as he pulled into the garage, he noticed a big package leaning against the front door.

After dragging his kit inside and dumping it in the laundry room, he went back to the front door.

The baby gates for Becca and Charlie's visit had arrived while he was gone. He dragged those boxes inside. The thud of the box against the wall in his foyer echoed through the house.

Thanks for the fucking reminder that I'm all alone tonight, he thought bitterly.

Well, he wouldn't be alone for long. Soon he'd have a toddler racing through the place, so he had some work ahead of him.

That was a project for the morning.

For tonight… He texted his brother.

Will: Want to get drunk and talk about women breaking our hearts?
Josh: I'll be there in five.

17

Even though Catie was only gone for three days, it felt like she had a week of work to catch up on Monday morning. Isla's bakery was closed on Mondays, so she went to Mac's for breakfast and filled Frank in on the official parts of the weekend.

Then she spent the entire morning returning messages Sam had collected.

One of them was a real bummer. She texted Bailey and Dilip on a group message, letting them know there had been an update on the motel.

Bailey showed up at the salon twenty minutes later. "Dil is in court," she said. "But he said I didn't have to wait until tonight to find out what the problem is."

Catie pointed to the seat next to her desk. "Well, it turns out the owner is a young person, and they aren't interested in selling it. There is a small chance they might be willing to have an investor, but selling it is off the table."

Bailey perched her elbows on the desk and planted her chin in her hands. "Interesting."

"You aren't too disappointed?"

Her friend shook her head. "Nope. If it's not meant to be, that's fine. There are other business opportunities. But tell me more about this mystery owner."

"That's all I know. They have owned it for ten years, and it's been held in trust. Now they're ready to take possession of it, so when someone shows up in town… we'll be able to piece it together at that point."

"Huh." Bailey's eyes sparkled. "Now, how was your weekend?"

"You saw we came in second?"

"I did. But like…how was the drive up with Will?"

"Yeah, fine." Catie busied herself with stuff on her desk. "He likes country music, but it turns out he likes other music, too." She told Bailey about Lore texting and Will seeing it. "So that was kind of awkward, but he was gracious."

"Is that why you can't look at me?"

Catie jerked her head up. "I'm looking at you."

Bailey nodded slowly. "Now don't look away." She gave Catie an unblinking stare. "What else happened."

"Nothing," Catie squeaked. Then she groaned. "Something. But it's messy and private."

"Will?"

"Yes."

"Enough said." Bailey zipped her mouth shut and threw away the key. "He'll get there eventually. Sorry that he was a jerk."

Oh, but it was Catie who had been the jerk. That was the problem. "It was me, actually."

"Then he deserved it."

She sighed. "No. I dunno. But no."

"You know who rarely gets taken down a peg or two?

Will Kincaid. Whatever your reasons, it will be a reflection on his character if he can handle you being a bit extra."

"Wait, why do you think I was extra?"

Bailey grimaced. "Too far?"

Catie waved it off. "Let's get back to real estate talk."

———

BUT THAT NIGHT, after she did a grocery run, she was consumed with the aside comment. Was she *extra?* She should have settled in for some good ole fashioned girl-friend truth instead of changing the subject.

She thought about calling Bailey and asking about it again.

Except she didn't want to talk about Will with anyone yet. So she put on music. The same playlist she and Will had listened to on the drive home from the competition.

The juxtaposition of the upbeat, retro pop music and the hollow, empty feeling inside her made her reflective in a bittersweet way as she tidied her house. As she prepped food for the week.

And then, once she was done with her chores, she drifted down the hall toward the bedrooms. Her room was on the left, overlooking the garden in the back. It had been her room when she was a girl, too. Across the hall, at the front of the house, was her home office, which had once been her mother's bedroom. Catie had an oversized armchair in the corner where her mother's pillow would have once been. Now she curled up there and pulled a blanket over herself, trying to think about what her mother would say, what advice she might have if she were here now.

She wasn't good at introspection. Wasn't patient

enough, or strong enough, to dig deep into these feelings. The sadness overwhelmed her too easily, and she gave in racking sobs.

Grief, it turned out, was not actually avoidable.

Catie spent most of her time in denial about that fact. She thought she could mind-over-matter a process everyone dealt with in one way or another.

When the wave passed, she took a sobering breath, and decided that was enough for one night. Time to lose herself in HGTV for a few hours.

The next morning, Catie's alarm went off at six because it was garbage day. Bleary-eyed, she rushed outside to get her recycling to the curb. Across the street, Frances's bins were neatly in a row and her neighbour was sitting on the porch, drinking a cup of coffee, watching Catie be a complete mess.

She waved with enough jaunty energy she hoped it landed as the Bruce County equivalent of a middle finger.

It was moments like this that really made Catie wonder what her mother had seen in this town when she first moved them there. Why was *this* the place she chose to settle down? Which, of course, then led to the next question of why on earth was Catie here now?

She'd left once, but she'd come back inexplicably. And now sort of loved it. Okay, really loved it. Everyone except Frances and the gossip network.

She'd learned to stop fighting herself and her natural impulses. They hadn't ever really led her astray. Sometimes they took her in unexpected places—like Will's bed, for example.

Which was not something she needed to think about right now.

Hustling back inside, she got ready for the day, then headed to work by way of *Bake Sale!*

The bakery smelled like pumpkin spice and hot apple cider, and Catie's mouth watered as she greeted her friend. "I went away for the weekend and I come back to fall vibes? Not that I'm complaining. Bring on sweater weather."

Isla tapped the menu for the day. "I couldn't resist. I have a new pumpkin muffin recipe that is just perfect. Couldn't hold it back until the start of school."

Which was just a week away. Not that Catie needed the reminder that in a week, she'd be spending even that much more time with Will.

Stop thinking about him.

But it wasn't quite sweater weather yet, as evidenced by the next customer being a teenage girl wearing a bikini top and cropped shorts.

"Welcome to *Bake Sale!* What can I get you?" Isla asked.

"What are the chances you have oat milk?"

She pointed to the plant-based milk options sign on the wall. "Pretty good. These are your options for vegan lattes."

"Are you kidding me? How cute is that? I'll take an oat milk PSL."

"Sure thing." Isla started steaming the milk and pressed the espresso as Catie tried not to laugh out loud at the assumption that the bakery wouldn't have anything other than dairy. "Are you visiting for the day, or up here for a while?"

"Just the day. We're going to the Grotto." She put a big emphasis on the location.

"Fun." Isla slid the latte across the counter. "Just up the

road from there is a taco truck that has the best vegan tacos north of the 401."

The girl's mouth dropped open. "Shut up."

"Okay." Isla said it so dryly, Catie started snickering, and had to cover it with a cough—which reminded her of Will's embarrassed, choking laughs.

He needed to get out of her head.

When the girl had paid and left, Isla sighed and leaned against the counter. "We were never that exhausting when we moved here, right?"

"No. Never." Catie paused for a moment. "I may have been that exhausting when I was eighteen and desperately wanted to *leave* here, though. I think that whole attitude is a layered mood, and not necessarily tethered to reality."

"Good point."

Catie cringed. "I've signed up to work with people that age every week for the entire school year."

Isla nodded sympathetically. "Sorry about your luck."

"You told me I should do it!"

"And you're going to be great." She put a pumpkin muffin in a paper bag. "Here's a thank you gift for your sacrifice and community service."

———

On Thursday, she breezed into the office of the Pine Harbour Community School and brightly introduced herself to the secretary at the desk. "I'm Catie Berton. Here to meet January Howe about the Junior Business Leaders Club."

She didn't look in the direction of the open door at the back of the office, the one marked *Principal*. She didn't try to figure out where Will's desk was, and if he was in there. The light was on, which probably meant he was.

All she could see was a plant and the corner of a chair.

Nice ficus, she observed.

Then she gave another bright smile to the secretary, who was telling her how to get to the library, like she hadn't attended this school herself a bajillion years ago.

In the library, January was meeting with another teacher, so Catie roamed the space, noticing how different it was from when she'd attended—because a bajillion years had passed. The wide window seats were still there, though, and she smiled as she remembered curling up in them with a book.

"Looking for something to read?"

She jumped at the sound of Will's voice. When she turned around, it was hard to look at him full on. *He looks good.*

He always looked good, that wasn't new. He was dressed down today, in school prep mode, wearing a cheery motivational poster t-shirt and faded jeans.

He looked guarded, too. But he'd approached her, and they were teammates and friends and now colleagues of a sort. So she tried not to notice the way his shirt stretched across his chest and how his jeans fit his thighs perfectly— were those the same ones he'd worn the night they slept together?

Instead, she lifted her chin and fixed her gaze on his face. "Reminiscing about my study periods spent hiding in this back corner."

"I did that, too." He held her attention for another moment, without saying anything, then glanced over his shoulder. January was just finishing up. "I'm heading into a meeting, but I just wanted to say it's good to have you on board for the business club."

"Thanks." Since he was being nice and mature, she decided to do the same. "See you at training tonight?"

It was their last official training night as trainees, and then they would shift gears and start prepping to take their basic searcher qualification test.

He shook his head. "I won't be there tonight. I have…" He gestured down the hall. "Back to school, you know? Meetings. That sort of thing."

"Oh, okay." She nodded, then waved at January. "Good luck with all of that."

As he left the library, she tried to ignore the pulse of disappointment beating deep inside her. She hadn't been looking forward to seeing him tonight. That would be ridiculous. She saw him all the time. She was looking at him right now as he stalked away. They'd just had a conversation.

A short one. A sad one.

Whew, crushes—and feelings—were rotten.

———

WILL's last meeting of the day was a tour of the junior hallway with an incoming grade three student who had autism and his mom. They were new to the community, and getting to know the classroom on the first day of school, with all of his classmates making noise, might be too overwhelming.

On the way to his new classroom, Max caught sight of a box of trains outside the kindergarten class. Will scooped them up and brought them along so the eight-year-old would have something he really liked as the grown-ups talked about communication and the school's safety plan.

"When will I get to meet his EA?" Max's mom asked.

"At drop off on Tuesday. We'll both meet you out front, and then she'll walk him around to find his class and teacher and they'll line up together."

She had other questions, too, and then Max wanted to know where the bathroom was, and the gym, and the climbers.

By the time they wrapped up, it was too late to catch the end of the SAR training, and well past dinner, too. He locked up the school and headed to Mac's to pick up something for dinner.

When he walked into the diner, a familiar blonde head was in front of him, waiting for a seat at the counter. The place was packed, so it would probably be a while before he could get a takeout order.

He had two choices. Turn around and leave, or step forward and make conversation.

"For two, was it?" the waitress asked as she flew past Catie.

Stepping forward, it was. He cleared his throat, and Catie jumped. Second time today he'd scared her.

"We aren't together," she blurted.

"I'm just here for some takeout," he added.

"It'll be about thirty minutes," Frank shouted from the kitchen. "Might as well sit with her. A booth just opened up."

Catie groaned under her breath. Maybe Will was the only one close enough to hear it. He was definitely the only one close enough to hear her whispered apology.

Him refusing to sit with her would probably cause a few tongues to wag. One part of why she didn't want to date him was the gossip factor—refusing to sit together would trigger the same issue for his prickly friend who didn't trust easily.

"I don't mind if you don't mind," he murmured. "I brought work with me."

That made her smile. "Do you ever stop working?"

"I could say the same thing to you. We can talk about business club stuff if you want. How'd your meeting with January go?"

"Great." She gave him a quick rundown of their first semester plans. "We're going to do a series of pumpkin sales to work on their understanding of cash flow, then use that as the basis for individual projects in the second half of the year."

He wasn't surprised that she had a neat, comprehensive plan that hit all the beats and then some. She always did.

The waitress pointed to the cleaned booth for them, and they sat down.

Catie sat down with a heavy sigh. "Whew, I'm beat. Roll me into a burger, then send me home to bed."

He'd love to do both of those things. Especially the bed part. His bed, preferably.

Bad Will.

Yep. Very bad. The absolute worst.

He changed the subject to her last night of training, and what came next. "Have you thought about what SAR skill you want to work on next?"

"I'm definitely joining Sharon's open water swim club next year. But between now and then? Probably first aid. Level up there."

"That's smart. Less flashy than some of the other courses offered over the winter, but more useful."

"It's a building block, right? I'm not in a rush to learn how to jump out of a helicopter or anything."

"You heard Jeong asking about that last weekend?" As soon as it was out of his mouth, he regretted it. He didn't want to think about last weekend. He thought about it enough—constantly, actually—when he was alone. Thinking about it in front of her was worse.

A flash of something passed over her face, then was gone. She laughed. "Yeah."

He dragged in a quick breath. "Helos are a lot of fun, though."

"I bet. Do you get to use them often?" She laughed again, sounding nervous now. "Use them? Fly in them. I really am tired, sorry."

He waved his hand. "I knew what you meant. A few times a year. Usually if we need something that requires a helicopter rescue, a dedicated crew from the city will do it. But I stay current on my cert just in case I—"

"Ms. Berton, may I have a word?" Frances Schmidt appeared beside their table, cutting Will off.

Catie's shoulders snapped back. "I haven't watered my lawn all week, Frances."

"This is about your hijacking of the Haunted Hayrides."

"My what now?" Three sharp syllables and a pointed look at Will.

He wasn't going to say anything. He didn't know what was going on, anyway.

"I was at the library this evening for a book club, and as I was departing, I overheard a discussion between..." Frances pivoted in his direction. "Your brothers, in fact."

Oh, shit. He racked his brain and came up with nothing.

Frances continued anyway. "They were talking about the permit changes for the Haunted Hayrides, and how it will be a *fundraising* event now—"

"It has always been a *fundraising* event," Catie pointed out evenly. "You don't need to say that word like it's *pornographic*."

"An interesting word choice, young lady."

For a second, Catie looked downright murderous. "What's your point?"

"You're just like your mother. A meddlesome little bitch who can't keep her legs together."

"Whoa there," Will said, not able to keep quiet about that off-side attack. "Frances, that's not okay. Apologize to Catie right now."

"You say that now because you're enthralled by her. You'll—"

Catie pushed herself out of the booth and headed to the kitchen.

"Wait—" Will was halfway out of the booth before he caught himself. She wouldn't want him to make a scene. People were already looking. He took a deep breath and stood more slowly. "Don't you ever speak to her like that again," he ordered under his breath. "Catie and I are colleagues. We were talking about *work* and *community service* when you interrupted us. I don't know what has gotten into you, or why you would think that was ever appropriate to say to anyone, but if you don't want me to publicly call you worse than you just said, you will keep your mouth shut. Not just to Catie. But to everyone. Do not speak to her like that, and do not speak about her like that. Ever. Do I make myself clear?"

Frances gasped. "Excuse me? How dare you speak to me in that tone? I don't deserve such disrespect."

Through the pass-through window, he caught Frank's eye, and the cook shook his head in dismay.

That was two of them who thought he'd fucked up, but he wasn't sure how.

"Respect is a two-way street, Mrs. Schmidt. You haven't earned it." He glanced sideways at the surrounding people. "Nothing to see here, folks."

Then he stalked back to the kitchen. Frank stopped him as soon as he was through the door.

"Where is she?"

The cook shook his head. "Give her a minute. She hates the attention."

The need to go and comfort her was overwhelming. Will rubbed his hand over his face. "What just happened?"

"Frances Schmidt just happened."

"I'm missing something. I've known that woman my whole life. I've never seen her speak to anyone the way she just spit at Catie."

"She's usually better at hiding her claws around certain people. People like you."

"What does that mean?"

Frank shrugged. "There are three kinds of people in this town. Those who were born here. The locals, you could say. Those who have enough money that it doesn't matter if they're local or not. And then there are those who are not from around here. Never to be trusted, especially when they're young, and beautiful, and catch the eye of local men."

"You're kidding me with this. Catie grew up here."

"I'm not talking about Catie, although she knows this better than anyone. I'm talking about her mother. That's who Frances hates. Catie is caught in the line of fire. And now she is the only target."

A horrible black hole opened up inside Will as he tried to process what Frank was telling him. As he started to comprehend just how little he understood about Catie's life. "What are you saying? That Catie's mom…"

"Suzanne died six months before Catie moved back. That's how she afforded to buy the house she grew up in. Suzanne had life insurance."

Will felt like a Grade A asshole for not knowing that Catie's mom was gone. For not asking about her once. "Shit, I didn't know."

"She didn't want anyone to know. She always had a funny relationship with this town, and how this town treated her mom. Suzanne was Catie's best friend growing up. More like an older sister than a mother half the time, but they liked it like that."

"I think she left town right around the time I came back from teacher's college? I guess I didn't think about her again, where she went from there."

"She followed Catie to the city. She gave her some space, but after two years apart, they wanted to be closer."

"How did she… Was she sick?"

Frank shook his head. "Car accident. She was hit by a drunk driver."

"I didn't know," he repeated, then cut himself off. There was no explanation necessary. Hurt was hurt. "I guess we have that in common now. We're both orphans."

But Frank winced, like there maybe was something else, and it might make the hurt even more compounded.

Fuck.

Will shook his head. "Tell me. What did I do?"

"Son, you didn't do anything. But when your parents died, the town came together. Not a person who lived here, including Suzanne Berton, missed their funerals.

Everyone made sure your brother had casseroles in the freezer to feed Josh and Adam for months. When Suzanne died? Catie ran an obituary in the paper. I was the only person from these parts who went to pay my respects."

"And then Catie moved back here anyway." Will's mouth was bone dry. The thought of never reconnecting with Catie tore something open in his chest. The thought of her grieving her mom's loss all alone ripped that jagged something clear out of his body.

"Pine Harbour was the home her mother tried to make for her. Now that Suzanne is gone, it's all Catie has left. This place where she never felt quite welcome."

"She's loved by many."

"I know that. You know that. But I promise you, the little girl who heard endless whispers about her mother does not know that." Frank jerked his head toward the office. "Now you can go to her. But you better not hurt her, or whatever you said to Frances out there will pale in comparison to how I'll come after you."

18

Catie was shaking. It had been years since she'd heard Frances say something like that. She had almost convinced herself those opinions were in the past, and her dislike of her neighbour was only an echo of that long-ago trauma.

And then, because of an overheard conversation that truly had nothing to do with Catie, the older woman had gone off on her. Not because she thought fundraising was inherently a bad idea, but because it was *Catie's* idea. That everything she touched was tainted because of who her mother was—and the happy, satisfied life her mother got to live.

What. Fucking. Bullshit.

Mac's wasn't the place, and when she was on the defensive wasn't the time, but there would soon be a time *and* a place for Catie to deal with Frances once and for all. Right now, she just needed to calm down.

The door to Frank's office creaked open, and she whirled around.

Will stood in the doorway.

Oh, she hated the look on his face. "I don't need your sympathy," she bit out.

He shook his head and stepped inside, closing the door behind him. "I get that. How about some empathy?"

She shook her head. "I don't... I can't..."

"She's a fucking bitch, Catie. With a clear need to hurt someone for her own twisted reasons that have nothing to do with you. Nothing."

Hot, frustrated tears spilled down her cheeks, like a dam burst. "Don't go there. You don't know what my childhood was like."

"But I want to."

She hated how gentle his voice was. "It was nothing like yours."

"We're all different. No question there."

"You wouldn't understand. The things people said..." She trailed off.

He didn't reply right away. He just stood there, handsome and popular, representing everything she resented about this town, and at the same time, also kind and caring and resilient, reminding her of everything she had come to admire about him individually.

Finally, he reached for the chair at the desk. "Can I sit?"

She nodded reluctantly. It wasn't like she wanted him to leave, and maybe it would be easier to talk if he wasn't quite so...big.

He sat down carefully, then leaned forward and braced his elbows on his knees. "Maybe my childhood wasn't like yours, but the years after my parents died were rough. We faced a good dose of judgement for Owen wanting custody of our brothers. We—no, he, because I fucked back off to school—struggled to take care of them, and that was pretty well known. Talked about. And the judgement I faced for not coming home? How much that hit me square in my own guilt? My life hasn't been the walk in the park you seem to think it was. And I'm not saying all of that to compare anything here. Just...there are always things we don't know about each other."

There was a weight to the last sentence, and that was reinforced when he lifted his head, his gaze searching her face.

"What?" She swiped her face. "I'm sorry about all of that. That's awful. What are you looking at me like that for?"

"Why didn't you tell anyone that your mom died?"

Fuck. "Frank told you."

"He loves you." Will's voice cracked there. "He read me the riot act for not knowing. Rightfully so. I'm sorry."

"You don't need to be—"

"Hey. I'm your friend. And I missed something big and awful that happened to you."

"That was before we were friends."

"Well, I'm sorry anyway. You once told me I could apologize to you any time."

That made her laugh a little tiny bit. "I did not."

"You did, in fact. After you called me on my shit, right out there, and then we stood in the parking lot outside. Full disclosure, I was thinking desperately about how much I wanted to kiss you, and then you said you wanted to thank me for letting you talk it out. I said, any time, and thanks for letting me apologize. And you said—"

"Any time," she breathed.

"Did you mean it?"

"Of course I didn't! It was a turn of phrase. I had gotten into the habit of snarkily repeating back to you what you had already said."

"But that wasn't snarky."

"No, I suppose it wasn't."

"I want to apologize, Catie."

"I don't need that now." She shook her head. "God, I didn't see this coming."

"What do you need, then? Just tell me, and I'll move heaven and earth to make it happen."

What she wanted was a big ask, given everything that had happened. She blew out her cheeks and shook her head.

"Anything."

Now it was her voice cracking. "Honestly? I need a hug."

He held his arms out to the side, and she laughed. But he didn't move, because he was serious. "As a friend. Orphaned kid to orphaned kid."

"I was a grown-up when she…" Her eyes welled up, and she swore.

He reached for her, and this time, she folded in against his chest. He was warm and solid, and his arms felt safe.

———

WILL EXHALED in relief as Catie burrowed in against him. She felt smaller than usual in his arms. Little and mighty at the same time.

"I was basically grown, too." His throat was tight. "It doesn't make it easier. Just different."

"I remember when your mom died," she said softly. "You were barely an adult."

Will thought back to that funeral, the second in a row for him and his brothers. "Your mom made a blueberry cobbler."

She gasped. "How do you remember that?"

"Most people made savoury dishes. They were convinced we weren't going to be able to feed Josh and Adam. Casseroles for days. I answered the door when your mom came by. She said the usual things, then gave me the dish, and told me my mom gave her the recipe, so she thought there was a good chance it might be something we liked." Fuck, his eyes were leaking.

She sniffled against his shirt. Good. It was good to not be alone in the memory.

"Your mom was one of the most thoughtful people in this town, to me, at the worst moment of my life. I don't know if that helps to hear tonight, but—"

"It helps." She hiccuped. "Thank you."

He smoothed his hand over her hair. She was so fiercely independent, and wary, and he just wanted to be protective of her, but he didn't really know where to start. Now wasn't the time to pick even further at all the secret vulnerabilities she was covering up. They weren't even any of his business, strictly speaking.

But he wanted them to be his business.

"What else do you need?"

She shrugged.

He squeezed her again. Another hug couldn't hurt.

And as she stepped back, he thought maybe he could lighten the mood a little. "Can we talk about how my brothers are part of your secret parking fundraising brigade and I am not?"

"They aren't!" She laughed and groaned at the same time. "I don't know what she was going on about. Tom would have submitted that permit change, adding the municipality as a co-sponsor of the event, and increasing the number of hayrides, ergo, needing more EMTs and firefighters there for safety control. I literally just suggested it as a trial balloon to see how people would react. I'm not organizing anything!"

He loved how exasperated she got. This was the worst moment for a surge of inexplicable desire, but there it was. He reached out and caught her hand. "It's a testament to just how much you do effect change around here. All for the better."

"Says my fiercest critic."

"Nah." He tugged her closer and brushed his lips against her forehead. "I'm your biggest fan. I promise."

She murmured her thanks, then pointed in the direction of their seats. "We should probably..."

"Yeah."

In the kitchen, Frank was waiting to give her a hug. "Your food's ready when you want it."

"Can I get mine to go?" Catie asked. "I'm ready for my PJs and some HGTV."

"Absolutely." He glanced at Will. "Yours, too?"

Will didn't want anyone to mistakenly think he was going home with Catie when that was the furthest thing from the truth. "No, I'll eat mine here, Frank. Thank you, though. I've got some reading to do, and I like the lighting over your booth."

A most unnecessary addition to the answer, he realized as soon as it was out of his mouth.

But Frank didn't seem to care.

Will walked Catie out to her car, just to make sure she wasn't going to be ambushed. "When you get home, text me that you get inside, all right?"

"She's a fifty-five-year-old lightweight, Will. I think I'll be okay."

"Just...humour me."

She gave him a half smile and nodded. "Thanks for tonight. That would have been even harder if I was alone."

———

FORTY-FIVE MINUTES LATER, after not really tasting much of his dinner and spending most of that time consumed by his thoughts, Will texted his brother a specific request.

Will: Do you have mom's recipe cards?
Owen: Probably.
Will: Great. I'm coming over.

Owen opened the front door as he climbed the steps. "Why do you need mom's recipe cards in the middle of the night?"

"It's ten-thirty, Betty White."

Owen frowned. "Betty White has never struck me as the early to bed type."

"Not the point."

"Also, you said that like some kind of insult, when it really needs to be pointed out that Betty White is a class act."

"We've derailed." Will paused, distracted by his brother's rabid but fair defence of the ninety-something-year-old actress. "But your point is taken, I meant no disrespect to Betty White."

"What about me?"

"You? Maybe I meant a little disrespect in your direction."

Owen yawned. "I'm going back to bed."

Will stood his ground. "First the recipe cards."

"Sure, okay." Owen wandered into the kitchen and dug

into the cupboard beside the fridge. "What is the cooking emergency?"

"Catie's mom died."

"Oh, shit." Owen stopped rifling and gave Will a sympathetic look. "I'm sorry. Is there anything we can do?"

"Go back in time and attend the funeral four years ago."

"Oh. *Shit.*"

"Yeah." Will sighed. "She never said anything—to anyone—when she moved back. And Frank read me the riot act tonight. Then we had a good cry together, and I told her about the blueberry cobbler her mom made for us after *our* mom died—which was apparently Mom's recipe."

"So you want to make her a cobbler."

"That was the idea. Yeah."

Owen pointed to the chair. "Sit. You need to think bigger than cobbler."

"I thought you wanted to go back to bed. Get all the sleep you can before the baby arrives."

"I can sleep when she turns eighteen. This is important."

Will blinked. "She? Did I miss a gender reveal announcement?"

Owen scrubbed his hand over his face, then grinned. "Fuck, that was a slip. Kerry wanted to keep it quiet, just in case...she's not big zon the gendered stuff anyway, which makes sense. But yeah. Another girl. I'm pretty fucking excited."

"I bet." Will clapped his brother on the shoulder. "That's great. And mum's the word."

"Thanks. Now go back and start at the beginning. How

did you find out?"

That was a mood ruiner question. "I ran into Catie at the diner tonight. It was jammed, so we decided to share a table—"

"Likely story, but go on."

"Hey, noisy peanut galleries don't get details." Will paused a beat, then swore under his breath. "Okay, it actually didn't start tonight. Because tonight, it really was a coincidence. I didn't seek her out this time. It's complicated, actually."

He poured his heart out onto the table. Without details, he told Owen what happened in Timmins, and Catie's resistance to dating when they got home. Then brought him up to speed on what Frances said, and some of what Frank added. "So all of Catie's feelings…I can't blame her, right? But I also hate that she's afraid to be with me because of what that witch thinks."

"It's probably not just Frances, though. There probably are other sour-faced, judgemental asses around town, and they bring back awful memories for Catie when she hears them whispering about anyone. Doesn't even need to be here." Owen shook his head. "That's awful."

"Yeah. So I want to do something. And you're right. Baking her a cobbler isn't the Big Idea, it's just…one thing. I want to do something for her now, and then more later, and then just keep showing up and trying to be something good in her life. So she…you know…"

Owen gave him a soft grin. "She makes you happy."

Will nodded, then screwed up his face against the hot, prickly feelings that roared to the surface. "But I'm not sure I do the same for her."

"It doesn't sound like it's *you* who doesn't make her happy as much as the circumstances. Sometimes there are barriers people need to work through, and Catie's perception of how people will see the two of you together is just that—a barrier."

"That's the exact opposite of what Josh said."

Owen snorted. "And what sage advice did the guy who chooses to live above a garage share?"

Will laughed—a little. It wasn't funny. "It's not supposed to be hard."

Owen grunted.

"You don't agree?"

"It's not supposed to be hard *all the time*, sure. But who ever promised us easy?"

"Josh said that if she's not all in, I shouldn't lose my head over her."

"He has some baggage. You don't need to carry it for him."

"Okay, sure, but…do I need to carry Catie's baggage, then? Isn't that what he's saying? If there's a barrier there, it's hers to break down. Not mine. Isn't that overstepping?"

"That's a lot of questions to say, *I don't know what Catie wants me to do here.* Can't you talk to her about it?"

Clearly not. "Yeah, I should. But she has these fucking walls, and I don't even see them until I ram up against them."

"So stop ramming up against them."

"I can't see them!"

Owen shook his head. "You're not listening to me. Take a breath. You say she's protecting herself, right? That's fair. We all do that. And when you try to get too close, boom, there's a wall. So maybe you're moving too fast. Take it slow. Slow enough that instead of ramming into a wall, you just graze against it. And when that happens, just make camp there. Outside the walls. But don't bounce off them or alert her defences or whatever imagery works there. Get close but don't try to invade. Wait until she invites you in."

It was a long speech for his brother. And actually, really fucking thoughtful. Will nodded. "So, blueberry cobbler is a first step. It gets me close. It's friendly."

"And then you do something else. Keep showing her how special she is to you, until she believes it."

Will frowned. "Frank said something along those same lines about belief. That she doesn't know how loved she is in this town."

Owen rocked back on his chair. "That's a tough one. Love is… You know what? Josh was wrong. It's not always easy. We think it is because we conflate like and love. Everyone likes Catie. But if everyone loved Catie, we would have known that her mom died, right?"

Will recoiled like he'd been slapped.

Owen kept going. "Maybe everyone, or maybe— Look, I'll be blunt. You're falling in love with Catie, right?" He didn't wait for an answer, which was good, because Will's throat went dry. "So you think how you see her now is how we all see her. And hey, I like Catie a lot. I feel shitty about the fact that we didn't know about her loss. But I think you're looking at this through some kind of rose-coloured glasses, because you want this to be easy for you. But falling in love isn't always easy. When I fell for Kerry, it was all about me. My feelings for her. And that *felt* easy, right up until the moment she found out I'd had a vasectomy. Which, by the way, she discovered as an aside after a condom broke. I mentioned it as an aside—and then things got really hard. Because the woman I was falling for wanted babies of her own, and I was done with all of that."

Will hadn't known the details there. "Fuck."

"Yeah. Right? So I had to come to terms with the fact that I had done something that was possibly going to be a barrier to us being together. I thought I was done after Becca. Long before I knew Kerry would come along. And then, I didn't share that with her at the first available opportunity. I never shared it with her consciously because it wasn't on the top of my mind." Owen sighed. "We can be selfish. All human beings can be selfish. And part of falling in love is coming to grips with the ways that we are selfish and learning to undo that, so that we can make room in ourselves to care for another person as wholly and as fulsomely as we care for ourselves. Falling in love *all the way* is inherently selfless, but that takes work, and a lot of people stop before they get there."

"Josh, for example."

"He doesn't open up to me," Owen grumbled. "So I don't know for sure, but yeah, sure sounds like. He spent three weeks in paradise with a woman. That's enough time to go head over heels, I suppose, but did they ever test that connection in real life?"

"No. You're right." There was so much for Will to think about next. "I see what you're saying about Catie. There's a lot to undo there."

"And you can't just wish it were easy, you can't just wish that Catie has always been loved and she's just wrong to perceive that she is lonely. She's guarded for a reason. That's not wrong. You don't need to prove to her that she's wrong. You need to show her that you see that she's right."

"I can do that." Will scratched his jaw. "Speaking of Berton women…what do you remember about Suzanne?"

———

THAT NIGHT, Will tossed and turned for a few fitful hours before giving up and going in search of coffee and guidance at the diner.

The door was still locked, but after he pounded loud enough to get Frank's attention, the cook let him in. "You better be here to peel potatoes."

"Sure." Will rolled up his sleeves and washed his hands. "This about Catie?"

"Sort of. Yes."

"She's fragile, you know. Strong, yes, but…"

Will nodded. "I know."

"Don't break her heart, you know?"

"I won't. But it's not Catie I wanted to talk about this morning. Not directly. I'm going to go slow with her. I think I have that plan figured out." He grinned, thinking about just setting up camp outside Catie's fortress of solitude. "This is about something else."

"Oh?"

"I was thinking we should do something to honour her mother. Last night, I went to my brother's house to get a blueberry cobbler recipe—long story—and we were talking about Suzanne. I remember her bringing that cobbler, my mom's recipe, over after Mom died. And Owen remembers Suzanne organizing a big yard sale for the hockey team, and it took over the entire town."

"I remember that, yeah. It was quite the thing."

"Did she do that sort of thing a lot?"

"Sure. She was never one for the formal organizations. Too stuffy, too many rules. But if there was something Suzanne could do directly, quickly, to help people out. She would throw a yard sale for any cause, and cook a meal for any family in need. She even got me hooked up with a halfway house that takes my leftovers."

"You still do that?"

"Sure do. Pack the meals up at the end of the day, stick 'em in the freezer."

"That's quite the legacy she had."

"There's more to it than that." Frank pointed to the pile of potatoes. "Don't stop."

"Sorry. Go on."

"Catie never had a father. Whoever it was, he was never in the picture, but also, Suzanne never wanted to marry. Some of her suitors offered, but she didn't love anyone like that. All her love was for Catie."

Will knew better than to stop peeling, but he had so many questions. He figured as long as he kept helping, he'd hear it all, so he kept his hands moving. "She must have been quite young when she moved here?"

"Young and beautiful, yep." Frank sighed. "It was a hard path she chose in some ways, but it was her path."

"Did people make trouble for her? This young, beautiful single mother who had a lot of suitors?" Will instinctively knew the answer to his own question, and hated it. He thought of Frances spitting a slut-shaming insult at Catie last night and his knuckles went white around the peeler.

"I suppose. But it wasn't all like that. Suzanne made a lot of friends, many who Catie never knew—that's something I tried to tell her at her mother's funeral, not that any of them were there. She did have some detractors, though."

Will's throat was tight. "Frances Schmidt?"

"Yeah, Frances always had a bit of jealously when it came to Suzanne. Something to do with someone in the Lion's Club, if I recall correctly. And that's the piece… that's why she always did things her own way. On her own terms."

"She had exes in those community organizations?"

"I think Suzanne maybe had an ex in every corner. She lived here for fifteen years, and was a single woman the entire time. If she were a man, she'd have been voted in as mayor."

"Wow." Will shook his head. "That's not right. It sounds like she *should* have been mayor. Catie doesn't know this?"

"She does, and she doesn't. It's hard, I think. Of course it is. But you're going to make it right, aren't you?"

"Yeah. Is there anyone else around I could talk to? People she once helped?"

19

―――――

September was always a weird month for Will. The first few weeks of school were a chaotic kaleidoscope of moments as classes got to know each other, as students and teachers settled into a routine, and behind the scenes, he juggled administration tasks with staying on top of threads that might need his attention all year. His afternoons were consumed with riding the buses—ten of them in total, and he rode each of them twice, to the delight of his students.

Some of them were on the bus for an hour each way. It made for a long day for them, and an even longer day for him, because when he returned to the school, he still had parent phone calls to return and incident reports to review and sign off on.

SAR training fell off his weekly schedule. His plate couldn't hold that as well, not in September, which was usually fine, but this year he missed it.

It was the easiest way to get close—but not too close— to Catie. So he had to slow his expectations for gaining her trust. He did make her the blueberry cobbler. His version was only okay, but she texted him a picture of it as her dessert-for-breakfast choice twice in a row.

As Owen predicted, it was a sweet gesture that didn't change much.

The other reason he missed training was the much-needed opportunity to burn off some energy.

And with the impending arrival of Kerry and Owen's baby—and Becca and Charlie planning to visit and stay at Will's house immediately thereafter—Will couldn't plan on working out in the spare bedroom of his house, either. Not with a toddler who napped and had early bedtimes.

So he moved his weights into the garage and started running hill repeats at the harbour with Josh. The whole time, he wondered if Catie was still working out with Isla, and if inviting her to work out with him would be a good "get close but not too close" strategy. He didn't act on it. He'd taken a step back, and now he was worried it was too far back.

Suddenly it was a week before Canadian Thanksgiving. The calendar flipped into October, and everything happened at once.

Catie's Big Pumpkin Plan for the business club was in full swing. School families were dropping them off by the truck full.

Kerry went into labour on the day Becca and Charlie were set to arrive. Will was stuck at school, but Josh drove to Toronto to pick them up, delivering them to Will's place just in time for dinner.

Seth flew down to join their vigil. Adam and Isla brought dessert.

Bedtime for Charlie came and went. Seth racked out next. Adam and Isla headed home. Will knew he needed to get some rest before school the next day, but Becca sat up, waiting for an update, and Will couldn't leave his niece alone.

"How are you holding up?"

She blew a raspberry. Now twenty-one, she was still a bit of a kid—but also a fully grown adult, with a family of her own. And she was about to have a baby sister arrive in this world. It was a lot. "I've done this before, remember."

Becca's mom, Rachel, had remarried earlier than Owen did, and she had half-siblings on that side of the family, too. "I know. But still, you and your dad have a special bond."

"Oh, yeah. But that's not going to change." She hopped up and down, shaking out her hands. "No, I'm nervous for Kerry. This is her first baby. Her first labour, even though she's a midwife. It's wild, and we haven't heard anything for hours, and…" Becca burst into tears. "It's just a lot, you know?"

He honestly wasn't sure he did. "Come here." He pulled her in for a hug. "Do you want to go over there? Take my truck. Go and check on them. They won't mind."

"Are you sure? Will you text me if Charlie wakes up? He's pretty good about sleeping through the night now, but if he gets scared…"

"I'll hang out with him. And if you're not back by breakfast, Seth and Josh can manage to entertain him between the two of them. We'll do our best *Three Men and a Baby* impression until you get back."

She flew to the front door, grabbing his keys. "Thank you!"

He headed upstairs, checking on Charlie before going into his own room. He tried to read, but that didn't work. It wasn't even that late. He glanced at the clock. It was just after eleven. What were the chances Catie would be up? He texted her, and she replied immediately.

> **Will: Top secret news.**
> **Catie: Is it baby news????**
> **Will: Soon. Kerry's been in labour since the after-noon. Becca arrived tonight, and she's over there now. I'm babysitting Charlie.**
> **Catie: That's amazing, Will.**
> **Will: I'll keep you posted.**
> **Catie: Lips sealed. If you need anything, let me know!**

He needed her. *One night, nobody needs to know.* How he wished that was an option for them. Sneaking around, sharing a private connection.

Before he could drift too far down that fantasy path, his phone rang. It wasn't Catie, though. It was Owen's name on the screen.

"What's the good word?" Will asked as he answered.

"Becca got here just in time. It's a girl. Lila Grace. She's perfect. Kerry was so strong." Owen laughed. "Fuck, man, I'm a dad all over again."

"Congratulations." Will was getting choked up right along with his brother. "Can we come over in the morning?"

"Sure. Becca's going to stay for a bit."

"Tell her I'll wait up until she gets back." He hung up so Owen could call Adam and Josh next, then went to tell Seth the good news. His brother waved in acknowledge-ment and went right back to sleep.

After months of Will's house being empty, it was good to have a home full of family again.

———

THE NEXT MORNING he went to school first thing, cleared his schedule for the morning, waited for the bus kids to arrive and make sure the day got started properly, and then told the secretary he'd be on his cell phone if there were any emergencies.

Then he swung back to his place to pick up Seth, Becca, and Charlie before heading to Owen and Kerry's house.

They promised not to stay long, but then Adam and Isla showed up with Josh, and food. Then Kerry asked Will to hold Lila so she could go take a shower. And Charlie came over to kiss the baby's toes, and it was all just so wholesome Will couldn't tear himself away, couldn't play the bad cop and kick everyone out so the new parents could have some quiet rest.

Owen didn't seem to mind, though. He looked shell-shocked, but happy. "I can't believe you made it over in time last night," he said to Becca, who was curled up next to him. "I should have asked you to come sooner."

"You were a bit busy." She leaned her head on his shoulder. "Next time."

He chuckled. "I dunno if Kerry wants to do it again. But yes."

Becca glanced at Will, then at her other uncles, her eyes sparkling. "Come on, look at the Kincaid tradition. You've got two kids now. Three more to go."

Owen shook his head. "Adam and Isla can bear that."

"Why are you looking at me?" Adam protested. "We're not having five kids. Or maybe any." He jerked his chin at Will. "That one can do it."

Will had always thought he'd wanted kids. Just like

he'd always thought one day, the Right Person would fall into his lap and everything would be easy.

Now he wanted Catie. Did she want kids? And just as that idea slid dangerously into his mind—cart way before the horse—he got a message from the subject of his endless thoughts.

Catie: Any baby pictures yet?

He sent her a snap of a tiny sleeping face, wrapped up in a blanket and nestled in his arms. She replied back with a heart emoji, then another text saying the lunch bell just rang.

Catie: Pumpkin selling time. Tell Kerry and Owen I say congrats!

————

HE MISSED the lunch time sale, but it was all anyone could talk about that afternoon.

"Ms. Berton is a genius," said Sam when he appeared in Will's office doorway during the last period.

Will smiled, noting that Sam—who had spent all summer calling her Catie—remembered to play by the school rules while at school. "She is. What can I do for you this afternoon?"

The genius poked her head around the corner behind Sam. "We're just waiting for Sam to use the office phone. Because we think we might sell out this afternoon. Your weird school rule about not using cell phones in class is very restrictive, you know that?"

Will gave her his sternest look. "I am aware. Those restrictions are for a reason. Did that occur to you?"

She straightened up. "Sam, you should go get back in line to use the phone."

He left, and she stepped inside, closing the door.

Will frowned as she took her time settling in the chair across from him. Then she gave him a deliberately innocent smile.

"No," she said breezily. "Not for a second. It would *never* occur to you that you might have a *reason* for doing something. Silly me."

"That's not what I meant."

"But it's what you said."

"You called my rule weird!"

"You're right, that was too familiar of me. But the cell phone rule really is a problem for the business club. Sam is currently missing math class because he's waiting in a line of kids to make a call. He's fifteen! Let the man child use his own phone."

Will sighed. "You're bossy."

"I am not."

"You are—"

"*You're* bossy. *I* have high standards and expect people to meet them or get out of my way. That's not the same thing."

It felt like the same thing, but Will wasn't interested in arguing. "I'll consider a phone exception for business calls. Put something in writing. But I *do* know what I'm doing. Here, in this school. With these kids. You don't need to come in here and change everything around."

She narrowed her eyes. "In this school? Your school?"

He nodded.

She nodded back. "And this town, maybe? *Your* town?"

Oh fuck. He'd walked right into that trap. "Whoa." He held up his hands. "Catie, I didn't—"

"Yes, you did. When I suggest anything remotely *new* or *different*, you're Mr. It Can't Be Done. For reasons. For tradition. You know what, Will? I am not a problem in your path that needs to be fixed."

"I didn't say—"

"Maybe I am bossy. Because I know how to get stuff done. The problem here is that you don't want me to do that." She stood up. "I—"

"No."

"Excuse me?"

He stood up, too, and marched around the desk, getting between her and the door. "You're not a problem that needs to be fixed. And I *do* want you to change things. I just asked that you put it in writing and not call it *weird* in front of one of my students. You breezed right past that. God, it's hard to just sit outside your walls and not try to scale them, you know that?"

"What are you talking about?"

"Sitting outside your fortress walls."

"I… What does that mean?"

"It's a long story."

"Well, I have a pumpkin sale to go oversee, so…"

He moved off the door. And closer to her. Close enough to lower his voice. "You have every right to be grumpy about the barriers thrown up in your path. Be mad about Frances. And if you want to talk more about the dickhead I was in the past, that's fine, too. But we're not going to fight about cell phone usage. Don't snap at me. Just keep talking."

"That's very…" She swallowed hard, and nodded. "Reasonable."

"I'm a reasonable man, Ms. Berton."

"You just want me to call you Mr. Kincaid."

He grinned. "I do like that a lot."

She rolled her eyes and brushed past him, sending a jolt of awareness through his body.

When she opened the door, January was standing on the other side of it.

Apparently, he wasn't going to get any work done this afternoon.

He gestured for her to come in and close the door, then he flopped back in his chair. "What's up?"

"My class is running laps outside with Mr. Sanders for Terry Fox Run practice."

"That's not a question."

"It's just what brought me here. And then there were… sounds…coming from in here."

He laughed. "Whatever you're thinking, it's not that. We were having a disagreement, because we're like oil and water sometimes, and cannot help ourselves. It was nothing. We're just too…opposite. I'm working on understanding her better."

January was staring at him. Bug-eyed.

Will grabbed his now-cold coffee and took a long sip, not sure he wanted to hear her opinion, but quite certain he wasn't going to be able to resist asking. He frowned, then put the cup down. "What?"

His friend rolled her eyes. "You're kidding me, right?"

"About what?"

"You think the problem is that you and Catie are too *opposite*? Mr. Responsibility and Ms. Take Care of Everyone, Mr. Give Back to the Community and Ms. Work Ethic." January sighed in an overly dramatic fashion. "Wherever might the two of you find common ground?"

"That's different."

"Is it?"

His frown pulled tighter. "Maybe we're similar, but we get there in very different ways."

"Uh huh."

"She doesn't understand me."

"And you clearly don't understand her. *Because you are both stupid boneheads.*"

"Language."

"Bite me."

"So professional." He fought back a grin. "You think she's a stupid bonehead, too?"

"Both of you are so fixated on the idea that the other one just could never understand the other, when it's pretty obvious you're just scared to try." January crossed her arms over her chest. "But you're a bigger bonehead than she is. You started this. And then you made it worse after the competition."

He could feel his face heating up. "She told you?"

"No. But the way you two stared at each other in the library the week after...it was like I wasn't even in the room. I assume you fucked it up."

He didn't answer the second part. "You were talking to someone else, and it's a big room."

"I can multitask."

"If you ever fall in love, I'm going to be deeply obnoxious about it." As soon as that was out of his mouth, he regretted it. January's face went soft, and she made a swooning noise.

"You're in love with her? Will, that's so cute!"

"You can leave my office now."

"I don't know. I feel like you kind of need my wisdom."

He probably did. But that was three people he'd now admitted his feelings for Catie to, and none of them were Catie. "This is a situation where I need to find my own wisdom, unfortunately. Out. Shoo. Thank you. See you later."

Will did think he was getting closer to some of that wisdom, cribbed liberally from advice from his brother and Frank. The key to Catie's heart wasn't going to be a brazen declaration. It was going to be him actually doing the work.

In his most pessimistic moments, he feared it might take longer than he wanted. It had taken twenty-five years for Catie to know without a shadow of a doubt that Pine Harbour was not a safe place for her to risk her heart in.

And he'd accidentally shown her over the last year that he was callous. That wasn't what he wanted to be going forward—to her or anyone else—so he was going to have to consciously repair that reputation. It might take a year to do that.

He sure as hell hoped it wouldn't take twenty-five years to fully restore her faith in Pine Harbour, too, but it was going to take some time before she knew with just as much sincerity that this place and its people valued her.

Going forward, he was going to be better, with purpose. He needed to show her the opposite of her past experiences. He needed to *be* the opposite.

When the end-of-day bell rang, he headed outside to say goodbye to all the students as they headed out to their buses or to meet their waiting parents.

And today, there were a lot of those parents, because the Great Pumpkin Sale was very popular. Will wasn't sure what magic Catie had woven, exactly, because pumpkins weren't hard to come by—in fact, the ones they were selling had been donated by some of these very same parents.

And yet the lineup was impressive. Kids telling their parents about the pumpkins they saw earlier. Parents pre-negotiating how many pumpkins they could take home.

And at the head of the line, the business club members —next to a selfie frame made of cardboard, and a poster board encouraging people to share photos of their pumpkin's new home.

Clever.

Will stood to the side and watched how it worked. One of the club members greeted each student and parent and invited them to find their very own special pumpkin to take home and be their special decoration. Another teen quickly took a family picture in the selfie frame—ensuring the pumpkin pile was well featured in the background, Will was sure—and then they were off to pick their pumpkin.

"This is very impressive," he said to Catie as she approached. "Truly. You aren't just selling pumpkins."

"You're never selling pumpkins. You're selling a pumpkin picking experience. It's an important lesson for them to learn."

"I like it." They walked down the dwindling line of pumpkins. "How long are you going to sell tonight?"

"We'll sell out before all these people get home and post their pictures on Instagram." She stopped next to Sam, who was counting pumpkins. "Isn't that right, Sam? And what kind of sales does that leave on the table?"

He glanced down the line, then did a bit more mental math before nodding. "That's right. If we think we could get another twenty percent of sales from word of mouth.

So we *could* sell maybe another fifty pumpkins, but we don't have them here."

"That's good data, though, right? You learned a lot from this," Will said. "So it's not all bad."

"It's not bad at all," Sam said emphatically. "But actually, I proactively connected with our supply chain to ensure we had all the data we might need to make the right business decision—" He paused for effect, and Catie beamed at him. "So if we want more pumpkins, we can have up to thirty tonight. And more tomorrow."

She waved over a few other students, and Sam recapped for them.

"What do you folks think?" Catie lobbed it right back at them, spreading her hands wide to include every available club member in the decision. "Come on, let's talk it out. What are the pros and cons?"

"We might end up with leftover pumpkins," one kid said.

"We can extend the dates of the sale," another pointed out. "Just keep going until we can't find any more pumpkins."

"What are the costs associated with extending the sale?" Catie asked. "Time, money, and effort."

"We'll all have to be here again tomorrow, and maybe for longer hours."

She nodded. "What else?"

"We need to factor in the effort of going and getting the pumpkins now," someone else said. "And we aren't allowed to leave school grounds."

"I can help with that," Will heard himself say. Everyone turned to look at him. He shrugged. "I'm cheap manual labour. And I don't need a parent permission slip to drive out to the pumpkin farm."

Catie frowned at him. "I'll go. I'm the adult in charge of the club."

Sam shook his head. "Ms. Berton, it doesn't make sense for you to go. You can't fit twenty pumpkins in your car."

Another kid glanced back and forth between them. "Logistically, it would make the most sense for them both to go, because then we get the pumpkins faster. They need to take Mr. Kincaid's truck. That's the most logical vehicle for transportation."

Will could tell from Catie's face that she regretted ever teaching them anything about logistics and the math of running a business. He was pretty sure they were all using that as a ruse to play matchmaker between their principal and the gorgeous business club advisor, a bit of mischief he wholeheartedly supported.

But then she shrugged, and gave him a shy smile. "If Mr. Kincaid doesn't mind…"

Yeah, he really liked it when she called him that. "Let's go."

20

CATIE CLIMBED into the passenger seat of Will's truck. All the memories from the weekend in Timmins slammed into her, and she felt a fresh wave of regret.

And then snapping at Will in his office… He was right. They weren't going to do that again. She was able to contain her feelings better than that, and he deserved better, too.

He hopped into the driver's side and started the truck. "Where to?"

"To the highway, and then one concession road north."

As he waited for the last school bus to depart in front of him, Catie glanced around the truck cab. "Did you get this detailed?"

He laughed. "I'll take that as a compliment. I gave it a good once over after our trip."

"It looks good." The console between them was completely empty, except for a card with a name and address on it.

She wasn't being nosy, picking it up. It was just right

there, and she was eager for anything to talk about other than the trip. "How do you know Patrick Hoffer?"

Will answered with a question instead. "Do you know him?"

"He dated my mom briefly. That's a blast from the past."

"He was a teacher there." Will pointed at the school, now receding out the back window as they drove away. "I did my first practicum placement with him, and he was a mentor to me."

"And now he lives in Collingwood?" She set the card down again.

"Yep. I'm going to see him on the weekend. It'll be nice to catch up." Will rubbed his palm on his thigh. "What was your impression of him?"

"Patrick? He was nice. He never taught me. I'd forgotten that he was a teacher. He was firmly in that grown-up world my mom existed in that I didn't care that much about, but I caught bits of here and there. They would go to dances together."

"Small world."

"It is, isn't it?"

"A thought I regularly have about Pine Harbour. Six hundred people and all that…"

He laughed. "Fair point."

The rest of the drive to the vegetable farm just north of town was quiet. Sam's supplier was his friend Hailey's dad.

"Mr. Kincaid, nice to see you."

Will shook the man's hand and inquired about his wife's health, then thanked him for the pumpkins. "And this is Catie Berton. She's advising the business club this year."

"You're the one who has my Hailey all fired up about cash flow." The man's face split into a massive grin. "It is a pleasure to meet you, ma'am. I'm Fred."

"The pleasure is all mine, Fred. Cash flows are my jam."

He chuckled. "Mine, too. The pumpkin patch is just around the side of the canning shed, Mr. Kincaid. We'll meet you there."

Catie fell into step with the farmer. "Hailey mentioned your canning business…is that year round?"

"Pretty much, but we freeze a lot so we can keep producing in the cooler months. She's all fired up to work for me this winter thanks to you."

And to think Catie almost threatened to quit the club in Will's office. Not that she actually would have. *Not that he'd have let her.* "I needed to hear that today, Fred. I'm truly glad that she's found a passion there and can help with the family business."

"Were you a farm kid, too?"

She shook her head. "But my mom was a real estate agent—among other things—and I learned that from her."

They stopped in front of the pumpkins just as Will backed his truck up to where they stood.

"Have at 'er," Fred said. "The big ones don't taste as good anyway, so they're all yours." He showed them a rough size with his hands. "Leave any that are yay big or smaller. Do you have shears?"

Will opened the back gate of his truck bed and lifted up a few cutting implements.

"Sounds like a plan." She held out her hand. "Thank you so much."

Will shook his hand again, too, and then they were alone in the field.

"Knife, knife, or shears?" Will asked, giving her the choice.

"Shears."

He handed her a pair of work gloves that were a bit too big, but would protect her anyway.

"This truck has everything in it, doesn't it?"

"Some basic tools." He glanced further down the back of the truck bed at a covered box. "And camping equipment, climbing ropes, a first aid kit..."

She laughed. "Like I said, everything. How often are you hit by a spur-of-the-moment need to go camping?"

He gave her a funny look. "More often than you might think."

She watched him stalk away, his long legs quickly carrying him out into the patch. He leaned over and cut two pumpkins clean from their vines, then lifted them up off the ground.

Right. To work.

She did the same, and after five trips into the field, the back of his truck was half full of pumpkins. "This is a great workout," she said as she passed him the biggest one she'd found yet. "And by great workout, I mean surprisingly hard, and I'm glad you're here to do half of it. Thank you for helping."

"How many do you think you would have fit in your car?"

She laughed. "Not many. Eight?"

He headed back into the field. "You'd already be done."

She followed. "There is that."

But it didn't take them long to finish, and before she knew it, they were done. "That's it," he said, as he closed up the back of the truck.

She turned to head to the passenger side, and he hustled around her to get the door. "Thank you," she murmured.

He didn't move away immediately. He gazed at her face for a moment, then smiled as he lifted his attention to the top of her head. "You have a..." He leaned in and plucked a crinkly dried leaf from her hair. "Pumpkin leaf."

She could breathe in the scent of him, he was that close, and now neither of them were moving. *Two dumb, horny chickens.* Well, Will wasn't a chicken. Not anymore. He'd made it clear what he wanted, and she'd turned him down.

One dumb, horny chicken, and a very patient man.

"Will..."

He brushed a strand of hair off her cheek. "I don't have any expectations of you. We're just getting some pumpkins."

She closed her eyes and nodded.

"Hold still," he murmured. His thumb brushed the corner of her mouth. "You've got a little dirt on your cheek."

That wasn't her cheek. But she didn't care. It had been too long since she'd had his hands on her skin, and now she was on fire. She breathed his name again, and he pulled her into his arms, pressing his mouth against hers.

A sweet, soft, too-short kiss that left her aching.

"Can I tell you a secret?"

"Yes," she breathed, her eyelids fluttering open.

His gaze was solid. Confident. "I thought about that camping equipment when we were driving home from Timmins. One more night, under the stars...we wouldn't be home yet, maybe it wouldn't count..." And then he stepped back, and was around the truck before she trusted her legs to climb in on her side.

He gave her a cocky grin as he started the truck up again. "Just getting some pumpkins," he repeated.

Maybe they needed to go on vegetable garden runs more often.

————

PATRICK HOFFER WASN'T the only former Pine Harbour resident Will visited over the next week. His secret project was growing now.

He was working on it at the kitchen table when Becca and Charlie came home from a walk with Kerry and Lila. Becca found Charlie a snack, then plopped down in the chair next to Will. "What's this?"

"A surprise for a friend of mine."

Becca looked at the sketches. "'Arms open in welcome.' That's really nice."

"Thanks. It's just one idea." He showed her the others. "How was your walk?"

"Great. Kerry mentioned that Dad has two folding tables for you. She said you can pick them up at five."

"Yeah, he texted me. Are you going to go over there with me?"

She shook her head. "Charlie and I are going to watch Hayden's game from last night, and maybe video call with him after practice."

Becca's boyfriend played professional hockey. He'd entered the league as a dad, and they all worried about the pressure that would put on the couple. But despite the odds being stacked against them, Becca and Hayden seemed to be making it work.

Will wasn't one to judge, anyway. He was still learning how to communicate with the woman he had feelings for.

Fate seemed to be of the clear opinion that he needed more practice, though. After a month of barely seeing her, Catie was everywhere he went now.

Including his brother's house late that afternoon.

There was a sticky note on the front door advising that a baby was sleeping, so please enter quietly. Instead of knocking, Will carefully turned the doorknob and stepped into the foyer—and saw a familiar blonde head resting against the couch cushions.

His brother and sister-in-law were nowhere in sight.

As Will toed off his boots and crept closer, he realized Catie was gently cooing to Lila, who was curled up on her chest.

Catie wiggled her fingers at him in a silent greeting, then pointed to the kitchen. The door was closed, and Will realized Owen and Kerry were on the other side of it.

"I didn't know you were coming over," she said softly.

He matched her quiet tone. "And I didn't know that *you* would be here when I did."

"Kerry invited me over to meet Lila."

"Ah," Will said. It seemed like everyone in Pine Harbour was now pushing them together. That was probably driving Catie up the wall. But at the same time, he couldn't be sure because they still hadn't talked. Maybe it was time to change that.

Seeing her with a baby in her arms definitely spurred him to speed up his timeline. He knew what that funny feeling in his chest was, he just didn't want to name it yet. Not when he was still working to get inside her walls. But as she smiled to herself and rubbed her nose against the top of Lila's head, the feeling grew. He liked that she had a soft spot for teeny, tiny, wriggly humans.

He liked that a lot.

Bad Will.

But his off-limits feelings didn't feel as bad as they had a month ago.

"Hey," she murmured. "I wanted to talk to you about the business club and the winter carnival."

"Sure."

Lila stirred on her chest, and she put her finger up. *Shhh*, she mouthed, then smiled.

He wanted to lean over and kiss her pursed lips and suggest they discuss the carnival at his house—which was full of people. Her house. Naked.

Lowering his voice to the quietest warning-a-kid-during-an-assembly voice he had, he suggested a more reasonable idea. "How about lunch tomorrow?"

She thought about it long enough that he knew *no* was one of the options she was considering. But after a moment, she nodded. "I have some showings in the afternoon, but I can do an early lunch. Eleven-thirty?"

"Great. It's a date."

Her eyes flared wide, and he was saved by the kitchen door opening. Kerry brought out a pot of tea. "Hey, Will." She set it down on the coffee table. "Do you want a cup?"

He shook his head, stopping by the couch to brush his fingers over Lila's back—and then along Catie's hand—before heading into the kitchen. "I'm just here to provide some requested muscle," he said as he gave Owen a focused glare.

His brother shrugged shamelessly. "The tables are out back. Did you take the turkey out of the freezer yet?"

"Yesterday." He was hosting the family Thanksgiving

on Monday, because they were still in babymoon nesting mode. But Owen usually cooked, and he was having trouble letting go of the reins. "It'll be fine."

"I know."

Will waited.

"I could come over and check on it, if you want."

"Mmm. You could. But you also could have brought the tables with you when you did that, so…I think I'm going to say since you summoned me here to pick them up, at a very specific time, while you had another guest, that you don't need to come and meddle in the turkey business."

"Hey now," Owen protested. "Kerry just thought you might want to see Catie in a neutral environment."

"I see her every week at school."

"Kerry's point stands."

Will decided not to let his brother know the ruse had worked, and now he was taking Catie out for lunch the next day. That—for now—was their little secret.

———

SUNDAY WAS a busy day at the diner, but Catie knew the sweet spot to arrive just before the church crowd, and just after the late breakfast people. Will, apparently, had the same idea, because when she arrived ten minutes early, he was already in line for a booth.

"You gotta beat the church crowd," he said, making her laugh. "What?"

"That's exactly my thinking, too."

"Great minds." He gestured for her to follow the waitress.

Catie accepted the menu offered, then craned her neck to see the board. "What are the pie options today?"

"Caramel apple and pumpkin."

"Thanks."

Once they were alone, Will asked her a silly question. "What's your favourite type of pie?"

She shook her head. "That's like asking who your favourite student is. An impossible choice."

"I'll let you in on a secret—we definitely have favourite students."

She gasped, slightly horrified. But also, vindicated. "I knew it. Then it's like…children. When I was a kid, I once told a classmate I was loved more than her, because I was an only child, and my mom didn't have to love a husband, either."

Will laughed. "Holy shit."

"I know. I had balls. But my teacher told my mom, and my mom explained that if she had another baby, she would still love me the same amount—with her whole heart—and the love for the other child would be layered on top of that, also with her whole heart."

"No conversation about the hypothetical husband?"

"Oh, no, we talked about that, too. She said if she ever did settle down with someone, they would get a sliver of her heart. In hindsight, I guess it's pretty clear why she never did." Will looked slightly shocked, so Catie frowned. "It wasn't a bad thing that she knew she wouldn't love someone the way she loved me."

He reached across the booth and covered her hand with his. "That's not what I was thinking."

Her hand was a tight ball. He didn't try to coax her fingers out of their tense fist, he just kept his hand there, steady and warm, until she relaxed. "I get defensive about her."

"I know."

She swallowed hard. "I don't want to do this here."

"That's okay." His thumb stroked back and forth over the inside of her wrist.

"I shouldn't have brought her up."

"I want to hear about her, though. Any time, any place." He smiled gently. "It's pretty awesome to know yourself that clearly. I'm still figuring out what I want in life."

"White picket fence, two point five kids?" She was joking, because humour was an excellent suit of armour she'd learned to wear well.

"Fence optional." He held her gaze as he slowly turned her hand so he could stroke her palm. "It was nice to see you with Lila yesterday."

She laughed out loud and pulled back. "Will!"

"What?"

"We haven't even gone on a date yet, and you're all like, you'd look good holding my babies."

He laughed with her. "Okay, I came on a bit strong there."

"You think?"

"But you would." He paused a beat, his eyes glittering. "If you wanted kids."

She was blushing now. "I thought we were going to talk about the winter carnival."

"We will." He really needed to stop looking at her like he wanted to take her home and make babies right now.

But she hadn't stopped thinking about the kiss in the pumpkin patch. Or how she really needed to stop caring about what other people thought about her private life. It wasn't like living as a model citizen had done anything to stop her critics from whispering about whatever lies they told themselves to feel better in comparison.

"I do want kids," she finally said. "I don't know about the point five, though. That seems cruel. Is that a deal-breaker for you? Half a child?"

"Everything is negotiable for the right person." He was teasing her now. They were playing a game. But it felt real, too. Like this was how they'd learn to share. "Although I'm learning that my assumptions about all of that were way off."

"What do you mean?"

"For a long time, I thought I was waiting for everything to fall into place. For everything to just happen to me, as it should."

"Befitting a man of your stature?"

His lips quirked. "It's rib on Will day, eh?"

"Every day is rib on Will day." Now it was her turn to reach across the table and squeeze his hand. "Just kidding."

"I can take it. What else?"

She shook her head. "No, that's it. Sorry. So you don't think everything is going to fall into place now?"

"Nope. Gonna to have to work for it. And I'm enjoying that a lot."

"This is an ongoing project for you, then?" She glanced down at the menu. They hadn't even ordered yet, and he was outright stating he was pursuing her. *It's a date.* He hadn't been joking.

"Open-ended. Might need to bring someone else on board to help me figure it all out together."

"Good luck with that," she murmured.

And then she rubbed her foot against his under the table.

————

By Wednesday, Catie realized she was cranky. Her period wasn't due, she wasn't swamped with too much work, and she'd been sleeping well. There was no reasonable explanation for her mood.

There was an unreasonable explanation, though. It had been three days since she'd had lunch with Will, and she missed him. She had a busy day at the salon, too, and she was grateful when Sam arrived after school.

"I've missed a few calls that went to voicemail," she warned him. "Can you pull those and return any that are just booking appointments? I have clients right up until close, too. The schedule is on the desk."

He nodded and quickly got to work.

The next two hours zoomed by, but her mood didn't improve. Every few songs, she asked Sam to put something else on, never getting quite into the zone.

Finally, she finished with her last client, who had a gorgeous new head of ombre highlights, and when Sam approached with the broom, she held up her hand to give him a high five. "I think we're almost done for the day."

But instead of clapping his hand against hers, he glanced toward the door.

"What is it?"

"You have one more appointment," he muttered. "Or you should..."

She frowned and crossed to the daily planner on her desk. "I didn't see it in the system at lunch when I wrote down the schedule."

"It was a last-minute addition I forgot to…" He trailed off as the door creaked open.

Catie glanced up, then understood.

"Don't be mad at him," Will said. "I pulled the principal card."

"Can I go?" Sam asked. "Because this is awkward and weird, and I regret being involved."

"I'm not mad," she said. "And yes, go. Thank you for your help today."

He grabbed his bag from behind the desk and headed out the front door. Catie followed so she could lock it behind him.

"Hi," she said quietly as she walked back to Will, her heart beating fast.

He grinned as she caught his hand and tugged him to her chair.

She put the cape on him, then smoothed her hands on his shoulders. Big, broad shoulders that she had missed more than she expected in just a few days. "What are we doing?"

"Slowly working our way towards a hard conversation."

"No, I know *that*." She tapped his head with her comb. "What are we doing with your hair?"

"Number two on the side, just a trim on top. Unless there's something else you'd rather try."

"Is that your usual?"

"Army standard."

"I heard they were shifting things up in that regard."

He caught her gaze in the mirror. "A lot of reservists come in here for trims?"

"Some. You never have before, though."

"I was a coward before."

She got her buzzers out. "Tilt your head away from me...just like that. You weren't a coward."

"In hindsight—"

"That's always twenty-twenty. We weren't ready before." She moved around him, carefully tidying up the sides before starting on the fade into the top.

The last thing she did was take the guard off and carefully shave a neat edge at the back and around his ears. Then she set the clippers down and picked up her scissors. Will didn't say anything as she trimmed the tips of his hair, then carefully made sure everything was neat and even.

"Speaking of the army, don't you have parade tonight?" She put the scissors down and picked up her brush, cleaning all the stray hairs off him.

"I had somewhere else to be." He watched her in the mirror as she swept up around him. She felt his gaze tracking her movements until she returned to him and removed the cape. Then he caught her by the wrist and tugged her to his side.

She didn't stop him. She couldn't.

And when he tugged again, she went willingly into his lap, her heart pounding a mile a minute.

"I missed you," he murmured as he cradled her in his arms. "And it's a perfect night for stargazing. Can I drive you home, with a stop in the country to look at the sky and try a bit more of that hard conversation?"

"Yes." She leaned in and brushed her lips against his. "I missed you, too. I was grumpy all day, and now I'm not."

After she locked up and they put on their coats, Will drove them north of town, past the provincial park to a gravel road that cut down away from the lake. It was dark at first, densely forested, and then the road started to rise.

The trees thinned, and suddenly they were on top of a rocky hill. The peninsula spilled out below them as he did a careful U-turn and parked on the side of the road, the back of his truck now pointing towards the view.

He came around to her side and helped her out.

In the bed of the truck, next to the toolbox and his usual box of could-be-useful-things, was a picnic basket.

"Dinner and a show?" she asked as she climbed in. It was cold tonight, nippy on the nose, but he was prepared.

"I picked up some pie and coffee. You have your choice of decaf, full caf, or hot chocolate." He spread out a couple of sleeping pads, then two blankets on top of that. He sat and patted the space next to him. "Care to join me?"

She snuggled into his side, and he pulled one blanket over them. She was well past pretending she didn't want him. "This is really pretty."

"The kids who lived here—well, they're in their forties now. I was a few years younger than them, but went to a few bonfire parties…" He pointed to a field halfway down the hill. "Over there."

"My generation, the bonfires were south of town."

He slid his arm around her. "Were you in that crowd?"

"I wasn't in any crowd. I went to a few parties, but mostly just worked at Mac's and saved money to get out of town." A pang of longing hit her square in her chest. This time, she didn't try to push the feelings away. "This kind of thing? The night sky, the country air, the peaceful-ness… This is what my mom loved. I didn't get it before."

"You didn't come back for the lack of light pollution?"

She tipped her face up to the heavens. No. Maybe she should have. "I came back in search of…understanding, maybe. Why did she bring me here when I was a child? What did she see here that would be better than a performing arts school in the city?" She reached for the thermos of hot chocolate and took a restorative sip. "That's all I could see when I was a kid. What I didn't have here, instead of what we did have."

"You wanted to act?"

"Dance, maybe. Model. Act, yes. Any and all of that." She exhaled before adding the real secret. "I wanted to be famous."

"And she brought you to a small town instead."

"I thought if I was famous, my dad might find me." Her voice cracked. "I never told her that. That was my secret. But yeah, I thought…she brought me here to hide me. To stop me from reaching for those stars. And then when I was a grown-up, when she moved back to the city to live close to me again, I confessed that part one night, and we had a good cry together."

"Your birth father wasn't a gangster?"

She laughed weakly. "Nope. Just a guy who didn't want a kid. But my mom made up for that. She wanted me with her whole heart. I never doubted that."

"What was it like, just the two of you? Did you fight?"

"Sometimes. Not often. I loved her fiercely. I think she knew that. No, she did know that."

Will dug out the pie options next. She picked cherry. He had pumpkin, and washed it down with coffee.

"What was it like for you? Seven people in a house?"

"All fighting, all the time. It would drive my mother bananas. She would snap at us at bedtime that we always needed to remember that we loved each other, even as we careened off walls and called each other names." He made a face. "I wish she could see us now. See how much we try to make sure everyone knows they are loved."

"Because she's not here to say it anymore."

"Yeah." She crawled into his lap and kissed him as he gently wiped tears off her cheeks.

"Grief is a jerk," he whispered against her mouth.

"Yeah? Tell me about that. I've managed to avoid thinking about it too much. Just…feel it. A lot."

"It's unpredictable. Confusing. Contradictory." He tugged her down so she was lying on top of him, so she could hear his voice rumble through his chest. "And it's different for everyone. Me and my brothers…we all grieved in different ways. To this day, we carry the loss of our parents very differently."

"I'm scared to let it out."

He kissed the top of her head. And then the tears flowed. Hard and fast, until his shirt was soaked.

When she lifted her head again, he met her mouth with his own. Gave her a drugging, healing kiss that turned desperate as she pressed against him. As if he ached, too, full of feelings that needed a place to go. A kiss so wild it could convince her to sink into the darkest depths in search of Atlantis.

It felt like their night together. When normally smooth Will, Mr. Always Knows What to Say, suddenly went quiet. And in that heady silence rose another side of him.

If he invited her home, she'd go. If he wanted to take her here, in the chilly night air on the side of the road, she wouldn't say no to that, either. She wanted that Will again. Wanted to be *needed* that way again.

But he eased back, breathing hard, and rested his forehead against hers. "Sorry," he whispered.

"Don't be. We both craved that." She smoothed her hand over his torso. They were warm under the blankets. "We don't need to stop, either."

"No, we do." He shuddered. "It was hard for me to

have you, and then not have you. I'm not racing ahead again only to find out you're not ready."

Oh. Her heart. Now it was her turn to whisper a broken apology.

He gathered her against him. "One day at a time, one kiss at a time, one quiet conversation at a time, I'm going to show you that I'm a guy you can trust with all of your secrets. All of your fears, all of your regrets, and all of your hopes and dreams, too."

"That's a lot."

"Yeah, but you're worth it." He brushed his fingers over her cheek. "It's not entirely selfish, you know."

"Oh?"

"You're there for me, too. Even when you don't want to be."

Her chest cracked open. "I do want to be. I do."

It was letting him in that was the hard part. Being his friend? That was easy. Being his lover? Magical.

But letting herself be loved terrified her to her core.

21

IT WAS AN ABSOLUTE RUSE. And a little bit of a fun game—he hoped. Might be more emotional than fun. He glanced at the clock. Catie was taking her sweet time getting to his office. He'd used the intercom to page her, waiting until the kids were almost set to leave. He pictured her excusing herself from the tail end of business club, rolling her eyes as she explained the principal needed to see her about something not at all important, and then sauntering down the halls of the school.

Making him wait.

When she finally appeared, he gestured for her to close the door.

He liked the way her eyebrows rose in surprise.

Well, he wanted some privacy for this conversation. He tugged his tie loose from his collar, noting the way her gaze tangled there, watching his hands work. "I need some advice. There's going to be a town meeting next week."

"Oh?"

"I want to put something on the agenda."

She paused, then strolled past his desk to the bookcase on the far wall. "Is this a trick?"

"No."

"Because January arrived as I came down here, so I know I don't need to go back and dismiss the club."

He spread his arms wide. "And you think I would manipulate you like that?"

"You've been acting sneaky. And the whole hair cut ruse…" She gave him a half smile. "I mean, I don't mind you wanting to have me all to yourself in your office. That's hot."

He groaned. "I promise that's not where this was going."

"That's a shame." She leaned back against the bookcase and crossed her arms. "All right. What is this agenda item you want to add? And what is the town meeting being called for? Is it Frances? Is this parking again?"

"I think that is on the agenda, but I have it on good authority that it's not Frances-driven." He stood and crossed to her. "I know you want us to be a secret."

"And you want to take things slow."

That was a very literal reading of their dynamic. What Will *wanted* was to toss her on his desk and break multiple clauses of his employment contract.

He settled for crowding her against his bookcase and bracing one arm on the shelf beside her head. "I'll get back to the town meeting in a moment, don't think you can distract me."

"I wouldn't dare."

He traced his fingers over her stubborn jaw. "Do you think this would be easier if we didn't sleep together before? More…straightforward?"

She sucked in a quick breath and gave him a look that

was halfway between *you've lost your mind* and *remember that thing we did on the edge of the bed?*

Yeah, he remembered everything.

"Maybe it was a mistake to rush," she whispered.

He nodded as he leaned in. "I know. Want to do it again?"

"What has gotten into you?" Her chest rose and fell quickly, but she didn't push him away. And she didn't answer him. Yes. The answer was yes. But also, it was no. At least for now.

"You," he said, then tasted her. Just a kiss, for now. They'd slid into this routine, just one hot kiss full of promise. And then he stepped back, as he always did. "That's not what I wanted to talk to you about. I just got…carried away."

He crossed to his computer, and gestured for her to sit in his chair.

"I have an idea for something I want to put on the agenda at the town meeting. I thought about doing it as a surprise, as a grand gesture thing, but I thought you might not like that. And this is something you deserve to control the narrative around."

He hit play on the video.

On the screen, Patrick Hoffer appeared. "I met Suzanne Berton at a singles' mingle she organized in Lion's Head, at the Green Hedgehog. When she found out I was a teacher, she asked me if I was good at proofreading, because she sometimes got sentences wrong. She didn't, not as often as she thought she did, but I was happy to help her. And that fall, I asked her if she could do me a favour in return. I had some students at my school—high school students—who struggled to read and write, and they didn't much like teachers trying to help them. Would she be willing to sit with them and read in the library? She came in. And for the next eight years, she never missed a week of reading support."

Will's attention was glued on Catie, whose face was carefully still. On the video, his voice could be heard asking Patrick why eight years.

The older teacher ducked his head. "That's when her daughter came to high school. Suzanne found other ways to volunteer after that. And she'd found me more than enough reading volunteers from the community. People like her who struggled with dyslexia."

Catie gasped.

Maybe this was cruel. Will hadn't thought about how that would sound to her. He hadn't known it was a secret, not really, but part of him had wondered. He reached for the mouse to pause it, and she stopped him. "It's okay," she breathed. "It's...please. Just..."

Off-screen, Will asked how else she volunteered. Patrick shook his head. "Every way you could imagine, man. Every way."

The next video was Frank, talking about community yard sales. Then Owen saying the same. Anne Minelli was next, explaining how Suzanne pushed for a women's business group, and then Raj Patel talked about how helpful she was to newcomers to the community. "We had that in common," he said. "She was the kindest person to us in those early days."

On and on it went. Will had talked to thirty people in total. Some of them didn't have much to say other than reiterating what Patrick and Frank had told him, but he found a way to splice them all together. There would be more once he made the video public—if Catie wanted him to.

He kneeled beside her. "Your mom was a gift to this community," he said quietly.

She nodded and threw herself at him. "You schemer." She wiped her eyes. "This is what you've been doing? I thought you were just...camping outside my fortress, right?"

"You remembered that. Of course you did. Yeah. But while I was waiting there, trying to be patient, I figured I might as well get to know your mom better. And it turns out, she was a really important person in this building. That's what I want to take to a town meeting. I want to raise the funds for a scholarship in her honour. And I want to be able to talk about you, too. You are your mother's daughter, in the best way possible. Everything you do for this community is an echo of, and an improvement on, all the things your mom did for this town. And to do it, you had to leave. You had to work all the way through high school to have enough money to go off and find your path. And then coming back was hard, too. I want to make that easier for kids like you."

"You sneaky, beautiful man. I thought when you paged me down here that you wanted more help to improve your winter carnival—"

"Our."

"What?"

He took her tear-streaked face in his hands. "*Our* winter carnival."

She wrinkled her nose.

Oh, that wouldn't do. "Catie Berton."

"Did you just full name me?"

"I sure did."

"Why?"

"Because this is your town as much as it is mine, so it's your carnival, too."

"Thanks, Mr. Magnanimous. But I know that. I just don't want to *call* it mine until it's better. Hence, the plan revisions."

He laughed out loud. "God, what am I going to do with you?"

"I would suggest something filthy, but you're also Mr. Take It Slow, so maybe we can revisit that —"

He rose up, lifting her bodily to sit on the edge of his desk. "You don't think I want you? I want you so much, I'm prepared to take you right here, right now, where I would fire anyone else who would try the same thing."

"Will..."

"I want you more than anything. You are all I want, all I can think about, and I'm terrified of pushing you too fast when I see you, Catie. I see how wary and worried and cautious you are, because you've been alone a long time. The only reason I don't push for more is because I'm vulnerable, too. I don't want to take too much and be left holding my feelings because you've run scared again. I want to be what you want. On your terms. So I'm trying to be patient, but God damn, woman. I *want* you."

She tangled her fingers in his hair, pulling him hard against her mouth. She tasted like fire, like nothing he'd ever dreamt of before. Pure passion, absolute need. He couldn't deny either of them a second longer.

He broke away long enough to hold her gaze. "Yes?"

"I love you," she whispered. "I'm not running scared again."

He made a wounded sound and kissed her again, ragged and desperate now. Fuck, the door. "Hold that thought. Do not move."

It took him three seconds to cross the room, lock the door, and get back to her.

In that time, she managed to move a lot, despite his order. She met him in the middle of the room, another clash of tongues and teeth and hands, their bodies moving against each other.

He caught her around the waist and turned her against him, her back to his front. He stroked his fingertips over her belly, along the waistband of her jeans. "Can I make you feel good? Everyone's gone. The door is locked. The drapes are pulled…it's just you and me. Let me show you how much I want you."

———

CATIE KNEW THIS WAS DANGEROUS. Foolish on many levels. But she needed to prove to this man that she was all his, however he wanted her. She arched her back and he unzipped her pants, then dipped his fingers into her panties, and groaned as he made contact with the curls at the top of her mound.

She rocked her hips, urging him to stroke lower, but he wouldn't be rushed. He cupped her whole sex next, whispering teasing thoughts about what he might do next. "Want to feel you all over my fingers. Make you all slippery and needy for me. I want you to come undone for me. Writhe on my hand, beg for my fingers."

"I want them now," she panted. "Inside me."

"Eager?"

"Yes."

"Me, too."

He bent her forward, pressing her torso flat against the

surface of his desk. Her toes barely reached the floor as he shoved her jeans down her hips, baring her ass.

His fingers returned between her legs, this time from behind, sliding effortlessly through the wet evidence that she was very much enjoying being manhandled like this. He leaned over her, his breath hot on the back of her neck.

"I'm going to fuck you with my fingers, Catie. As many as you want. But you don't get my cock until I get you in my bed. When we fuck for real, it's going to be *for fucking real* on every level. My bed, taking all the time in the world, where I can hear you scream *my name*."

"Will," she gasped, because yes, that, all of that.

She was his.

But then his fingers were inside her, at least two of them, and the next sound out of her mouth was a groan, a desperate deep whine.

White heat raced through her, coiling low in her belly, as he worked her ruthlessly towards an orgasm. She swallowed as many sounds as she could, desperately aware he could get in so much trouble for this moment.

It didn't take long for her to get there, for her legs to start trembling as her pulse raced just as fast, out of control and then she was lost, free-floating and wild in the night sky. A shooting star.

And then darkness. Shaking.

Kisses on the back of her neck and the warmest, sweetest words.

As soon as he tugged her jeans back up over her hips, she twisted around, reaching for his belt. He let her hook her fingers into his waistband, but then he shuddered and wrapped his fingers around her wrists.

"No." He licked his lips, his eyes hooded and heavy.

Full of lust. "I want your fingers on me, God damn I do, but I can't. Not here."

Her heart bounced, a little giddy-up, at the realization that he'd risk a lot to get her off, but not for himself. As far as ethical bounds went, it probably wouldn't pass anyone else's squint test, but she thought the world of him for it. She shimmied off the desk and pulled him right against her. "Then we should probably make our way to your bed —or mine—so we can talk more about what you mean by *for fucking real?*"

He cupped her face in his hands. "Ab-so—"

The pager on his desk cut him off. A loud, piercing alert.

22

———

CATIE'S HEART stopped as the pager vibrated behind her. Will closed his eyes, swore long and hard under his breath, then nodded. "Excellent timing, universe."

She reached for the interrupting device and passed it to him, then dug out her phone. In a few months, she'd have a pager of her own, but for now, as a trainee, she might get invited along for the search or she might not.

As Will read the message on the pager screen, a text came in for her.

Tom: SAR team call out. All volunteers needed. Missing hikers. Meet at the Emergency Services Building.

The address followed.

Will gave her a tight look. "Do you want to drive together?"

She shook her head. "Let's take two cars. You might need to go in a different direction than me."

He caught her gently and tugged her in, his hand cupping the back of her neck. "We'll continue this later."

She nodded. Then she headed out to her car to grab her bag. She needed to change into her Day-Glo-iest outfit for a night search.

————

THIS WAS A BIG ONE. One of the hikers had a medical condition, details not known yet, but it had been flagged by the bed and breakfast owner who reported that her guests didn't return from a planned outing. Time was of the essence to find them. In addition to the SAR turnout, the volunteer fire brigade, off-duty full-time firefighters like Adam, and OPP officers like Rafe Minelli were also arriving.

They were divided into groups that had someone from each type of first responder. They would be travelling from this central spot to a designated search quadrant.

Will was the team leader for her group. They all hovered and watched as he did a quick map review. He talked under his breath, practicing what he would tell them. Making his time assessment for each phase of the search, and setting an initial plan.

Then he looked up, glanced around to find a decent briefing area away from the noise, and motioned for their group to follow him. "All right. Here's our task. We're driving over to this concession road. The hiking paths diverge here. This is where we'll enter the woods. We'll do this together, as one group. I'll give you a more detailed briefing when we arrive there. Who has first aid knowledge?"

The EMT raised her hand. "And I have a complete advanced first aid kit on me."

"Excellent. Thank you. We're looking for two hikers, a man and a woman in their late twenties. We're going to be covering a densely forested area with multiple trails. The plan is that our search could take six hours, but make sure you have enough food on you for twenty-four just in case. Understood?"

They all said yes out loud at the same time.

"Check your gear, grab extra batteries, and be ready to roll in five minutes. Here are your copies of the map."

To her horror, Catie recognized the area where they would be searching. It was the same area she'd gotten lost at the start of the summer.

The way Will gave her a grim look, he was thinking the same thing.

"Catie, can you sign out two radios and a GPS unit?"

"Yes."

"I can do that," the young OPP officer said.

Will frowned at the cop. "I asked her. Check your gear."

Catie hustled over to the truck that Yolanda had driven over from the SAR training centre. She carefully put in her supply order.

Yolanda handed it over, and gave her an extra head lamp, too. "You never know when someone thinks they've tested theirs but they haven't."

"Thanks."

As she returned to the group, the EMT and the cop were arguing over how to read the map.

Will returned at the same time. "Is there a problem?"

The cop held up his phone. "The map looks different from what I have."

Catie put on her helpful face. "If you turn on—"

"Look, lady—"

"That *lady* knows how to read the damn map," Will bit out. "Either you listen to her or you get the hell away from this search."

Catie spun on her heel and gave him big eyes. *What?*

It wasn't like him to overreact like that.

He grimaced. "Someone else will be taking over as your team leader. Sorry, everyone, tensions are running a bit high. Catie, can I talk to you for a minute?"

She followed him around the side of the communication truck. "What's wrong?"

He tugged off his gloves, his breath puffing between them. "I want you to have this." He carefully peeled up her sleeve. "It's a compass for your watch," he murmured. "So you don't need to rely on your phone app or the one on your pack."

Her breath caught in her throat as his fingers brushed the inside of her wrist.

"It may rain or snow. Keep your wet weather gear close to the top of your packs." He was just firing tips at her for her first search, but she didn't understand what was going on.

"Will, where are you going?"

He pointed to the sky as she became aware of the heavy whirring of an approaching helicopter. "I have to catch a ride."

"Will—"

He caught her hand. "Stay safe. Don't let those dickheads think they know more about searching than you do. They don't have anyone else who can rappel out of a helo, so I'm up."

She kissed him hard on the mouth, then watched as he

sprinted to where his pack sat next to his truck. He grabbed it and made his way to the road, where the helicopter set down.

———

THE HELICOPTER FOUND the hikers before the ground searchers did. They had found a clearing, and spread out light coloured and reflective things.

They circled the area twice, looking for vehicle access, and when they couldn't see any in the dark, Will hooked his harness to the winch and stepped out into the night.

On the ground, he took a quick assessment of both hikers, who were conscious and unharmed. But the woman reported that she did have diabetes. "It's just diet controlled. I mentioned it to our host when we checked in. She remembered?"

Will nodded. "She did. Let's get you up there first, then."

He put her in a harness, told her friend he would be right back, and hooked them up to be lifted to the bird above.

Her pulse was higher than he liked for someone who was just standing on the ground, even someone stressed by being lost. The EMT on board agreed, and after doing a blood sugar test, made the judgement call they should leave as soon as possible, so Will was lowered back down to stay with the other hiker. As soon as he hit the ground and was unclipped, he radioed above that he was free, and the helicopter took off, heading south to the hospital.

"Hey man," Will said, sitting down heavily next to the remaining hiker. "How's your night going?"

That got him a weak laugh. "I'll be better when I know she's okay. This has never happened to us before."

"My girlfriend got lost on these trails earlier in the summer. And she's trained SAR, too. It happens to the best of us."

"What are we going to do? Wait for the helicopter to come back?"

Will shook his head. "They'll get a hasty team close to our position, and then we'll hike out once they find us."

"Okay." The man shook his head. "This is wild."

Will dug out his pack of snacks and a spare water bottle. "Hungry?"

"Starved."

It wasn't long before his radio squawked, but the news wasn't great. They were almost an hour on foot away from the nearest access road. Will dug out his survival blankets and gave the guy one and wrapped the other around himself. "We're here for a bit, bud."

He pictured where Catie was right now. They'd have just gotten the heads up that the hikers had been found, so their team could return to search command base. She'd been trekking back through the woods with that cocky cop on one side and the EMT on the other. Probably being upbeat and cheerful.

Thirty minutes passed before he got another update. "Hey man. Your partner is at the hospital getting checked out. All looks good."

The sound the other man let out was unholy. Pure relief. And for the first time in his life, Will could truly identify. If something was wrong with Catie, he'd be beside himself with worry.

And then it was a countdown of sharing girlfriend stories until Tom and Tobin's hasty team search found them. They retraced the men's steps to get to Tom's truck, and then it was a quiet, grateful drive back to Pine Harbour.

By the time he returned, the original search teams had been debriefed and sent home. His own debrief was quick. Tom had heard about Will snapping at the OPP officer, and that was the piece they talked about the most.

"I didn't like him thinking he could be rude to Catie," Will confessed.

Tom gave him a steady look. "And who is the best person to deal with that directly?"

"Catie." Will groaned. "I know. I *know.*"

"Maybe going forward, we should be more mindful to put you on separate teams."

He shrugged. "It can't hurt."

Tom laughed.

"I thought we could keep it separate."

"And what is *it,* exactly?"

Will shook his head. "Too early to say, man. But you'll be the first to know once we have a name for it."

As soon as he humanly could get away, he was in his truck, calling her.

"Hello?" She sounded tired, but not sleepy. Like she was in bed but wide awake.

"Are you wired?"

"Yeah." She sounded relieved to hear from him. "Are you done?"

"Yep."

A silence stretched before either of them said anything. He listened to her shift, then exhale. On either side of the road, dark trees and shadowy fields flashed by.

"I was thinking—"

"Do you want to come over?" She asked it at the same time as he started to speak.

Silently, he pumped his fist in the air. "I'll be there in five minutes."

She was waiting for him, swinging the door open as he walked up her step. She was wearing sweatpants and a long-sleeve t-shirt, and she had a half-drunk bottle of beer in her hand.

He followed her inside, and as soon as the door was closed, he had her pressed against the wall. She tasted like hops, like victory. Like utter fatigue and pure bliss.

"Want one?" she asked as she led him through a living room that looked magazine perfect. The next room was an equally gorgeous kitchen.

He shrugged out of his coat and hung it on the back of one of two chairs at the kitchen island. "Sure. A beer would be great."

She grabbed him one from the fridge, then leaned against the island.

He couldn't read her expression. So he set aside all their personal stuff and went to the big thing she'd just experienced. "How do you feel?"

"Antsy."

"You did well."

"It got dark pretty fast." Her gazed darted away from his face, then back again. Down to his hands, then back up. "That took me by surprise."

"Yeah. You were focused on your grid search. And we trained in the summer. Longer days."

"I'm glad we were in a line." She started to peel the label off her bottle, then stopped. Gripped it tighter, until her knuckles turned white. "I started to…worry."

When she hesitated before the final word, he wondered

if she was going to say she panicked. It would be normal if she did. Starting to panic, recognizing those feelings, then working through them and getting the job done was commendable. He told her as much.

She shook her head. "It's not that. But yeah, I could see that. No, I started to go negative in my head. Think we weren't going to find them. Went straight to the worst outcomes. It was like flashes in my mind."

Shit. He moved closer, and she swayed into him. He set his bottle down and hugged her tight.

"Why did you want to come over?" Her question was muffled by his shirt, but he understood it all the same.

He exhaled roughly into her hair. "Because I didn't want to be alone tonight. Not just because of earlier. We have unfinished business, sure, but it's also just a search thing. I'm antsy, too. I'm anxious, too. Even when it goes well, I think about the what-ifs."

She kissed his neck, then his jaw. "Can we burn off this energy for an hour or two?"

He was already hard for her. He slid his hand into her hair and tugged so he could see her face. "Do you have to work tomorrow?"

"Not until noon."

He hovered his mouth above hers. "Then we could stay up until dawn if you want."

She pressed up, bringing them together. Her lips were feather light, soft and sensual, as she moved against him.

"Let's start in the shower," he rumbled against her mouth.

She nodded and led him down the hall. They kept their bottles of beer, but discarded their clothes as they went. In the steam, she kept kissing him as he soaped up her back.

Then he turned her around so he could carefully wash every inch of her front.

When she was done, she pushed him back against the tiled wall and knelt in front of him. She washed up one leg, then the other. And when she got to his cock, she wrapped her soapy hand around him, and serviced him in a whole different way, until he was throbbing with the need to be inside her.

He wrapped her in the largest towel he'd ever seen, then carried her to her bed as she gave him directions.

It was only when he was on top of her that he realized he was utterly unprepared for actually being inside her. "I didn't bring anything," he muttered into her neck as he rearranged his horny thoughts into alternate ways to get off.

"I bought a pack of condoms with your name on it two weeks ago," she said, sounding very proud of herself. "Economy sized. Because I don't want this to be a one-off."

She looked at him almost shyly, and he kissed her until they were both panting. "Fucking genius." Heat swirled low in his belly. "It won't be a one-off, I promise you. You can't get rid of me a second time."

"We'll figure it out?"

"Over and over again." He claimed her mouth. "Get one of those condoms."

She rolled over, and the curve of her bottom and the slice of her sex peeking at him from between her thighs undid him completely. With a growl, he caught her hips and lifted her up on her knees.

"Just let me taste you," he panted as he got behind her.

She cried out his name as he buried his face against her pussy. He breathed in her scent, the sweet animal essence of her blooming heat, and suckled on her clit until she was grinding back against him.

When he reared up to take the condom from her, she tackled him, flattening him onto his back, and crawled down his body. "I need to taste you, too," she said, locked her gaze onto his as she swallowed his length.

He throbbed against the warm, wet heat of her mouth. She slicked him up, then focused at the slit on his crown, where he was leaking seed for her now.

"Get on me," he growled.

Together they rolled on a condom, their fingers sticky with the lubricant, and then her pussy was on his and their fingers were tangled. She pressed him down into the mattress and rode him, slow and fierce.

It was part exorcism, part prayer, and all love.

"Catie," he said, panting her name. "Fuck, you're gorgeous. I love you. Yes. Ride me. Just like that, my love. God, I'm going to fill you up. Pump you so full. Always."

She threw her head back as he gripped her hips, taking over the rhythm. Her first climax took him by surprise, suddenly milking him, pulling him with her. Into a storm, and then through it, to the calm on the other side.

She slumped on top of him, and he stroked his fingers up her back. "That's one," he whispered. "How many more times can we do that before dawn?"

23

Nothing could pierce the floating high Catie woke up on. Not even opening the front door, after making Will breakfast and coffee to take with him to school, to realize Frances Schmidt was sitting on her porch across the street.

Evil eye locked on Will's truck.

"What do you want to bet she noticed you were here all night?" She grabbed her coat and shoved her feet into her boots, now intent on seeing Will off properly on her front step.

Will tugged the door closed behind him and slowly kissed Catie's temple. "So what if she did?"

She squirmed. He was right.

He turned and leaned in, wrapping her in a much-needed warm hug as she shivered. "Catie, did Frances ever say anything mean to you about your mom when you were a kid?"

Hot, surprised tears appeared behind her eyelids. She ducked her head and blinked them away. Nope. Uh uh. "She gossips about a lot of people."

"But you lived here when you were little, and she's a

nosy bitch. Has been since she was a young housewife and there was a pretty single woman living across the road, right?" He was vibrating now, and it suddenly occurred to her that Will was angry.

Not with Catie.

For Catie.

"How did you—"

"A little bit from Frank. A little bit from Owen. Most of it from you. In what you say, and what you don't say." He brushed an errant strand of hair off her cheek, tucking it behind her ear. "I don't usually care about gossip. I don't care who knows I want to spend every night in your bed. But if you care, then I will care, too. I'm sorry that she's watching us right now. But I'm not sorry for last night."

"Neither am I." Her voice was small. "I hate that she's my neighbour."

"Want to move in with me?"

She laughed. "You're funny."

"Or I could move in here. I mean, we have all those kids to make."

Now she was giggling. "Right, I forgot."

He waggled his eyebrows. "I never forget."

She reached out and patted his shirt. "You're amazing, you know that?"

He stilled, then leaned in. "You know what? I didn't know that. Thank you. If you think so, that's going to carry me far today."

"Shut up."

"You shut up."

"Make me," she whispered.

"The neighbours might see."

"That one already thinks we did terrible things all night."

He laughed and brushed his lips against hers, lightly at first, then again, pausing to deepen the kiss with a growl before stepping back.

She pressed her fingers to her mouth, and he grinned.

"Come here," he said, hooking his arm around her shoulders. "We're going to get there." His next kiss for her was gentle and sweet, on her forehead.

A promise.

She closed her eyes and leaned in to his warmth.

Then, after he had safely pulled out of her drive and was on his way to school, she flipped Frances the middle finger.

———

AFTER WILL LEFT, Catie crawled back into bed for a couple of hours. When she woke up again, she went to the bakery for a late breakfast.

As soon as she walked through the door, Isla's eyes grew big and round.

"Oh no," Catie groaned. "Seriously?"

"Frances just left," her friend said.

"That woman is a menace to society."

"So it's true? Will spent the night at your place?"

Her pink cheeks would betray her even if she wanted to hide the truth. Which the more she thought about it, the less she wanted to. "Yes," she finally said. "He sure did."

"Was this a heat of the post-rescue moment, or…"

"Or." Catie tried to contain herself, but she couldn't. She hopped up and down and did a little dance. "We've been circling each other for weeks, and then we kind of… and then…"

Isla swooned. "I love *and then…*"

"Right?" Catie shrugged. "So okay, people know now. I guess we'll see what they say when they know we're sleeping together."

"Is that what it is? Casual?" Isla held up her hands. "That's cool. Whatever floats your boat. I'm just bracing myself to manage the Kincaid brothers and their expectations."

"It's not casual." Catie shook her head. "I mean...I guess everyone will find out that we're dating."

She laughed out loud.

Isla looked thrilled. "Hey, maybe if you get serious, we would be sisters-in-law."

Catie stopped laughing. "Holy shit."

Isla blinked at her. "Are you okay?"

She wasn't ready to tell her friend about the baby talk. Or the moving in together talk. That had just been...jokes. Of a sort.

A serious sort.

———

THAT NIGHT, Will came over to her place again. He waved cheerily at Frances as Catie opened the door for him. He had a duffle bag on his shoulder.

She kissed him deeply before closing the door. "We're wicked," she whispered.

"Wicked people don't whisper about perfectly reasonable joy when they're alone," he whispered back. "Missed you today."

"Does your niece mind that you're not there again?"

"Nah, Becca's happy to have the place to herself. And Josh is there for dinner tonight, anyway."

"Speaking of that, I didn't know what you would

want." She gave him a complete rundown of the options from her fridge, and he told her it was her choice, but he wanted to help cook.

It was an absolutely perfect second date.

She told him that when they were tucked into bed for the night, naked and sated after a slow, emotional fuck.

He trailed his fingers over her collarbone. "Speaking of dates."

"Mmm."

"I need a date for the winter carnival."

"Aren't you going to be working?" There was a school dance component to the community event. It sounded like a mess, but the business club was now in charge of the snack shack at least.

"All work and no play makes the principal a very sad man."

There was no avoiding the point he was making. "You want to go legit legit. Out in public together legit."

"You make it sound like our relationship is a criminal enterprise. I'm not Josh."

"Does Josh do—"

"No, that was just a knee-jerk Kincaid snark attack, ignore I said that." He rolled her onto her back, and the sheet slipped down her body. He cupped her breast with one hand as he braced his weight on the other. "Come with me to the carnival."

She caught his hand in hers, and nipped at his fingertips. "I was thinking about this earlier."

"What?"

"You and me. Being serious. It freaked me out a bit."

"Just a bit?" He smiled. "That's progress."

"It occurred to me that you have this big family, and

your expectations for a relationship—your understanding of what that is—it might be different from…"

He waited.

She shrugged. "I don't know what I'm saying."

"You're nervous."

"Yep. But I love you. So I'm in for exploring what this is. I want to be clear about that. I just also have some tiny bits of stress around anyone thinking I'm trying to snare you."

"So snare me. Yes, please."

"Will—"

"What? We're not back to this, right? You don't see us going anywhere?"

Of course she did. It was just scary. "Are you ready for that?"

"To get serious with you? I'm so ready for that it hurts." He jumped out of bed and pulled on underwear, then jeans.

Catie pushed herself upright, then slowly stood, gathering the sheet around her.

He held out his hands. "I'm messing this up."

"What is *this*?"

"I'm asking you out on a real date. A serious date. Not our first one, but our most important one. The kind of date that people notice, because I want people to know I'm head over heels in love with you. The kind of date that gets people whispering about how *I* feel about *you*, which is the only narrative anyone in this town needs to worry about. I love you, Catie. I want to ask you to marry me one day soon, but before I do that, I need to take you on some better dates."

"Serious dates."

"Yes."

"Okay." She smiled, but it was tremulous.

"Fuck, are you crying? Baby, don't—"

"It's all right. Not all tears are bad," she whispered.

"I'm head over heels for you," he repeated. He scooped her up and planted her butt on the bed, then pressed his face to her belly. "In. Fucking. Love. Got it?"

"Got it."

He crawled on top of her. "Lemme prove it to you again."

———

THE SCHOOL WAS DECKED out with balloons and streamers and both Halloween and leftover Thanksgiving decorations. It was a chaotic aesthetic, one that would have prompted Catie of the Past to immediately volunteer for next year's organizing committee so the *winter* carnival could have a proper *winter* theme—

"Are you redecorating in your head?" Will asked as he wrapped his arm around her waist, maybe to hold her back from taking a horn o'plenty helium balloon out of a skeleton's hand and putting it anywhere else. The garbage, maybe.

"Did they raid the clearance rack at the dollar store?"

He laughed. "Yes."

"Will."

"Catie." His voice was rich with laughter, no disguise.

She sighed and leaned into him, letting him tighten his possessive hold on her. Because maybe he was holding her back, but he was also holding her close. "I love it. It's very Pine Harbour."

"You can be on the planning committee next year."

"Just an advisory position. I can attend a few meetings and get them on the right track…"

He stopped under what looked like a glitter bat holding…mistletoe? "You can take the whole thing over if you want." Then he dipped her backwards, leaning over her as he planted a kiss right on her mouth, a good lingering smooch, before swinging her back up and spinning her around.

Maybe she didn't care.

Maybe the horror show decor was some kind of good luck.

Inside the gymnasium, Will made the rounds, holding Catie's hand the entire time. They had two slow dances together, which Sam informed her after had been well documented and shared on Instagram by at least six students.

She took a sneak peek when Will went up on stage to make some announcements, and just about died in the best way when she realized they were all using the hashtag #PrincipalBae and #FutureMrsKincaid.

They weren't wrong on either count.

There was nothing conventional about how she and Will were diving into their relationship. He pointed out regularly that he was no spring chicken. She figured one day they would decide to elope, like his brother Adam did, and that would be that.

One day soon, probably.

She snapped a picture of her handsome boyfriend up on stage, then put her phone away so she could focus on what he was saying.

"The final part of tonight's official winter carnival celebrations is an unveiling of a plaque. As most of you know, this fall has brought some significant changes to Pine

Harbour Community School. I've learned a lot about what it means to be a principal to a school population that ranges from kindergarten to grade twelve. There have been challenges along the way, but many rewards. One of those rewards has been in reinvigorating our Reading Where You Are program, which was first implemented more than twenty years ago by Suzanne Berton."

Catie pressed her fingers to her mouth and willed herself not to cry.

"There are not very many people who have the patience and the understanding and the relatability to sit down with a teenager who is struggling to read because of a learning disability or a second language or lack of reading material at home and relate to them on a peer level. Suzanne Berton did that and more. She found other volunteers and brought them in, and worked with my mentor, Patrick Hoffer, to build this program. That wasn't properly recognized in the past. I'm rectifying that tonight."

Someone had pushed a fabric-covered stand forward, and he lifted the cloth now. "Everything that I have heard from former teachers at this school and from some people in our community who read with her on a weekly basis is that Suzanne Berton set the bar exceptionally high. She was non-judgemental, funny, and supportive. And she did all of that without ever asking for any recognition. This year, her daughter Catie filled a similar role by becoming our business club advisor."

Someone yelled out, "The Future Mrs. Kincaid."

Will leaned in to the mic. "I sincerely hope so. If you know her, please put in a good word for me."

That got him a laugh.

Beside Catie, someone appeared with a tissue. She

glanced sideways at Sam, who had sprouted up over the last month and was now taller than her. "Thanks," she whispered.

"He's probably marrying material," the teen muttered. "Responsible and all that."

She giggled and nodded. "Yeah."

Will glanced in her direction. "Catie, do you want to come up here?"

She shook her head no. Then nodded, yes.

With a deep breath, she climbed the stairs and joined him on the stage.

"Tonight, we are announcing the Suzanne Berton Memorial Scholarship. The scholarship is in two parts. One thousand dollars for moving expenses for a student to move away from Pine Harbour to attend college, university, or a vocational or trade school of their choice. And another thousand dollars will be available to them, at any point thereafter, for them to move back to Pine Harbour should they wish to. It's a unique scholarship designed to honour a unique woman who gave this town more than we ever appreciated."

The gymnasium erupted into deafening applause. It seemed spurred on by the business club, not that Catie minded.

Will gave her a tight hug before leading her off the stage. The DJ returned to playing music, and they drifted to the edge of the dance floor.

"No more surprises," she whispered to him as they swayed back and forth. "But I'm so very happy right now. Thank you."

"Then I should warn you that I'm going to propose tonight when we get home."

She smiled happily. "Spoiler alert. I'll say yes."

It was the best school dance she'd ever attended. One of those forever memories that she would hold precious for the rest of her life, in this place that she had once had more complicated thoughts about.

Now there was nothing complicated about how much she loved this town.

Some of that was about the man beside her, who regularly brushed his lips against her forehead, just to remind her how much she was adored.

But it was also because Pine Harbour was full of memories of her mother, more than she had ever known. And Catie knew that one day, it would hold memories of her for her children. Hopefully mostly good, very few bad, and if any were confusing, that they might lead her kids on wild adventures of their own.

EPILOGUE

the following August

THIS YEAR, the drive home from Timmins was different. A lot about the trip was the same—the Pine Harbour SAR held on to their second place position in the competition, Tom bought a round of drinks at the bar after, and Catie climbed Will like a tree once they got back to their room.

Deja vu all over the place.

But the conversation they had when they woke up was different.

The drive home was *very* different.

This year, they were going to stop and camp for the night after they got off the ferry. It was a fantasy role-play that stemmed from a conversation earlier in the summer about how hard it had been to want each other and think the other one was off-limits.

"You featured heavily in my fantasies, anyway. I couldn't help it," Will confessed.

"Tell me more."

"Any chance you're ever been a swimsuit model?"

She climbed on top of him, doing her best—not great—attempt at a model pose. "Like with my legs spread, covered in sand?"

He groaned. "Sure. Yes."

"Little bikinis?"

"Yes. And a swimsuit with zippers."

"Is that what you pictured me wearing when you took me to the Grotto?"

That night, Catie had ordered a swimsuit with a zipper down the front of it. Now it was carefully tucked in her extra bag for camping.

On the ferry, Catie felt Will watching her as she made small talk with their teammates. They hadn't told anyone they would be stopping. It felt like their little secret.

They needed those lately. Life had been a chaotic whirl in recent months.

Will was basically living at Catie's house, because his place had become Kincaid Central. First Becca and Charlie came back for another visit, and then in the late spring, Seth decided he wanted to stay at Josh's apartment at the garage, to be close to the marina—and January Howe. That hadn't gone unnoticed, either, not that either of them were talking about whatever was going on at night after her niece and nephew were asleep.

Catie loved that Will was happy his brother was back in town, even if it was only for the summer. But it made for a weird game of musical chairs. Josh didn't want to have a roommate, so he moved into Will's house—"because you're never there, anyway". Which was true, but Catie's house really only had room for Will to visit.

Not for Will's stuff to move in, too.

Her house was a girl's house, all soft and pretty and full of comfy spots to read.

Will had more army, camping, and climbing gear than could ever fit her garage. Plus workout equipment, and his beloved Duster. Her single drive couldn't contain all three vehicles.

So they had been putting off the question of how to merge their households, but it loomed ahead of them, suddenly urgent. They were getting married in less than a month.

It would be nice to have Will fully moved in, somehow magically, before the autumn wedding of their dreams.

"You're frowning," her fiancé murmured as they climbed back into his truck.

She smoothed out her brow. "I was actually thinking about how happy I am that we have one more night together before we need to tackle the move again."

"It'll work out."

"I don't see how."

"We could build an addition." He chuckled as her frown deepened. "Or a shed."

"I like a shed. It's more doable in four weeks."

"An excellent point." He lifted her hand to kiss her knuckles. "Let's worry about that tomorrow."

"Agreed."

"Tonight is a moment outside of time. Just you and me, nothing else."

"Is that what you wanted to do last year?" She stroked her fingers up his arm. "Pause time and take me camping?"

"I wanted to pause time and get back inside your body. Camping was just the opportunity in front of me." He smiled as her questing fingers rubbed over the back of his neck. "No, not *just* the opportunity. It was my last chance, I thought. But I could see the whole night.

Walking out to the Grotto. Piecing together dinner from the camp store."

He turned off the highway and into the national park.

A tremor of excitement rippled through Catie's belly.

After checking in, Will stopped at the store. Inside, they bought the s'mores pre-requisites of marshmallows, graham crackers, and chocolate, as well as a pack of over-priced hot dogs, buns, mustard and relish, and a quarter watermelon, already sliced.

"Dinner of champions," he said as they loaded their groceries in the back of the truck.

"We came in second again."

He caught and held her gaze. "I'm not talking about the competition."

Whoosh. Even after almost a year of being on the receiving end of his earnest love, Catie still got weak in the knees when Will said things like that. And they weren't lines. He wasn't smooth like that. He was smooth in other ways, but when it came to his feelings for her, he was rough and raw. So when something landed like a line, it was just a bit of kismet.

And tonight, maybe a bit of role-play, too.

This is what he wanted last year. Another night to cele-brate with her. Another night to devour her. The bare minimum for food and equipment, a spontaneous pause before they had to return to real life.

Next they grabbed firewood, then headed to their campsite. They set up the tent first, changed into their swimsuits—Catie making sure to dawdle, so Will was done and out of the tent before she actually changed—then locked up the truck and set out on the path to the Grotto on foot.

Catie had been here once before, but it was different

tonight. The last of the day pass visitors had already arrived, so while they passed some people heading back to the campsite, they were alone in their walk *to* the Grotto along the wide, winding path through the soaring trees.

Will held her hand the whole way, and didn't let go until they reached the rocky outcropping above the spectacular cove.

The crystal clear water glittered over wide, flat rocks not far below the surface, making Georgian Bay appear turquoise in the fading light—a slice of landscape that looked right of the Caribbean.

The water temperature was significantly cooler, though. Not like that stopped anyone. Below them, people of all ages splashed in the shallow pools, and further out, at the mouth of the cove, young folks hollered as they leapt off the rocks and swan dived into the darker, deeper water there.

But instead of climbing down the natural stairs formed by rocks, Will led her down a narrow path back into the forest. The noise of the tourists faded into the distance, and when they emerged into the late afternoon sun again, they were above another, similar cove. This one was more narrow, without an obvious path down to the water. It was also blissfully quiet, and it looked like they had it all to themselves.

"Can we climb down there?" Catie heard the nerves in her voice. *Is it safe?*

Will brushed a quick kiss on the corner of her mouth. "I wouldn't ask you to do anything dangerous."

And he proved that he knew what he was doing, carefully leading her down the rocks in a precise pattern he seemed to have memorized. "I've been coming here since I was a teenager," he confessed when they got to the bottom. "When my brothers were back at the Grotto, leaping into the Bay, I would explore further. This is my favourite spot."

A secret he had wanted to share it with her last year. That hit her right in the feels.

"I love it." She caught his hand and pulled him for a tight hug. "Thank you for sharing it with me."

"Up for a brisk swim?"

She shivered. But not because the water would be cold. "Yes."

Will shrugged out of his shirt as Catie peeled off her cotton t-shirt dress. She wasn't posed like a swimsuit model, but when he glanced back to see if she was ready and did a double-take at her new swimsuit, that made her feel like a star all the same.

"Holy shit, look at you..." He prowled towards her and tugged at the zipper. It slid down an inch with ease, and he groaned. "This is a nice surprise."

"I'll do my best to look like a pin up as I burst out of the water."

He caught her around the waist and pressed a hot, questing kiss into her mouth. "You'll succeed," he panted when he broke away.

She swayed against him. "Where should we swim to?"

He pointed to a rock bursting through the water twenty feet out.

"Let's swim to that."

She sat down on a rock that hung like a ledge over the water, then twisted, dropping herself into the cool water. The heat of the day fell away immediately, and she pushed off, her stroke stronger now than it had been a year before.

Will still caught up to her in a few powerful strokes,

then pulled past, and she let him go, watching him churn his way to the rock.

He was beautiful. Kind, and smart, and self-deprecating around those he trusted. That had been a big learning point for her. It wasn't that he didn't know humility, he just was careful about what adults he bared his soul to.

Not kids, though. Kids of all ages got the real Will. Over the last year, he'd done even more work to connect with the high school students.

His beauty was inside and out, and a year ago, she hadn't seen all of him. She'd known parts of him, and shown him parts of herself. Fear had stood in her way.

Not anymore.

He was holding on to the rock with one hand, lazily paddling with the other, when she joined him.

"I didn't mean to race." He pulled her into his lap. Through the clear water, she could see that he could touch out here.

She nestled into his body, warm and taut. "I didn't think you were racing. I was admiring your form."

"Is that right?"

"Mm-hmm." She kissed his neck, her mouth open. Tasting, searching, wanting. "Just how private is it here?"

His grip on her tightened. "What are you thinking?"

"Could go skinny dipping."

She was prepared for a lecture. *School principals don't go skinny dipping.* And she would reply, *but do they fantasize about watching their lovers float naked in the sunlight?* She knew the answer to that. Yes, he did. And he could be talked into a little fun.

But he surprised her, reaching for the pull on her

zipper again. This time, he didn't stop after an inch. "You read my mind."

"It really is designed to be unzipped," she whispered as his fingers slid down the bare skin between her breasts.

He shuddered as he got to the bottom of the zipper, low on her belly. "That's something straight out of my fantasies just like that." He shifted so he could slide a muscled thigh between her legs, crowding her as he kissed a drop of water on her shoulder. Then he pushed that strap off her body, baring her whole breast to the water.

He repeated the careful ministration to the other side, then peeled her suit off her lower body. Extra handsy with this part, cupping her ass and sliding his fingers against her slit.

She revealed in the attention as he stripped her bare, turning her into a naked mermaid.

Then he shoved his shorts off and lofted them up onto the rock, next to where he set her suit.

Will Kincaid, naked in the late summer sun. Nothing but tan skin, barely obscured by the rippling water surface.

He pulled her back into the warm circle of his arms, their limbs sliding together as he kissed her. "Race to the next rock?"

She dove under water, kicking a big splash in his face, and he let her go. This time, he didn't pass her, and when she tagged the rock and turned around, he was waiting for her to pull him in for the next kiss.

They played like that, two naked nymphs in a private cove, until Catie started to shiver. Will pulled her tight against his body and kissed her to warm her up, then they made their way back to their swimsuits.

"Getting dressed under water is easier said than done,"

Catie huffed as she tried to yank her swimsuit back up her thighs.

Will braced himself against the rock, then helped her, his fingers warm and sure against her skin as he untangled the straps and smoothed out the fabric. It wasn't entirely necessary for him to check the lie of the seams all the way around, especially where her thighs met, but they both enjoyed it.

Once they were both decent, they swam for shore, and she crawled onto a big, flat rock to dry off in the sun. Will collapsed next to her, his hand landing on her thigh. Big, fat water droplets clung to his skin, glistening in the sunlight.

And then the sun dropped behind the forest, and the cove fell into shadow.

Will rolled onto his side, his hand covering more of her now. "The things I want to do to you," he murmured. "But back at the camp."

"Cove sex is a bridge too far for the upstanding principal?"

He laughed. "Let's save that for after my retirement."

"Deal."

She scrambled up and pulled on her dress, and once Will had his shirt back on, they carefully climbed back up the secret vertical path to the trail above.

Dusk had fully descended by the time they were back at the campsite. They got a fire started, then cuddled as their hot dogs cooked. S'mores were next, and watermelon last.

"Enjoying our dinner of champions?" Will asked her, an indulgent smile dancing across his face in the firelight.

"It's delicious." She sighed happily after taking another bite.

Will lazily reached over and swiped an errant drop of juice off her chin, and she caught her wrist, holding his hand so she could lick it off his thumb.

The feral groan he uttered was perfect. She liked the True Real Will so much it hurt. He was deeply dirty and not uptight at all. This Will hauled her off the picnic table bench and sat her on the tabletop, kissing her until she was grinding against him.

"We have to put everything in the truck," she panted.

"Fifteen seconds." He groaned and tore himself away. They worked together, then he hustled her into the tent, leaving the door open, only the mesh up, so they were lit by the remnants of the fire. He stripped her down to nothing at all, then covered her body with his so they would stay warm.

She felt the swift rise of his cock, nestled against her sex as their thighs moved together. This was effortless and perfect, how their bodies fit like a jigsaw puzzle. She hadn't believed it a year ago. She'd thought their night together—and then the next morning, their endless hunger for each other, the wild passion—had been an aberration. That there was no way their lives could fit together just as perfectly.

How wrong she had been.

When they were both warm, he sat up. When she brought her knees together, he caught her calves and stilled her, shaking his head.

"Spread your legs for me." She slid her thighs apart, holding his gaze. Enough to give him a peek at her swollen flesh. The hungry look on his face said he wanted more than a glimpse. "All the way."

"Come up here and kiss me." But she knew what wasn't what he wanted.

"I want to kiss you there." He pressed his mouth to the inside of her knee. "I want to feast on your beautiful pussy."

"Mmm." She relaxed more, still watching him as he kissed his way up her inner thigh.

Then, just as he reached the core of her, he lifted her by her hips and rolled them, so he was on the bottom and she was scrambling for purchase on top.

She laughed and cried his name out, and he urged her spin around.

"This was the second part of my Catie in a swimsuit fantasy. Catie, peeled out of it, and riding my face." His breath was hot against her inner thigh.

She couldn't see what he was doing, could only feel his touch and then his tongue, but she could see what it did to his cock. He throbbed, thick and ready, and as his mouth worked against her folds, his heavy tip started to gleam.

In a month, this man would be her husband. She would spend the rest of her life knowing just how much he enjoyed pleasuring her. What a glorious thing that was.

She carefully flattened out, lying down on his solid body, and rocked her hips back against his face as she carefully took his cock into her mouth. He moaned at the wet contact, bucking up from below. A burst of his seed spurted against her tongue.

Swallowing it down, she wrapped her hand around his base.

Between her legs, he latched on to her clit, and everything started to narrow. Blood rushed through her ears as her body's natural need took over, an otherworldly charge to please and be pleased, to find a mutual release with her other half.

And then she was there. Her back arched and she lost

Will for a moment as her body seized, then a beautiful feeling rippled through her, from her core all the way out to her fingertips and into the night around them.

Will turned her again, rolling her onto her back. Then he was inside her, urgent, and she found her clit, riding the aftershocks straight into another climax. This one milked him, too, and he finished deep in her belly.

"Ah…" He smoothed his hand over her hair. "So good."

"As good as your fantasy?"

"Better. So much better." He stretched his arms wide. Then he lifted his head and glanced out the tent. "The fire's still going. Want another s'more?"

An hour later, well fed in all the ways that mattered, they were tucked back in the tent. Fire carefully out. Will's breathing evened out quickly.

Somewhere in the distance, an owl called out. Closer, trees rustled in the wind, and night creatures skittered through the underbrush. There were other distant sounds, too, campers settling in for the night.

Part of Catie's brain catalogued all of that, mapping it on to this moment in a way that felt indelible. But most of her conscious awareness was centred on Will's heartbeat thumping beneath her ear, and the warmth of his arm wrapped around her back, the sure squeeze of his fingers on her shoulder as he held her tight.

She could still feel his mouth between her legs. As hungry as the first time. They had the rest of their lives together to satisfy that need, and explore where it came from. Her lovely, beautiful man.

"I love you," she whispered.

He didn't reply. He was fast asleep. She turned her face

and buried it in his skin. He smelled like sex, like campfire, and the lake.

She laughed softly to herself, and he shifted, rousing a little.

"Shhh," she murmured again. "Go back to sleep."

"What's so funny?"

"How happy I am. How thankful I am."

He mumbled something that sounded like *that's good*, and drifted off again.

"Thank you for never giving up on me," she breathed, barely saying it out loud. Then she closed her eyes and let him pull her into dreamland.

THE END

Want more Pine Harbour?

Fearless at Heart is coming in June 2022

For twenty years, Seth Kincaid has kept his visits to his home town brief. He's not avoiding January Hill, exactly—he's giving his high school girlfriend space. But that distance evaporates when she takes over her family's marina for the summer. Which means every time he flies his floatplane into the harbour, she's there, and the temptation to fall into her sunny smile and forget about the past is stronger than ever. He can't resist lending a hand, though. Not when she needs the help.

January has a lot on her plate. She's temporarily raising her niece and nephew while her sister is overseas, and running the family business, too. The last thing she needs is the dangerous risk of pretending a fling with Seth could be simple. Except the grown man version of the boy she once dated is…perfectly easy. He helps with the kids, no questions asked, and then once they're asleep, satisfies her in ways her eighteen-year-old self couldn't have imagined.

But two decades of distance is a shadow layered on top of complicated, long ago memories.

Whatever this temporary magic spell they are under, it can only be for the summer. Any chance of something else between evaporated the day Seth joined the Air Force—and broke her teenage heart.

ACKNOWLEDGEMENTS

This book took a village. I had wonderful editorial support as I wrote it. First from Hudson Lin, who I hired for book coaching about an entirely different project, and then we fell into talking about Will and Catie for the better part of three months. I love where our conversations took this project.

And then my developmental editor, Kristi Yanta, who has worked on eight Pine Harbour novels now, and always reminds me about the heart of this small town series, read an early draft and helped me figure out where I went off the rails.

As the book came together at the end, Kimberly Cannon saved my butt with the copyedit on this project. (Any errors were inserted by me revising things right up to the last minute.)

And speaking of unexpected changes, I must give a grateful nod to a friend on Twitter. Keri Stevens tweeted about characters not finishing ice cream cones, because they've become overwhelmed by their passion—a trope I had literally just written in chapter fifteen! I laughed out loud, then went back and revised the chapter because Catie wouldn't toss a perfectly good cone of rainbow sorbet. No matter how soft Will's lips looked... Will, on the other hand, would probably toss a hundred dollar bill if he got a chance to kiss Catie, so I think the trope has some validity, but he contained himself because he knows how important ice cream is to Catie. Keri has my eternal gratitude for reminding me about my protagonist's core values and priorities!

I also saw a tweet from an account called @DevinNunescow (don't ask, if you don't know), that read: "Is there anything better than coming to a place you've lived before, embraced by memories, secure in the knowledge you're about to make more?" And that's where the first and last lines of the book came from. (Don't let anyone tell you that faffing about on Twitter is a waste of time.)

As always, much thanks to The Viking, my own authoritarian freak, and the little Vikings (not so little anymore), who love real life Pine Harbour just as much as I do. We spent a lot of time there this summer, and they made every minute of that a joy.

Finally, I dedicated this book to my mother. This fall was the twentieth anniversary of her death, and this book was written with that grief heavy on my shoulders. Like Catie, I didn't understand my mom's choices when she was alive, and have grown into wanting to make them my own choices, too. I think about that often, and ache to tell her how right she was.

ABOUT THE AUTHOR

Zoe York lives in London, Ontario with her young family where she writes romance novels set in the places where she grew up and fell in love herself. She's currently chugging Americanos, wiping sticky fingers, and dreaming of heroes in and out of uniform.

www.zoeyork.com

facebook.com/zoeyorkwrites
twitter.com/zoeyorkwrites
instagram.com/zoeyorkwrites